Twisted at
the Root

Twisted at the Root

ELLEN HART

MINOTAUR BOOKS · NEW YORK

Published in the United States by Minotaur Books, an imprint of St. Martin's Publishing Group

www.minotaurbooks.com

Library of Congress Cataloging-in-Publication Data

Names: Hart, Ellen, author.
Title: Twisted at the root / Ellen Hart.
Description: First edition. | New York : Minotaur Books, 2019.
Identifiers: LCCN 2019008879| ISBN 9781250308429 (hardcover) |
    ISBN 9781250308436 (ebook)
Subjects: | GSAFD: Mystery stories.
Classification: LCC PS3558.A6775 T88 2019 | DDC 813/.54—dc23
LC record available at https://lccn.loc.gov/2019008879

Our books may be purchased in bulk for promotional, educational, or business use. Please contact your local bookseller or the Macmillan Corporate and Premium Sales Department at 1-800-221-7945, extension 5442, or by email at MacmillanSpecialMarkets@macmillan.com.

First Edition: August 2019

10   9   8   7   6   5   4   3   2   1

For J. M. Redmann,
with admiration and great affection

Cast of Characters

Jane Lawless: Owner of the Lyme House restaurant in Minneapolis. Part-time P.I. Peter's sister.

Cordelia Thorn: Creative Director at the Thorn-Lester Playhouse in Minneapolis. Hattie's aunt.

Raymond Lawless: Criminal defense attorney in the Twin Cities. Jane and Peter's father.

Gideon Wise: Corporate attorney. Marlo's father. Rashad's husband.

Rashad May: Senior vice president of sales at MRTL. Gideon's husband.

Marlo Wise: Owner of SwankyNotes greeting card company. George's wife. Gideon's daughter.

George Krochak:	Men's clothing salesman. Marlo's husband.
Eli Chenoweth:	Fine Art Consultant at the J.H. Chenoweth Gallery. J.H. Chenoweth's son.
Kit Lipton-Chenoweth:	Fine Art Consultant at the J.H. Chenoweth Gallery. John Henry's wife.
Peter Lawless:	Documentary filmmaker. Jane's brother.
J. H. Chenoweth (John Henry):	Owner of the J.H. Chenoweth gallery. Married to Kit. Eli's father.
Charles (Chuck) Atchison:	Lawyer. Marlo's cousin.
Harper Tillman:	Hotel receptionist. Eli's girlfriend.
Dr. Julia Martinsen:	Jane's girlfriend.

Twisted at
the Root

1

It was during that no man's land between Christmas and New Year's, when few really wanted to be at work, when most everyone was still in a party mood and rarely made an effort to get anything done, that Marlo Wise left her business early and headed for a coffeehouse not far from her midtown condo.

As twilight settled over the city, she sat by a tall window, nursing her macchiato and watching fat snowflakes flutter down onto the parked cars along Nicollet Avenue. Less than an inch had fallen in the last couple of hours, and yet it was enough to slow the rush hour traffic outside to a crawl. It wasn't hard to read the aggravation in the faces of the drivers, which made her glad that she could retreat from the pre-New-Year's hurly-burly for a few minutes. She wished she could retreat from her thoughts as easily.

A bright turquoise-and-yellow neon sign in a second-story window across the street advertised MELINDA'S PSYCHIC READINGS. Over the years, Marlo had watched many strangers enter an odd little door sandwiched between a Vietnamese dentist's office and a donut shop. She'd often laughed to herself, wondering how stupid someone had to be to pay good money to such an obvious charlatan. Except that now here she was, thinking of doing exactly that.

Marlo was frustrated. She'd been married for exactly three years and nine months to a man she adored, and yet, in all that time, she'd failed to conceive. She wanted a child more than just about anything on earth, but month after month, year after year, it didn't happen. She hadn't been able to share this frustration with her husband, George, because, to be honest, she feared rocking the boat. Her marriage wasn't exactly conventional. If George felt pressured to do something he wasn't completely comfortable with, he might jump ship. Then again, he'd once commented that his first wife had never wanted children. When he'd made the statement, he'd seemed sad. Marlo had taken it as a sign that there was hope.

Marlo wasn't usually so passive/aggressive about her life, and yet, in this instance, it seemed the only way to move forward. George was a beautiful, elegant man who looked and sounded like a British aristocrat. He wasn't an aristocrat, of course—though he did have an upper-class British accent. Over the past few years, Marlo had been amazed by how many Americans conflated the two. She could have said George was an ambassador and nobody would have batted an eye.

Marlo, on the other hand, while reasonably attractive—with luxurious dark blond hair her best feature—wasn't in the same league. Fashion challenged, plus-sized, and tomboyish, she felt deeply put upon if she had to wear anything other than jeans and a sweatshirt. In contrast, her husband dressed like a *GQ* model. George was seventeen years older and sold clothing at an upscale men's store. He had no degree. Wasn't ambitious. He hadn't even owned a car when she first met him. But he was a catch. Everyone said so. She also assumed that people looked at him, then looked at her, and wondered what the hell he was doing dating such an obvious frump.

Marlo recognized the disparities in her marriage but generally ignored them because she brought something of value to the union herself. She was a graphic artist who'd begun creating a line of artistic/humorous greeting cards right out of college and had parlayed it into a successful and growing business. More to the point, she was the beneficiary of a sizable inheritance from her father, part of which was a penthouse condo in the heart of the city. As far as she was concerned, she and George were pretty much equal. Well, except for one important fact: Marlo loved George more than he loved her.

If she had to be honest, she'd never been entirely certain that he loved her at all, not the way a husband normally loves a wife. The marital arrangement they'd agreed upon didn't require it. To be sure, they were good friends. More than that, they were willing lovers and companions. Still, she desperately wanted a child—a child with him. She berated herself for being such a wuss, for conniving behind his back—for tossing out her birth control pills and forgetting to mention it. She was a bad person. Naughty, naughty Marlo, as George often said. He didn't know how right he was.

Doctors had informed Marlo, much to her relief, that she was fully capable of conceiving. Perhaps, as one doctor suggested, George was the problem. If he was, then that was the end of it. Or was it? She'd recently concluded that she wanted a child a tiny bit more than she wanted George, and thus, she was willing to gamble and even connive. The doctor had urged her to stop stressing about it and relax. He offered some practical advice and then sent her on her way. Time, he'd assured her, as his parting shot, was her friend.

Time, in Marlo's opinion, had never been anybody's friend.

The neon sign across the street glowed even more brightly as the winter's early twilight faded to night. Steeling herself for what she was about to do, Marlo rose, lifting her puffy parka from the back of the chair. On her way to the light at the corner of the block, she was seized once again by the feeling that she was being ridiculous. Did she really think she'd learn anything by consulting a crystal-ball gazer?

Standing in front of the door, she hesitated. What was the worst that could happen? She might be wasting a few bucks, but it wouldn't be the first time. Turning the handle and pushing the door in, she proceeded up a dismally dark, narrow stairway that smelled of onions and decades of accumulated dust. Just perfect, she huffed. The psychic didn't even have the foresight to realize she could be sued if someone fell because they couldn't see the steps.

At the top, she found another door. Next to it was a sign:

MELINDA DEYASI
Psychic Healing
Readings Available by Appointment

Rats. She didn't have an appointment. She knocked on the door and waited, digging a fingernail into the palm of her hand. It didn't take long before the door drew back and a middle-aged woman in glasses and a fringed flowery shawl stood peering at her. She cradled a black cat in her arms. Right out of central casting, thought Marlo acidly.

"Can I help you?" asked the woman.

"Are you—" Marlo looked back at the sign.

"Melinda Deyasi," said the woman. "Rhymes with sassy."

"I'd like to talk to you. To . . . get . . . you know, a reading?"

"Of course," the woman said, stepping back to reveal a somewhat cluttered living room. The furniture straddled the line between junk and genuine antique.

"Have a seat and I'll be right with you." The psychic walked over to the corner of the room and deposited the cat at the top of a tall cat tree. Two other felines adorned the lower branches.

Marlo lowered herself onto a lumpy couch cushion.

After adjusting her shawl, Melinda sat down next to her.

"So, how do we do this?" asked Marlo, inching away. She didn't like people who violated her personal space. "Do I pay you up front?"

The woman explained that her fees depended on how much time she spent with each client. If she couldn't "connect," as she called it, she simply charged a flat fee of twenty-five dollars.

Marlo doubted the oracle ever had trouble "connecting."

"So, how can I help you?"

"Well," said Marlo, glancing down at her wedding ring. "My husband and I desperately want a baby, but . . . we're having trouble conceiving."

"How long have you been married?"

"Almost four years. Can you look into my future and tell me if I'll ever have a child?"

"Possibly."

Marlo felt her face grow warm. She might as well have found herself a gypsy at some tacky carnival and had her palms read. Every instinct she had told her to get up and run.

"Give me your hand," said Melinda.

Marlo's expression must have betrayed her thoughts because the woman face softened and she said, "I won't hurt you. I promise. I must have your left hand. It's closer to your heart."

"Um, okay."

The psychic closed her eyes. Marlo wondered if she should shut hers, but before she'd come to a firm conclusion, the woman let out a cry and dropped the hand as if it were a burning cinder.

The cats jumped off their jungle gym and fled into the kitchen.

"What?" asked Marlo.

"I can't help you."

"Why not?"

"I'm sorry, but I need you to leave."

The woman was clearly shaken. Was this part of the act? "You must have seen something. Just tell me. Do you see a child in my future?"

"I'm sorry but I can't continue."

Maybe the oracle's "clients" liked this sort of cheap melodrama. Marlo didn't. "Come on, Melinda. If nothing else, you could at least lie."

The woman seemed shocked by the comment. "I don't lie. I never lie in my readings. All I do is explain what I see."

"So tell me," said Marlo, her voice dripping sarcasm, "What was in your vision?"

Melinda seemed to take the question as a challenge. "All right. I saw darkness. Blood. Violence. It surrounded you. Swirled like a fog. I saw no children."

Marlo stared at her. And then a thought occurred: The psychic was probably talking about the death of Marlo's dad. He'd been the victim of a homicide and, yes, it had been bloody. But for the psychic to pick up on that meant that she really was . . . psychic. "A relative of mine died a few years ago. You're probably seeing that."

"Perhaps," said Melinda. "But much of what I see isn't in your past. It's in your future."

"Excuse me?"

The psychic stood, pulling the shawl more tightly around her shoulders. "I want you to go. Please."

"But you can't just leave it at that. I need details." Marlo reached out her hand. Melinda shrank back.

"If something terrible is going to happen, I have to know what it is. You can't just drop a bomb like that and then push me out the door."

"I'm sorry. When I see this kind of malevolence, I have to withdraw. I made a promise to myself long ago."

Marlo studied the woman's face. It had to be an act. "Fine. You want more money? Is that it?"

"All I want is for you to leave," said Melinda, walking over to the door and yanking it open. She stared straight ahead, refusing to make eye contact with Marlo.

"This is a ploy, isn't it," said Marlo. "Your dramatic way of getting me to come back."

The woman said nothing, merely stood by the door, her hand on the knob.

"Fine, Melinda Deyasi, rhymes with sassy. I'll go. Just don't expect a good review on Yelp." Marlo snatched up her gloves and swept past the woman. It was just as she'd expected. A total waste of time.

2

Tuesday
Four Nights Later

New Year's Eve was an extra busy night at the Lyme House, Jane
Lawless's restaurant in south Minneapolis. By five-thirty, the second-
floor dining room was already packed with customers hoping to get
an early start on their evening. This was also the night her best
friend—Cordelia Thorn—gave her biggest bash of the year.

Cordelia invited everybody in her vast orbit, which included em-
ployees from her theater in downtown Minneapolis, neighbors
from every part of the city she'd ever lived in, a couple of her favorite massage therapists, her gardener, every bookstore owner in
the metro area, a beloved veterinary assistant, old high school and
college chums, her favorite local drag queens, as well as the mayor,
the governor, various local TV personalities and celebrities, well-
known writers, actors, artists—anyone and everyone she knew
who might be traveling through town and happened to be in need
of some serious New Year's Eve glitter. For Jane, it was a command
performance.

Cordelia had phoned around five to ask her to bring over an extra case or two of champagne, just in case. Jane was happy to help out and had carried the boxes to her new—used—truck, a Honda Ridgeline, placing them in the rear seat of the cab. By the time it was needed, the frigid night air would have chilled it to a perfect temperature. Cordelia was experiencing her usual pre-party meltdown. The event was catered, though when it came to entertaining, Cordelia was a micromanager. Jane was happy to be missing the drama.

She'd just shut down her computer and was about to run up the back stairs from her office to the kitchen to check in one last time with her executive chef and her night manager, when her cell phone buzzed. Assuming it was Cordelia again with some new crisis, she fished it out of her back pocket and said, "What now?"

"Jane? Hello? Is that you?"

Oops. Not Cordelia. Instead, the voice belonged to Sigrid, Jane's sister-in-law. "Sorry. I figured you were someone else." Sitting back down, she offered a cheery, "Happy New Year."

Silence. Then, "Yeah, same to you."

Sigrid, Jane's younger brother, Peter, and Sigrid and Peter's daughter, Mia, had all moved out of the country several years back, first to live and work in Brazil. Peter, a documentary filmmaker, had been hired to shoot the footage there for a piece on South America's shifting political winds. After his work was complete, the family moved to England, where Sigrid managed to snag a terrific job that allowed her to apply for a work visa. She'd been a family therapist for many years, but this was something new for her. Moving to London gave her the opportunity to learn from an expert in cognitive behavioral therapy, a professor she'd met somewhere along the line—Jane didn't have all the details. This man

not only wanted to hire her for his practice, but was also instru-
mental in getting her into a cutting-edge program at King's College. While Sigrid was busy with her new life, Peter had been off
shooting another documentary in Eastern Europe. Jane kept in
contact with them, though because of schedules and the time difference, it was somewhat sporadic.

"How are you?" asked Jane, leaning back in her chair.

Another pause. "Actually, not good."

"Really? What's going on?"

"Listen, Jane, have you heard from Peter?"

"No, not recently. Why?"

"He . . . he left our flat three nights ago. I haven't heard from
him since."

"Isn't he still shooting that documentary?"

She cleared her throat. "No. It's . . . a long story. He's been
home for a while."

"Did something happen?"

"We had a fight. When he left he was really upset. He won't
answer my calls, won't respond to texts. It's bad, Jane. We've had
fights before, but nothing like this. He usually goes away for a few
hours, blows off steam, and comes home. But he didn't this time.
I get it, I do. We have some stuff to work out. But I'm worried
that something may have happened to him."

"Like what?"

"Anything. A car crash. A mugging. I called around to the local
hospitals, but . . . nothing. I phoned friends. Nobody's seen or
heard from him."

If Sigrid was calling hospitals, it really was serious.

"He was so angry, Jane. I blame myself. It's all my fault."

Jane's mind began to race.

"Do you think he could have called your dad?"

Peter and Jane were both close to their father, less close these days with each other. "He might have, if you want to call him."

"I just don't know what else to do. I feel so helpless. If he'd just come home . . ." The sentence drifted off.

"Does Mia know what's going on?"

Sigrid sighed. "No. We've tried to keep it from her. She's away right now, staying at a friend's house in Bricket Wood."

"Do you think Peter might have contacted her?"

"I doubt it. I didn't ask when I talked to her last night. She never brought it up, so I decided not to worry her."

It was Jane's turn to hesitate. "Sigrid . . . you don't have to tell me if you don't want to, but, I mean—"

"Oh Jane, it's such a mess. I wouldn't know where to begin. I just can't get into it right now. Will you call me if you hear from him?"

"Sure. You do the same, okay?"

"I just keep telling myself that he could walk back in the door any minute."

"I'm sure he'll come home soon." Jane was trying to stay positive for Sigrid's sake—and for her own.

"Love you, Jane. Bye."

After they'd hung up, Jane quickly punched in Peter's number. It rang five times before it went to voice mail. Instead of leaving a message, she texted him, telling him that he needed to get in touch with her right away. He might be angry with Sigrid, but his family was worried and needed to hear from him. She stared at her phone for a few seconds, hoping he'd text her back. When he didn't, she rose from her chair and headed up to the kitchen.

3

Shortly after six, Jane pulled her truck up to the curb across from her father's law office in Saint Paul. She was early, so instead of waiting in the truck, she got out and dashed across the street. It was after hours, which meant she had to use her key to get in. Finding the reception area and the desk-filled room behind it empty and dark, she headed for the stairs, taking the steps two at a time. She rounded the top of the stairs into the second-floor waiting room. Three of the office doors were closed. The only one open belonged to her father, who was at his desk. Two people, a man and a woman, sat in chairs on the other side.

Not wanting to intrude, Jane sat down and picked up a magazine, leafing through it absently, waiting for the meeting to end. Every time she saw her father these days, she was struck by how thin he'd become. He wasn't frail exactly, though he wasn't the robust man he used to be either. His hair, for so many years a shiny silver mane, had turned completely white. He was still as handsome as ever, at least in Jane's opinion. That was something that would never change.

Raymond Lawless was in his midseventies. He'd been in semi-retirement for a number of years—that is, until CNN contacted him, asking if he'd be interested in appearing on the network as a contributor. They wanted his take on criminal justice reform. It was the year before the election, when the Black Lives Matter movement had been gaining steam. The exposure he'd received caused his law practice to become even more sought after, both locally and nationally. Thus, as time went on, it became clear that he would either need to lean on his partners to handle the extra load, hire new associates, or return to work full time. Much to Jane's dismay, he'd chosen the last.

Hearing the old wood floors creak, she looked over and saw that the meeting was breaking up. The man and woman, both African-American, were on their way out of the office.

"I'll be in touch, Ray," called the man, nodding to Jane as they passed her.

Motioning for Jane to come into his office, her dad returned to his chair. As Jane settled across from him, she couldn't help but notice that he seemed a million miles away.

"You look tired," she said.

"Do I?" It took a moment for him to focus. "No, I'm good."

"Who were they?"

"You remember Rashad May? I represented him in a homicide trial a few years ago. He was accused of murdering his husband, Gideon Wise."

"Oh, sure," said Jane. "Rashad was a good friend of Cordelia's."

"That was Rashad's brother, Sherwin, and his wife, Dessa. He called earlier and asked if they could stop by after he was done with work. The upshot is, he thinks he's found evidence that could get his brother a new trial. He asked me to look into it."

"Will you?"

Her dad appeared to mull it over. "Sherwin's really pushing hard. He's a program director for a radio station here in town. He knows a lot of the local news people. Apparently he gave a TV interview that hasn't aired yet but will soon. He's doing everything he can to get the word out that his brother is an innocent man."

"Have you seen the evidence?"

"Some of it." He tapped a finger against the arm of his chair. "You interested?"

Jane had signed a contract a couple years back to work as a part-time investigator for her father's law firm. As odd as it sounded to those who didn't know her, she had two careers going—restaurateur and private investigator, both longtime passions. Sometimes the needs of one collided with the other, though Jane made every effort to perform the balancing act necessary to make them both possible.

"Come around here and I'll show you." He waited until she'd pulled a chair up next to him and then plugged a thumb drive into his laptop. Clicking on an icon, he brought up a series of crime-scene photos.

"Before I look at them," said Jane, "refresh my memory." Unlike Cordelia, she didn't know Rashad and only vaguely followed the trial in the newspapers, so even the basics were hazy.

"Gideon Wise and Rashad May had been married for half a dozen years when it happened. Shortly after eight on a hot July evening, Rashad came home to find Gideon submerged in the bathtub. He was fully clothed and the bathwater was stained red. Rashad was, of course, shocked—out of his mind with panic. He checked Gideon's vitals, though he later said it seemed obvious to him that he was gone. The cut marks on Gideon's wrists were clearly visible so it wasn't unreasonable for him to conclude—incorrectly, as it turned out—that Gideon had taken his own life. That's what he said to the 911 operator. When the first two officers arrived, both uniforms, they found Rashad on his knees in the middle of the bathroom floor, holding Gideon in his arms. His shirt, by then, was wet and covered in blood."

"How did Gideon actually die?" asked Jane.

"Blunt force trauma to the back of his head, inconsistent with a fall. The investigator assigned to the case arrived a while later, assessed the scene, and jumped to the conclusion that Rashad had been trying to mislead them with the 911 call. He maintained that Rashad should have known it wasn't a suicide because of the head injury. Rashad said he saw the head wound, but figured Gideon had tried to get out of the tub but was too weak and fell back. The fact that he'd pulled Gideon from the tub and was holding him was also deemed suspicious."

"Because?"

"The investigator felt he was attempting to hide physical evidence resulting from the murder—evidence on his clothing. Everything Rashad did, from the moment the primary arrived on the scene, was seen through that filter. The investigator's name was Louie Zandler. He testified later that his gut had led him straight to Rashad. You've probably heard me say this before, Jane: Picking a suspect in a murder investigation can be a little like falling in love. The object of the investigator's affection takes over all of his or her waking thoughts. I'm sad to say that type of tunnel vision on the part of law enforcement professionals isn't unusual. As far as I could tell, the investigation barely looked at anybody else. They had their man and they used all their resources to prove he was guilty."

"What was Rashad's motive?"

"Money. Freedom. Gideon was a wealthy lawyer in his mid-fifties. Rashad was a black man in his early forties. He was the senior vice president of sales at MRTL Worldwide. It paid well, but nothing like Gideon's income. Oh, and believe me, Rashad's race was underlined every chance they got—before and during trial. The prosecution put several of Rashad's so-called friends on the stand to undermine his professed love for Gideon. They all indicated, with almost the same words and phrases, that the only reason Rashad married Gideon was for his money."

"They were coached."

"That was my assessment. We, of course, put on our own witnesses, who testified that the two men were deeply committed and had been for fourteen years—eight of those years before they were legally married. But it didn't matter. The prosecutor made every attempt to dog-whistle and character-assassinate Rashad into a guilty verdict."

Jane remembered her father saying that the side with the best story, true or not, often won the day. While that might not seem like justice, it was the way the judicial system all too often worked. "What was your theory?"

"In talking to Rashad, it came out that Marlo Wise, Gideon's daughter, and her fiancé, a guy named George Krochak, had potential motives. Marlo had started a greeting-card company in her late twenties. Apparently, she was constantly after Gideon to invest money in it. She wanted to expand but couldn't do it without more capital investment. Rashad said that Gideon tried to be diplomatic with her, but eventually just got sick of the conversation and gave her a flat no. That was a couple of weeks before his death."

"I'm not sure that rises to the level of a motive for murder."

"Granted. But there's more. Gideon was vehemently opposed to Marlo's marriage to Krochak. The guy was almost the same age as Gideon. That was a huge sticking point. The other was that Krochak wasn't employed. Gideon figured he was a parasite and said as much, loudly. He refused to pay for the wedding. As I understand it, Gideon and Marlo were both terribly stubborn, and in this instance, they both dug in hard. At one point, Rashad said Gideon threatened to disinherit her if she didn't send Krochak packing. That, in my opinion, could be a motive for murder—not just for Marlo, but for George, too."

"How did that go over when you presented it to the jury?"

"We never got the chance. I was hoping to bring it in when I put Sherwin May on the stand, but the prosecution objected to my initial question. That first objection was overruled, but as it became clear where I was going, the prosecution objected again, and the judge sustained. That effectively shut down our alternate theory of the case."

Once again, Jane remembered why she never wanted to be a lawyer.

Her father leaned back in his chair. "When you think about it, their involvement makes a certain sense. Both Marlo and Krochak had the key code to get them past the security in the condo. Marlo likely knew her dad's schedule. I'm not saying she did the deed herself. Or that Krochak did."

"They hired someone."

"It's possible."

"Any other suspects?"

"Well, I did get wind of some problems at Gideon's law firm. Just rumors, you understand. My investigator was never able to nail anything down."

"So?" said Jane. "What happens next? Will you take the case?"

He took a breath, held it, then let it out with a long sigh. "I don't know, Janey. I'm just about to start another major trial. My time is limited. I did promise Sherwin and Dessa that I'd look back through our files. If the new evidence Sherwin's investigator found turns out to be a Brady violation, which I think is possible, then yes, I could file a habeas petition claiming the prosecution withheld exculpatory evidence, thus materially undermining the result of the trial. At this point, after two failed appeals, it may be Rashad's only real shot. And even then, even with what many might consider unassailable evidence, a new trial is rarely granted."

Jane believed, as did her father, that truth existed and mattered. It was why she was drawn so powerfully to criminal investigation. Itching to see what Sherwin had brought for her dad to look at, she nodded to his laptop, leaning in as he scrolled through a series of photos.

"Let me preface this by saying," continued her father, "the prosecution contended that the only person in the condo that night, other than Gideon, was Rashad. We had no way to disprove it. I should mention that a couple of hairs, one with the root still attached, were found in the bathroom. They were never tied to anyone. The prosecution maintained that, since Gideon and Rashad entertained fairly frequently, the hairs could belong to anyone. We saw to it that the hairs were preserved, so if we do find a suspect in the future, they might prove useful."

"What about security cameras?"

"Gideon and Rashad bought the second condo to go on sale in the rehabbed upper stories of the Finnmark building."

"The Finnmark? I've got a friend who opened a restaurant there."

"The first-floor courtyard under the three-story atrium is sur-

18

rounded by stores—a small inner-city grocery, a wine store, a Starbucks, a bank, various restaurants, etc. The fourth and fifth floors are office space. Gideon and Rashad moved into one of two penthouse suites early, as did the woman across the hall from them, before the rest of the condos had been finished, and before much of the upper-floor security system was in place. The only working cameras in the building that night were located in the courtyard and in the parking garage. Gideon got home around 5:20, if I recall correctly. He was visible on the parking garage video."

"Was he alone?"

Her father nodded. "He generally worked until after seven but had gone to the dentist that afternoon. He did go back to work, but because he was in pain, he went home early. Rashad arrived home that night at around 8:15, again, visible on the video. He was alone. His 911 call came in twelve minutes later. The prosecutor painted a picture of a man quietly letting himself into the condo, grabbing for a preselected weapon, a small bronze sculpture as it turns out, luring Gideon into the downstairs bathroom and murdering him there, then attempting to cover up what he'd done by dumping the body in the tub, switching on the cold water, spending a few seconds cutting Gideon's wrists so it would look like suicide, and finally washing the blood off the sculpture and putting it back in the living room."

"Could Rashad have done all that in twelve minutes?"

"Unlikely if not impossible."

"If there weren't any working cameras on the top floor," asked Jane, "couldn't people have come and gone from the condo without being seen?"

"I would think that was obvious. But because I had no proof to back up our contention that someone else was in the apartment that night, no sign of a break-in or a burglary, it was a dead end. During discovery, we believed we'd received all the relevant information the police had assembled about the case. We made multiple discovery requests, which is normal. It's never wise to assume that everything is being turned over in a timely way. I remember looking at the security video. Nothing stood out. My team also carefully combed through the photographs and video taken by the police that night, mostly of the interior of the condo. Again, nothing. Now," he said, pulling up a shot of an open living room filled with mid-century modern furniture. "Look here," he said, pointing at a chair that sat a few feet from a long, exposed-brick wall. "See anything on the floor next to that turquoise armchair?"

Jane squinted. "No."

"Me neither. Now take a look at this shot."

The second photo was taken from a similar angle—almost straight on—but this time there was a canvas tote resting on the carpet just inches from the chair. "Why wasn't it there in the other picture?" asked Jane.

"Good question. I can tell you this much. The police never turned that last photo over to us. I know because, if we'd come into possession of it before trial, it might have helped us prove our contention that someone, other than Rashad, had been in the condo that night."

Jane was confused. "Maybe it belonged to someone in the crime-scene unit."

"Look at this." Ray clicked out of the photo file and brought up a video. "This was taken in the parking garage at 6:25 by one of the security cameras. You see an individual from the back, walking up to the elevators. He's careful to keep his face averted from the camera, which suggests to me that he knew it was there and he was hiding his identity. He's wearing dark pants and a hoodie pulled up over his head, unusual clothing for a hot July night. Now look at what he's holding." He paused the video.

Jane leaned close. "My god," she said. "It's the same tote bag." It was easily recognizable. The bottom part was black, the upper section white, with the letters JHC written across the front in big block letters. "Any idea what the initials stand for?"

"None. And I have no idea who the man in the hoodie is, but Sherwin May and I agree on one thing: We may be looking at Gideon Wise's killer."

She switched her gaze from the computer screen to her dad's face. "Wow."

"I know."

"Why didn't the prosecution hand over that photo with the tote?"

"You tell me."

"An oversight?"

"Possible, but unlikely."

"How did the guy get into the condo?"

"I assume Gideon let him in. There was no evidence of a break-in."

"Did Sherwin have anything else to offer?"

"His investigator's final report should've come in today, but because of the holidays, it was delayed. Sherwin thinks there might be something else in it. He said he'd call as soon as he knows anything."

Jane shook her head and kept shaking it. "Doesn't smell right. Any of it."

"I agree." Closing his laptop, her dad began to stuff papers into his briefcase. "I think we better get over to Cordelia's."

"Oh lord, I completely forgot about that."

"We don't want her to send out a search party." After shrugging into his heavy topcoat, he picked up his briefcase. "Come on, sweetheart. Let's go celebrate the new year."

They linked arms and walked out of the office together.

4

The traffic on I-94 on the way back to Minneapolis was more congested than it had been on the way out. While her father sat quietly looking out the window, Jane had some time to reflect. Tonight would be a special night for her; the first time in many years she would be celebrating with a special woman. She'd reunited with Julia just over a month ago. Cordelia, as always, had warned against it, saying Jane could never trust a woman like Julia, a manipulative liar, a narcissistic user. Cordelia rarely minced words when discussing the good doctor. Jane, on the other hand, saw a more nuanced woman, a flawed though still admirable human being. Jane also saw that she was never going to win the argument with Cordelia, so she gave up trying.

Shortly after eight, Jane pulled the Ridgeline into the circular drive in front of Cordelia's Kenwood mansion. Cordelia lovingly referred to the place as Thornfield Hall, christening it, as she put it, "with the full Charlotte Brontë." Snow had blanketed the city two nights before and the walking, even on shoveled sidewalks, wasn't good. Jane let her father out, waiting as he entered the house, then went in search of a parking spot. She found one on the next block over and picked her way carefully through the side streets back to the house.

Once inside, she was met by a meaty Marlon Brando lookalike in a leather jacket and jeans, aviator shades, and a cotton canvas cap, straight out of the fifties flick, *The Wild One.* He was probably meant to be the bouncer.

"You got an invite?" he asked. His Brooklyn accent sounded fake.

"I do," said Jane. She pegged him as an actor, someone Cordelia had hired as a joke. Not that a little muscle at the front door was unwarranted.

"Good. Mind your p's and q's, otherwise, me and you, we gonna have a problem."

That was friendly, she thought as she stepped past him. He was clearly enjoying his role, creating it one threat at a time.

Inside, the party was in full progress. As she stood in the hall looking around, Hattie, Cordelia's eleven-year-old niece, followed by four kids about the same age, surged out of the dining room, each holding a plate stacked high with cake.

"Janey," cried Hattie, rushing over to give her a squeeze.

Jane couldn't believe that Hattie was getting so big. Sixth grade. Where had the time gone? "Are you having a good time?"

"Cake first," whispered Hattie, giving Jane a serious look and then another grin.

"Where's your auntie?"

"Who knows?" She glanced back at her posse, giving them a thumbs up.

"You go," said Jane. "I'll catch up with you later."

"Okay. But . . . did you bring Mouse and Gimlet?"

24

Hattie adored Jane's dogs. Much to Cordelia's continuing frustration, Hattie adored all nature, including bugs.

"No, they're having their own party over at Evelyn Bratrude's house." Evelyn was a retired neighbor who often took care of the dogs when Jane was gone for the evening.

As Hattie raced back to her buddies, her blond curly hair bouncing, Jane turned her attention to the great room. Julia had texted her about an hour ago, saying that Carol, a retired nurse administrator who was now her assistant, would drop her off. The house was so huge that it could easily swallow up several hundred people with room to spare. Jane nodded to a man who looked so much like Armistead Maupin that she did a double take—could it be? As she turned, the crowd in front of her parted ever so briefly, allowing her a glimpse of a woman in a glittery pink T-shirt and matching hair. She stood on a low platform directly under a gothic tryptic of stately stained-glass windows. In front of her was a table filled with electronic equipment.

Jane recalled now that Cordelia had said she intended to hire a DJ for the evening. For the moment, a mixture of sixties oldies blared from four strategically placed loudspeakers. Cordelia had planned the music down to the second. There would be a short David Bowie retrospective; Broadway show tunes, most going back decades; a Lady Gaga set; some techno-pop and other dance electronica; an hour of big bands, swing, and old standards; seventies rock; a periodic novelty, such as the original "Here Comes Peter Cottontail" sung by Gene Autry, one of Cordelia's all-time favorites; and finally, lots of doo-wop generously stirred in.

Jane said hello to a few of the revelers but didn't allow herself to get dragged into any conversations. Her main objective was to find Julia.

As she stretched her neck, trying to see over a knot of tall football linemen types, she thought she caught sight of the back of a familiar head. "Peter?" she whispered. She snaked her way through the throng, pushing past a crowd gathered around the mayor, and escaped to the base of the stairway that led up to the open second-floor mezzanine. Midway up the steps she stopped. From this vantage, she had a better view. He could be anywhere in the house by now. And then she saw him. He was talking to Fiona McGuy, the stage manager at Cordelia's theater. Much to Jane's disappointment, it wasn't her brother. It seemed likely that she would see him everywhere until he turned up.

Glancing around at the sound of applause, she watched Cordelia make a grand entrance into the great room wearing the gold-and-black headdress of an Egyptian pharaoh and a gold-lamé gown. With her height and girth, even in normal clothes, it was impossible for her to "blend," as she called it. Waving a fan made of faux black feathers in front of her face, she proffered a hand to her minions, bestowed a few air kisses, fluttered here and there spreading her New Year's cheer. The heavy makeup she wore was straight out of a King Tut playbook. Jane waved and caught her eye. Cordelia nodded, winked, and made her way toward the stairway. They met on the second-floor landing.

"You made it," said Cordelia, eyeing Jane's less-than-thrilling costume. "A navy blazer, a red cotton shirt, and jeans? Really, Jane? *Really?*"

"I came directly from work. I would have gone home and changed, but Dad's car is in the shop and he needed a ride, so I invited him to stay the night at my place and—"

"Enough." Cordelia held up her hand for silence. "At least your father can pass for an aging Perry Mason."

The music changed to the Beatles' "Come Together." As the bass notes pumped through the air around them, Jane asked, "Have you seen Julia?"

"She's upstairs in the Redgrave bedroom. When she arrived she said she wanted to lie down."

How anyone could nap through this noise was difficult to comprehend. "Did she seem—"

"Just tired," said Cordelia.

When it came to Julia, worrying was a great part of what Jane did these days. "I think I'll go check on her."

"Did you bring the champagne?"

"Of course. I'll go bring my truck around if you need it."

"Good woman." As Cordelia floated regally back down the stairs into the throng, Jane headed into a broad hall. All the bedrooms in the house had been named after famous actresses, with one exception: Hattie insisted on naming her bedroom for the originator of quantum theory, Max Planck. Cordelia didn't much like such a strange idea, but because it was Hattie, she gave in. Cordelia's room was, of course, the Hepburn bedroom. Other bedrooms included the Gloria Swanson, the Bette Davis, the Claudette Colbert, and the Olivia de Havilland. Octavia Thorn-Lester, Cordelia's sister, when she was in town, always stayed in the Meryl Streep. And Jane, on occasion, used the Kathleen Turner.

Jane found Julia asleep in the middle of an ornate French chestnut bed, a pillow pressed to each ear. Sitting down next to her, all Jane wanted was to enjoy the moment. Julia's face seemed so peaceful, so serious.

Dr. Julia Martinsen, an internationally prominent oncologist, had been diagnosed last spring with a rare tumor, an optic-nerve glioma. In children, tumors on the optic nerve were common, usually slow-growing and benign. In adults, they were more often cancerous and aggressive. Late in the summer, Julia had confided the facts to Jane, admitting that her greatest fear was living through it—or dying—alone. Meaning, without Jane in her life. In a moment of weakness, Jane had promised to be there for her.

When Julia's sight began to worsen, she'd moved into Jane's home. And from there, even though Jane had set boundaries for herself, she'd allowed Julia into her life again—and into her bed. Through it all, she kept asking herself: What was the harm? What was the worst that could happen? Julia was ill, probably gravely so. She likely didn't have long to live. Jane had no illusions about who she was. She'd entered the relationship—for a second time—with her eyes wide open.

Julia turned on her side. Smiling up at Jane, she said, "Hi."

"Hi, yourself. How are you feeling?"

"Just a little tired."

"What about the pain?"

"Manageable."

Jane took her hand and held it to her lips. "You want to go downstairs? You feel up to it?"

"What time is it?"

"Around eight thirty."

"Lie down with me for a few minutes. It's a long time until midnight."

"And what's happening at midnight?" asked Jane, stretching out on the bed and drawing Julia into her arms.

"I'm going to kiss the woman I love."

"Does she have to wait that long?"

Nuzzling Jane's hair, Julia said, "That's a good question. Why don't we discuss it?"

5

George worked at the kitchen counter, wiping the marble down, making sure it would be clean for the morning. He'd just finished the dinner dishes. Marlo was upstairs taking her nightly bath. They had a routine, one that varied only slightly even on New Year's Eve. Since Marlo didn't like to cook and George did, and because his job at a men's clothing store had regular hours, he would arrive home around six, shower, change into something more casual, pour himself a glass of wine, and begin preparing the evening meal. It was his form of meditation. Soothing. Understandable. Something the world often refused to be.

As he poured himself another glass of Viognier, the landline rang. Scooping it up off the counter, he said hello.

"George? Is that you?"

"Who's calling please?"

"It's Chuck Atchison."

Chuck was Marlo's cousin. George found him dull. Not that it mattered. He was family now. "Nice to hear from you. Marlo tells me you're going to stay with us for a week or so. Flying in from Fort Lauderdale on Friday, yes?"

"A change of plans," said Chuck. "I'm here a little early, hope that's not a problem. I booked a room at one of the downtown hotels for tonight. I'm wondering if I could come by tomorrow. If it's not convenient—"

"It's fine," said George, picking up the bottle of wine and holding it up to see how much was left. "I'll tell Marlo."

"Great, great. Well, I look forward to seeing you."

George spoke to him for another few seconds, settling on a time. He didn't want Chuck arriving too early, since both he and Marlo were planning on sleeping in tomorrow. After hanging up, he carried his glass into the media room and sat down on the leather couch facing the TV.

Very little had changed in the condo since the days when Marlo's father had owned it. George had been surprised when Marlo suggested they move in. If *his* father had been found murdered in the first-floor bathroom's vintage claw-foot tub, he would have unloaded the place immediately. When it came to domestic affairs, however, Marlo usually went for what was easy. Along with cooking, she didn't much like cleaning or decorating. They both knew they wanted out of their town house. Marlo had thus concluded that it was better to try to forget that one awful night than it was to sell the condo, look for another property, organize a move, etc.

The condo was in a converted commercial building built in the early twenties. Their top-floor, twenty-three-hundred-square-foot unit was a two-story, brick-and-concrete inner-city penthouse with a state-of-the-art kitchen; deep, oversized windows with views of midtown; and a long gallery wall of paintings. The furniture was functional and uncluttered, with a kind of mid-century, cool-jazz vibe that could easily have served as a set for the TV show *Mad Men*. While it wasn't George's taste, he didn't feel it was his place to suggest a wholesale redecoration.

Picking up the remote, he turned on the TV. The idea was to watch a movie and then go to bed early. He'd made a light dinner so they'd have room for popcorn while they watched.

George had always craved comfort, the kind he couldn't afford. His parents had emigrated from Kharkov to Israel when he was a baby. They'd only stayed a few years before moving to the UK, where his father had taken a position teaching biochemistry at the University of Cambridge. It didn't pay very well, though both George and his older brother had gone to good schools, and for that he was grateful.

They'd moved again thirteen years later, when his father took a teaching position at the University of Minnesota. George had just turned sixteen. Minnesota was a culture shock, one he wasn't prepared for. By then, he thought of himself as thoroughly British. He didn't like the swagger and aggressive braggadocio he saw in so many of his new American friends. The flat, thudding Minnesota accent was thoroughly distasteful, as were the inflated comments he kept hearing about American exceptionalism. Rather quickly, the US began to feel like a circus, a sideshow on every corner. By his senior year, George had concluded that much of life was, simply put, absurd.

George's brother viewed the world more flat on, more practically, which allowed him to fit in far better. He'd gone on to distinguish himself in college, becoming a business major and eventually going to work for a prestigious financial firm in New York. But not even his brother could afford a place like this. The irony never failed to amuse.

"So," said Marlo, coming into the room wearing her favorite flannel bathrobe. She carried her own glass of wine along with the bottle. "Have you thought about a film?" she asked, sitting down next to George on the couch.

He put his arm around her. "You smell wonderful." He sniffed her hair. She looked lovely, too, skin all pink from her bath. "What about watching an oldie? *Vertigo*? Or perhaps *All About Eve*?"

"*Vertigo* would be great. Haven't seen that in ages." She touched his brow, tracing his hairline. "You know, I realize you hate to hear it, but you and Hugh Grant could have been separated at birth."

The only thing he could see that he and Grant had in common was the English accent. Even though George's had faded over the years, most Americans still pegged him as British.

Halfway through the movie, Marlo reminded him about their "snack." If it had been up to her, they would be eating out of one of those godawful microwave bags. He couldn't abide the taste or the smell. When he brought out a big bowl of fresh popcorn drenched in just the right amount of butter, she purred. He loved that. Cooking for her was a pleasure because she was such an appreciative audience.

When the movie was over, he switched to the local news.

"Wait, wait," said Marlo, sitting up and leaning forward. "Don't change the channel. I know that guy. Him," she said, pointing. "The black guy."

Two men sat opposite each other in what looked like the living room of a family home. George thought the man seemed familiar, though he couldn't place him.

"That's Rashad May's brother," said Marlo. "I think he's talking about my dad."

They both listened as the man explained that he'd found proof that Rashad was innocent, that he should never have been convicted of Gideon Wise's murder.

"What on earth is he talking about?" demanded Marlo. "Everyone knows Rashad murdered my dad. How can he go on TV saying things like that?"

"Quiet down," said George, straining to hear over his wife's protestations. The man was saying he'd found new evidence. The interviewer asked if he'd retained an attorney.

"Raymond Lawless," he said without missing a beat. "He knows the case backward and forward. He never believed my brother was guilty. Now we're going to prove it."

"Interesting," said George, resting his elbows on his knees.

The man continued, "If anyone out there has even the smallest scrap of information that could help my brother, please, *please*, contact Raymond Lawless."

"This is crazy," said Marlo. She stiffened and pushed off the couch, pacing in front of the screen.

George switched it off. "Calm down."

"How can I? He outright lied."

"They're a long way from reopening the case. If it happens, we'll have to live with it."

"Maybe you can, but I can't go through that again. The whole thing was torture, waiting for the verdict, thinking Rashad might get off. That man is in prison for a reason. He was unfaithful. He was seeing someone behind my dad's back. He wanted out of the marriage without losing his cash cow. That's all my dad was to him. Rashad broke up my parent's marriage, you know. It's why my mother died such an early death."

"Your mom died of kidney disease."

"Made worse because of the divorce. I hate that man. He's right where he belongs."

George had heard the same litany of grievances dozens of times. Rashad was guilty and that was the end of the story. "Your father was gay, Marlo. His marriage to your mother was bound to come apart. If it hadn't been Rashad, it would have been someone else." George didn't enjoy defending Gideon Wise. He'd found the man pompous, with a rich man's view of the world. Gideon had done everything in his power to force his daughter to cut George out of her life. When Marlo announced, out of the blue—and much to George's surprise—that they were engaged, Gideon had pitched a fit, threatening to disinherit her. At times, they were like two bulls, pawing the dust, grunting and snarling, eyeing each other with blood in their eyes.

What truly amazed George was that Marlo had never come to terms with her dad's sexuality. She wasn't an unreasonable woman. There were no religious issues. She did, however, have a tendency to see only the parts of people she wanted to see. And when it came to men—which likely included her father—she could be willingly blind. George wasn't about to examine that part of her personality too closely because he'd been a major beneficiary of that blindness.

"Come sit down," said George. He patted the couch.

Marlo began to cry. She dropped down next to him. "I thought this was over, that we could put it behind us and move on."

"I know," he whispered. "I know."

Looking him full in the face, she said, "I'm so glad I have you."

"I'm glad you have me, too."

"I don't know what I'd do without you."

"You'd be just fine, Marlo. You're a capable woman."

She searched his face. "What are you saying?"

"Just what I said." She was always looking for subtext. Not that he blamed her. Most of life was lived in the kingdom of subtext.

"Don't leave me."

"I'm not going anywhere."

"Really, George? Truly?"

He drew her against his chest. "We should finish our popcorn. And then you should head upstairs and take your sleeping pill."

"That man on the TV really upset me."

"Better living through chemicals."

She snuggled close. "You always know the right thing to say."

No doubt about it. He was a whiz. Lucky Marlo.

6

The gallery had evolved. Once upon a time it had been a single room in a crumbling building in the warehouse district, scrubbed and polished to within an inch of its life by Eli Chenoweth's father and mother. The year it opened, 1977, was the year Eli was born. He'd grown up in the gallery, crawled along the wooden floors, been tickled by his mother and tossed in the air by his father under the newly installed track lights. He knew these things not from actual memory, but from the hundreds of photos his parents had taken of their first child. Even now, the floors felt unusually friendly to Eli, and oddly exciting.

After ten years of eking out a modest living, Eli's parents had bought the building, which included the shop next door, with money from his dad's inheritance. They'd torn out an adjoining wall and enlarged the gallery from one exhibition space to three. Eli had been in awe of that gaping hole, the most vivid, violent piece of art he'd ever seen. He remembered how relieved he'd been when the gallery was repaired and put back in order. Many years later, back down on the floor once again, in a corner under a Jackson Pollack knockoff, he'd made love to Kit for the first time.

As Eli walked through the darkened galleries, he thought about last New Year's Eve, a night when he hadn't been alone. He'd had such high hopes that his life was finally on track. He wasn't interested in doing a year-end retrospective, and yet it was hard to escape what had gone down, what he'd said, and most importantly, what he'd done. He craved a drink, or a hit of something that would alter his consciousness as fast as possible. Except he wasn't that man anymore. He was the new and improved Eli, cleansed of his former bad habits. His peace was found through a slower, more difficult means—meditation, stillness, quieting the mind, the Noble Eightfold Path. Wisdom dictated that he go home, cook dinner, and spend the evening in some principled pursuit—or, at the very least, something normal and healthy; anything to distract him from all the things crowding the edges of his mind that decidedly weren't either.

He tapped ash into a paper cup, then took another drag. He'd been told that to be a good Buddhist he should quit smoking cigarettes. A man should be open to his cravings but not give in to them. Eli's much-beloved Camels represented "giving in" multiple times a day. Even so, it was the one drug he refused to give up. As he stood at one of the bay windows, watching an occasional car go by outside, his cell phone rang. The picture of an angel popped up on his screen.

"Hey," he said, trying to work some cheer into his voice.

"Where are you?"

"I'm still at the gallery. How about you?"

"Home."

"You two celebrating?"

She groaned. "He had a few too many Manhattans and fell asleep on the couch. Listen, did you catch the local news tonight?"

"No. Why?"

"Sounds like the murder case against Rashad May may be reopened."

For a moment, he was almost too stunned to speak. "No," was all he could squeeze out.

"Ray Lawless is taking the case again."

It was freakin' four hundred below outside, and Eli was sweating.

"We're fine, Eli."

"You're sure of that?"

"We did nothing wrong."

He let out a snort. "Right."

"The point is, we had nothing to do with what happened to Gideon."

He backed up against a wall, sliding down until he hit the floor. "If they reopen the case, that means they'll be looking around for someone else to nail for his murder."

"But not us."

"Peter Lawless. He lied on the stand. And then he got real weird around me, don't you remember?"

"You're not listening. Peter can't hurt us. Besides, he left for parts unknown years ago. And even if he did come back and tell the truth, what does it prove? Nothing."

She was overconfident as usual, but he didn't have the energy to argue.

"You were a different person back then, Eli. We all were. If we stick together, we'll be fine. Look, I just wanted to let you know. I didn't want you to hear it from someone else and freak out."

"You mean like I'm doing right now? Maybe we should come clean to the police, Kit. Tell them what happened."

"Are you out of your mind? It would point a finger directly at us."

She was probably right. Why raise your hand and wave it around if you maintained you had nothing to do with the crime.

"You okay? We in agreement?"

"Yeah," he said.

"So I gotta go."

"No. Kit, please. Just talk to me a while longer." He ached to tell her that he still loved her. That he'd never stopped. But what was the point? She'd moved on. So had he, though unlike her, his new life had crashed into a million pieces.

"Oh, baby, just chill. Everything will be fine."

"Yeah," he said weakly.

"I'll see you at work. We're going to get through this."

As he tucked the phone back into his jacket, his thoughts turned to the restaurant down the street, the one with the long, shiny, ever-so-inviting bar. No, he told himself. Baby steps. Enlightenment might be beyond his ability, but he should definitely get up and get the hell out of the gallery before he did something he'd regret.

After making sure that everything was properly locked up for the night, the security system on, he exited out the back way to his car. As he unlocked the door with his remote, he heard a tiny cry, something that sounded like it came from a small animal. Using the flashlight app on his cell phone, he swept the lot, which was mostly empty of cars, and then turned it on the alley. Under an icy drain spout, he saw two shiny eyes staring back at him.

Switching off the light, he approached cautiously. Whatever it was, it had to be nearly frozen.

"Hello," he said, crouching down. "Who do we have here?" It was a small cat with white paws and terrified eyes. Since it was wearing a collar, he assumed it wasn't feral. His mother had been a veterinarian, so he'd grown up with animals around the house, though they'd never had a cat because of his sister's allergies. They had dogs. Mostly schnauzers. Eli didn't really understand cats. This one wasn't much past kittenhood. He remembered his mother railing about people who gave kittens and puppies as Christmas presents to their kids—and how many of them were dumped shortly thereafter.

If this little thing were a dog, Eli would have offered his hand for it to sniff. He wasn't sure how a cat would respond.

It squeaked again, or cried, or mewed. Whatever it was, the sound was so desperate and lonely that it sliced right through him.

"Will you come to me?" he asked softly. "I'd like to help you."

Very gingerly, the cat stood and moved a few inches away from the brick wall. Eli could see now that the poor thing was shivering.

It was another full minute before the cat moved toward him again.

"Are you hungry?" he asked, making sure he kept his voice low and soothing. His bent knees were starting to scream at him. He held out a finger. The cat moved toward it, allowing Eli to scratch its head. All of a sudden, it leaped into his arms. Eli couldn't quite believe it. He tucked it inside his coat and carried it to his car, feeling it tremble against his chest. Tomorrow he would check around to see if anybody in the area was missing a pet cat. If nothing else, he'd put up a note on Craigslist and find it a home.

7

The sound of Cordelia's New Year's Eve party was still reverberating through the neighborhood when Jane ducked out the front door around one A.M. She'd insisted that Julia and her dad, both drooping pretty badly, wait inside until she brought the truck around. Hopping over a snowbank, she skidded her way down the center of the street, the night air feeling deliciously cold against her flushed face. Unlike Cordelia, Jane found crowded parties oppressive, overstimulating, and often downright boring. Nonconversations shouted over loud music made no sense to her at all. Perhaps it was the curse of the introvert. Whatever it was, Jane was glad to leave.

After buckling her seatbelt, Julia closed her eyes, and Jane's dad did the same. Glad to finally be free of the doo-wop, Jane rode home in glorious silence.

When she pulled into the drive along the side of her house a while later, she saw that both her passengers were asleep. She ahem-ed a couple of times, finally waking them. As they headed inside, Jane took a moment to kick off the packed snow that had accumulated in the Ridgeline's wheel wells. She was almost done when she heard a familiar voice call her name. Turning, she saw Evelyn standing on her stoop in bathrobe and curlers, waving to get her attention.

Trotting across the street, Jane called softly, "What are you doing up so late?"

Before she could respond, Mouse, Jane's brown lab, charged out from behind Evelyn making a beeline for Jane.

She crouched down to greet him.

"I'm so sorry," said Evelyn, catching Gimlet, a small black poodle, before she could make her own jailbreak.

Jane had assumed Evelyn had already brought the dogs back. "Is everything okay?"

Moving slowly down the steps, Evelyn said, "The dogs are fine. But when I opened the front door around midnight to bring them home, I saw this car parked in front of your house. The headlights were off, but there was exhaust coming from the tailpipe, so I knew someone was inside. Mouse started to growl, so I closed the door and watched from the living room. The car sat there for another ten minutes or so before the lights came on and it drove away. I have to say, it scared me. I decided to keep the dogs here until I saw lights go on in your house and I knew you were back."

Patting her thigh and telling Mouse to stay close, Jane took Gimlet from Evelyn's arms. "Did you get a look at the guy's face?"

"I could be wrong, but it seemed like he had on a hood. Not one that covered his entire face, just the top and sides."

"Like a hoodie?"

"Yes, that's what they call it. The streetlight gives off good light, but I couldn't make out much more than that."

"What kind of car?" asked Jane. "What color?"

"It was light colored," Evelyn said, looking distressed. "Maybe silver or gray. A four-door sedan, and I could be wrong, but I think there were some odd light-gray stripes down the front and back."

"Like racing stripes?"

"I'm not sure what that is. Sorry."

"You did exactly the right thing."

"Do you have any idea who the man might be?"

"None," said Jane. "I do know that sometimes on holiday nights like tonight, people are out casing houses."

"Goodness, I hope that's not it." Evelyn hesitated, crossing her arms over her chest. "Well, I shouldn't keep you. The dogs were perfect, as usual."

"Thank you," Jane called to Evelyn's retreating back. She waited until the door was shut and locked and then carried Gimlet to her house, with Mouse leading the way. She entered through the back door and found Julia in the kitchen.

"I wondered where they were," said Julia, getting out a box of treats. When the dogs saw the box, they instantly sat down and waited for Julia to toss them their nightly Milk-Bones.

While they crunched away, Jane tugged on Julia's belt and drew her close. "Happy New Year."

The kiss they shared gave Jane hope that Julia might be up for more, but Julia begged off, saying she was beat.

Jane held her. She wished she could do more. "I'll join you upstairs in a little while."

Julia whispered into Jane's ear, "I have only one New Year's wish. I want one year with you. One good year. And then I'll go quietly."

Jane increased her grip. "I don't want you to go at all."

"Mustn't be greedy." She pulled back, gave Jane's nose a kiss and then left the room.

Julia might be ill, but they still had time. And who knew? Perhaps there was a chance she could beat the disease. Julia spent most of her time these days searching the internet, talking to doctors— to researchers all over the world—looking for a magic bullet, a recent study, a new drug trial. She thought she'd found one in early December, though it hadn't worked out. Barely two weeks after beginning the new drug protocol, she'd landed in the hospital with a mild but terrifying stroke. Nothing was going to be easy from here on out.

After letting the dogs into the backyard, Jane went in search of her father. She found him in the living room, sitting on the couch.

"Use the small bedroom," she said. "Towels are in the linen closet. If you need anything else, just let me know."

"Thanks, honey."

She kept Evelyn's story from him. No point in worrying him over what was likely nothing. She also kept her conversation with Sigrid to herself. They could talk about it in the morning.

As her father rose to go, Jane wished him a good night's sleep. She loved it when he stayed over. Tonight, she was especially glad for his presence.

After letting the dogs in, Jane walked around checking all the windows to make sure they were locked and the blinds were drawn. The dogs trotted along beside her as she stopped in the front hall to switch on the security system. Gimlet was hard of hearing, so she wasn't much of a watchdog, but Mouse—with his deep growl and a mountain of natural protectiveness—made up for it. And yet, even with all the precautions, Jane removed a baseball bat from the front closet before she went upstairs to bed.

8

As tired as she was, Jane's mind wouldn't stop churning. Checking the clock on the nightstand, she saw that it was just after two thirty. Julia was sound asleep, as was Gimlet, who was snoring away on the dog bed. Mouse was stretched out on the rug next to it. As Jane slipped out from under the covers, she caught his eye. Together, they descended the stairs into the living room.

She spent a few minutes assembling logs, paper, and kindling in the fireplace. If she was up, she figured, she might as well be entertained. Once the birch bark had caught, she went looking for whiskey. She returned with the bottle and a glass. Hunkering down on the Oriental rug, with her back against the couch and her arm around Mouse, she sipped her drink, watching the logs spark and listening to the birch bark crackle.

The act of worrying always made her feel like she was doing something, when in reality, she was wasting her time and emotional energy. Still, she couldn't seem to stop. She gazed around the darkened living room, listening for any sounds that didn't belong. She was going to feel jumpy for a while, she supposed, so she might as well get used to it.

Sipping her whiskey, her thoughts turned to Peter. The longer she went without hearing from him, the more concerned she became. Where had he gone? Why didn't he answer her calls or texts? Perhaps even more importantly, what was going on in his marriage to Sigrid? Jane should have kept in better touch. Once upon a time, she'd been close to her brother. After their mother died, they'd returned to England, to Lyme Regis, where they'd grown up. They had craved that connection to their mother and to her family, people they'd left behind when they moved to Minnesota. Neither Peter nor Jane had regretted the time they'd spent in England, even though it had caused a falling-out with their dad that had taken years to heal.

Jane had friends who didn't get along with their siblings. She remembered feeling a little smug, sure she and Peter would always be close. And yet a year before he and his family had left the country, a rift had developed between them. Jane hadn't been able to get a grip on her anger at his behavior—behavior he seemed proud of. They'd eventually worked their way through some of it, tried to bury their differences, and for the most part they'd succeeded, at least on the surface. And yet, before he left for South America, she'd felt that something was still amiss. In the end, Jane had put it down to a residual sense of disconnection. She let it go because she had no idea how to fix it.

As the fire burned down and one glass of whiskey became two, Jane felt herself finally growing sleepy. She got up to stoke the last of the fire and then stretched out on the couch, pulling the quilt off the back and covering herself. Mouse moved over to the rug and gave a deep sigh. It wasn't long before they were both asleep.

The familiar smell of coffee and toast woke her the following morning. Kicking off the quilt, she sat up, rubbing her eyes. Bright morning sunlight seeped in around the edges of the window shades. Mouse had disappeared from his rug near the hearth. Only one reason he'd leave she thought as she passed through the foyer into the dining room and then into the kitchen: food.

"You're up early," she said, seeing her father at the kitchen table. He was already dressed in a pair of comfortable old jeans and a navy cardigan.

"Had a phone call. Couldn't get back to sleep." His laptop was open in front of him. He gestured to the coffee maker on the counter. "Just made a fresh pot."

Mouse was working his way through a bowl of morning kibble and only looked up briefly.

"Has he been out?" asked Jane, getting a mug from the cupboard and pouring herself some coffee.

He nodded. "You know, being around Mouse always makes me miss my old dog."

"You could adopt someone new. I could help."

He sat back and thought about it. "I'm gone too much. Wouldn't be fair."

"Want some eggs? Bacon? Hash browns? I could even be persuaded to make blueberry pancakes."

"This is fine for now," he said, brushing toast crumbs off his sweater.

She leaned against the counter, sipping from her mug. "So, have you heard anything new from Sherwin May?"

"Actually, I have. He was the one who called me."

"And?"

"It's pretty interesting. You up for another bit of legal history?"

"Absolutely."

He pushed his empty toast plate away. "Okay. Let's go back to Rashad's trial. Toward the end, we were blindsided by a last-minute witness, someone who really put the case to bed for the prosecution. His name was Trevor Loy. He and Rashad had once been lovers. Trevor testified that several months before Gideon's death, Rashad had come to him to ask if he knew anyone who could 'take care' of Gideon for him, that he was willing to pay."

"Take care as in . . . murder?" said Jane.

Her dad nodded. "Trevor told him he might be able to find a guy, but in the end, he never did. And that was why, the prosecution maintained, Rashad had been forced to do it himself."

"The jury believed this Trevor?"

"They ate it up. Trevor had photo evidence that they'd met—a couple of selfies he'd taken in Rashad and Gideon's condo the afternoon he said he and Rashad had the conversation. Up until Trevor's appearance, I felt we had a good chance at a hung jury. Maybe even an acquittal. There was a lot of hearsay, in my opinion, and the case was thin. I don't believe I'm overstating matters when I say that it was Trevor's testimony that sent Rashad to prison."

Jane stepped over to the table with her mug of coffee, pulled out a chair, and sat down. "If Trevor was telling the truth, Rashad was guilty. Did that shake your opinion of him?"

"My job, Janey, was to defend him, not to judge him. Rashad denied—absolutely, categorically denied—asking Trevor to find someone to murder Gideon. As for the meeting at the condo, Rashad said that Trevor was the one who asked to get together."

"Tell me again how this Trevor knew Rashad."

"They'd been together for a short time when Rashad was in college and Trevor was working at a business supply store over by the U. According to Rashad, it was nothing serious. When Trevor was arrested for holding up a 7-Eleven with a loaded twenty-two, Rashad walked away. Trevor was tried and sent to prison. It was his first offense, so he served, as I recall, maybe a couple years. Rashad knew Trevor was a liar, and that he occasionally stole from people—even friends—to make ends meet. After Trevor got out, he'd occasionally hit Rashad up for a loan. Rashad felt sorry for him, so he'd give him something and send him on his way. He thought of him as a hard-luck case.

"When they met at the condo a few weeks before Gideon's murder, Rashad said that Trevor looked better than he had in years. But he was so talkative, almost crazy upbeat, that Rashad figured he was on something. Trevor eventually blurted out that he wanted to get back with Rashad. He painted this word-salad picture of a rosy future together. Before Rashad could shove him out the door, Gideon came home. Rashad began to explain who Trevor was and what he was doing there, but as he did, Trevor threw his arm around Rashad and said they loved each other and were getting back together."

"That must have gone over well," said Jane.

"Rashad finally convinced him to leave. There were a few heated words, but Gideon eventually said he believed Rashad and the matter was dropped."

"But there was no way to prove any of this," said Jane.

"None. It was Rashad's word against Trevor's."

"Did you put Rashad on the stand to tell his side of the story?"

"I advised against it, but, yes, he did take the stand. He's an intelligent, articulate man, but he was no match for the prosecutor. The woman carved him to pieces. I tried my best to rehabilitate him, but the damage was done." Jane's father folded his arms and looked down into his coffee mug. "You asked if I thought Rashad was guilty. I could be wrong, of course, but in my gut, I never did. The fact that Trevor came forward at the last minute—when the trial seemed like it could go either way, when the prosecution's slam dunk didn't look quite so certain—well, let's just say it was too convenient for me."

"You think someone pressured Trevor to testify?"

"That was my theory at the time, but I didn't know who. Sherwin May's PI has apparently come up with a possibility. If we decide to take this on, I'd need you to go talk to Trevor, get the full story. One last point: If you work on this with me, it would all be pro bono."

The mystery had already taken root inside her. She wasn't about to let it go until she had some kind of resolution. "I'm in."

Her dad smiled. "Good. Better go get a notebook. We need to start making a list."

9

Dragging a hand lazily through her hair, Marlo glanced at her watch before snuggling close to George. "Wake up, sleeping beauty," she whispered.

He turned on his back and yawned. "What time is it?"

"Almost eleven."

"I'm staying in bed until at least noon." He shut his eyes.

"You came to bed late last night."

"Did I?"

"Where were you?"

Another yawn. "Watching TV. And then I went up to the roof deck to smoke my pipe."

After moving in, she'd proposed that there should be no smoking in the condo. George had agreed, though she sensed he wasn't entirely happy about it.

"Beautiful night," he said, scratching his chest through his undershirt. "A full moon."

If she hadn't taken that sleeping pill, she could have gone up with him. But as George had pointed out last night, if she didn't take one of her magic tablets, it was unlikely she'd ever get to sleep.

For the last couple of days, Marlo had been toying with the idea of telling him she'd seen a psychic. She wouldn't mention what had motivated her decision, at least not right away. Still, the charlatan's vision of her future had upset her and she needed to talk to someone about it. The problem was, George probably wasn't the right "someone."

Marlo could easily predict his reaction. He'd tell her she'd wasted her time and money, that she was silly to believe in fantasyland crap like that. He would, as usual, allow that humans could be deeply silly and still walk upright. He would end his screed, as he often did when they entered this sort of territory, by announcing that he didn't believe in religion or ghosts, numerology or alien abduction. She'd asked him once what he did believe in, and he'd replied, "A chicken sandwich and a glass of scotch." She had to agree. It was hard to be cynical about food.

"I'm going downstairs," she said.

"Have a wonderful trip." Flipping on his side, he added, "Oh, I forgot: Chuck called last night. He's already in town. Booked himself a hotel room for the night. He wanted to know if he could come to stay a few days early."

Marlo padded to the door, hands in the pockets of her robe. "Like today?"

"Like today. I told him it was all right with me as long as it wasn't early."

"I wonder why the change in plans."

"He may have mentioned it, but I'm too sleepy to remember." He began to mock snore.

On her way down the open stairway, her stomach growled. She

hoped there might be some leftover popcorn. It was a favorite breakfast of hers, one that had sustained her through college and beyond. But when she saw the empty bowl on the counter, she knew she had to look elsewhere.

Digging through the pantry shelves, she found a package of instant oatmeal pushed behind a bag of dry pasta. Oatmeal with apples. And cinnamon. She popped it into the microwave and then remembered she had to remove the cover, dump in some water, and stir it first. Bother. Once that was done and it was heating on high—she detested waiting for food, especially when it was labeled "instant"—she filled up the electric kettle and set it on its base to heat. The next decision was coffee or tea. She preferred real coffee, not instant, so the question was moot. Taking down the wooden tea chest, the one George had given her on her last birthday, she was faced with ten slots crammed with teabags. She sighed and lifted a hand to her hip. It was simply too early for all this decisive action.

Before the microwave dinged and the kettle boiled, the security buzzer alerted her that someone was down in the lobby. Had to be Chuck. Picking up the phone, she said, "Yes?"

"Hi, Cousin. It's me."

She wasn't dressed, but she was reasonably well-covered in plaid flannel. "I'll buzz you in."

Marlo spooned oatmeal into her mouth as she waited in the hallway for the elevator doors to open. When they did, Chuck stepped off, his brown hair now a pointed pompadour with shaved sides. She groaned internally, thinking how untrendy the trendy haircut made him look. More Hitler Youth than Abercrombie & Fitch. Of course, she was more Lane Bryant than she was Ann Taylor, so who was she to cast stones.

Chuck bared his blazingly white teeth as he dragged two rolling suitcases toward her. "Thanks for letting me come early."

She held the door open for him. "I made tea," she said brightly. She didn't offer him oatmeal because she wasn't sure there was another instant cup in the pantry.

He removed his coat and scarf and tossed them over a chair. "You look wonderful," he said, squeezing her arms.

Little lies were necessary to grease social interaction. She'd put on a good twenty pounds since she'd last seen him. She smiled, her eyes rising to his pointed pompadour. "You look wonderful, too."

"Thank you. Where's George?"

"Still asleep. He works such long hours that I didn't want to wake him."

"Really? Last time I saw him, he wasn't working at all."

Her eyes lost some of their brightness and her lip curled, nothing someone as socially inept as Chuck would notice.

Marlo had never really liked her cousin. He'd been in and out of her life when they were kids. His mother was her dad's older sister, a woman whose voice sounded like it was being squeezed through a tiny electronic megaphone. Chuck's honking vocalizations were only marginally less screechy. The condo was spacious. Marlo figured she could lose Chuck in the square footage while he was a houseguest. Now that he was here, she could see it wasn't going to be so easy.

"I'll bring the teapot into the living room."

"Wonderful," he said, rubbing his hands together.

"How come you guys decided to leave Fort Lauderdale?" she asked, returning to the kitchen as he made himself comfortable on the couch. "I thought you loved it there."

"I do," said Chuck. "Amy can't stand the heat."

"She prefers the frozen tundra?" In Marlo's opinion, the only difference between Minnesota and Siberia was the occasional gulag. Minnesota didn't have any. Yet.

"She's from Bemidji," offered Chuck.

"Ah," said Marlo. Case closed. She carried a tray into the living room and set it on the coffee table. "Why don't you pour?" she said, dropping down heavily on a chair. There was no reason she had to do everything. "So," she continued, "you're looking for a new job."

"I've got five interviews lined up."

"I'm sure my dad gave you a glowing letter of recommendation."

"Oh, yes," he said, handing her a cup.

"Refresh my memory. Why did you leave the firm?"

"Oh, you know. I needed a change."

"Uh huh." She'd gleaned, mostly from her father's body language, that there might be a bit more to it than that, but she had no idea what the problems were, just that Chuck had made a hasty exit. Maybe she'd get the details out of him now that he was her captive.

Chuck smiled over the rim of his cup. "Bought this luxury cabin cruiser last year. A small yacht, really. I'm having it shipped to Minnesota. I'll need to find a marina somewhere close. You know any?"

"Um, no," she said flatly, completely uninterested in the topic. "I don't travel in the company of people who need marinas."

"I just need a slip. This thing is a total beauty, Mar. You should see it."

"How can you afford a luxury cabin cruiser?"

He laughed. "You sound like Amy." He went on to describe all the places he'd taken it, the fishing he'd done, the kind of motor it had, the leather this and decorator that.

"Sounds like a floating palace."

"Oh, yeah," he said, lowering his voice. The gleam in his eye suggested that it was used for more than family outings.

It had never occurred to her before that Chuck might be unfaithful. He was such a schlub, such a tedious, awkward, sweaty little man, that she couldn't imagine anyone being attracted to him.

Chuck appeared oblivious to her scrutiny. He segued from the boat to some of his new friends, millionaires all. Marlo had forgotten about his penchant for braggadocio, as well as his ability to dominate conversations. She decided to make a subject change. "Ever gone to a psychic?"

He seemed nonplussed by the question. "Me? No. Amy did once. Before we were married. It was a fortune teller at the Renaissance fair. She wanted to know if the man she was dating was the one she was going to marry."

"Were you the man?"

"Some guy from her church. The fortune teller told her that she would definitely marry him, and that they'd live happily ever after."

Marlo played with her cup, turning it around in its saucer. "What if I told you I went to see a psychic the other day?"

It was his turn to seem bored. "Really?"

"And what if I told you she wouldn't even talk to me?"

"Why?"

"When she touched me, she said she saw darkness, evil, blood."

"Holy crap."

"Yeah."

"You think she was talking about your father?"

She'd finally captured his attention. "That's exactly what I thought. But she said the darkness wasn't just in my past, it was in my future."

He cleared his throat. "I see. Well. If someone said something like that to me, I'd run like hell."

"But it makes you wonder, doesn't it? She wouldn't even take my money."

"Honestly, Mar. You get yourself into some of the weirdest shit. Just forget about it. Put it behind you."

"You think?"

"Absolutely. As a lawyer and your cousin, that's my best advice. Now" —he craned his neck toward the kitchen—"you got anything to eat around here?"

"Sure. There's microwave popcorn in the cupboard above the Vitamix. Help yourself. Oh, and while you're cooking, make a bag for me, too."

10

On New Year's Day, the Lyme House served a special brunch until three P.M. Instead of preparing a meal at the house, Jane took Julia and her father over to the restaurant, a building that rose from the edge of Lake Harriet like a Northwoods log cathedral. The table, where they ate prime rib and Yorkshire pudding, overlooked the water, now covered in a layer of ice and snow.

Even after twelve plus hours of sleep, Julia seemed tired and out of sorts. Jane and her dad kept up a lively conversation, one that Julia checked in and out of, never entirely connecting. For Jane, it was becoming more and more difficult to navigate Julia's moods. Neither of them wanted her illness to absorb all the air in the room, and yet there were times when that's what it did. Jane's worry caused her to take Julia's physical and emotional temperature more often than necessary, which annoyed Julia and made her retreat into herself even more. They were developing a weirdly negative feedback loop, one neither of them seemed able to crawl out of.

After dropping Julia back home and then taking her father across the river to his house in Highland Park, Jane returned to the restaurant, where she spent a couple hours working quietly in her office. By five, she was up in the dining room greeting customers for the dinner meal. As she was making the rounds with the coffee pot, Cordelia loomed in the double doors, waving frantically. "Just a second," Jane mouthed. She walked over to the wait station and set the pot back on the warming plate.

Cordelia was dressed in her new Gatsby coat, a vintage, green-velvet kimono style, with three-quarter sleeves finished in brown faux fur. Her fur-lined hunting cap with ear flaps didn't fit with the rest of her ensemble, but in winter, Cordelia was never one to sacrifice comfort on the altar of fashion.

"Where's the fire?" asked Jane as she finally reached her.

"Come with me," said Cordelia, grabbing Jane's hand and dragging her toward the stairs.

"Where are we going?"

"It's a surprise."

"I don't like surprises."

"Sure you do."

Jane managed to pry her hand from Cordelia's grip as they entered the pub.

"This way," said Cordelia, leading the way to the less noisy, darker, more intimate back room.

As they approached a table near a round, open fireplace, a man stood and turned to face them.

Jane stopped dead. "Peter?"

He grinned and opened his arms wide.

"I can't believe it," she said. Rushing to him, she held on tight. "I can't believe you're here."

"Come on, you two," said Cordelia. "I need a hug, too."

They opened their arms and let her in.

After they took their seats, Jane drank in every feature of her brother's face. He looked so different than before he left. His chestnut hair, the same color as hers, was now blond, though the dark roots were visible. His beard—not quite a beard, but more than a scruff—was dark. "Your hair," she said.

"And yours," he said in mock astonishment. "You cut it so short. Is that what they call a pixie?"

"Not in this century," said Cordelia, carefully removing her hunting cap to reveal one of her favorite wigs.

"And *your* hair," said Peter, turning to her. "It's pink."

"With oodles of Roaring Twenties finger waves and an occasional bobby pin for decoration. I predict a resurgence of the style."

"Are we done talking about hair?" asked Jane. "Because if we are, and I mean, I hate to be a downer, but Sigrid called me yesterday."

Peter winced.

"She was worried about you."

Cordelia sniffed the air. "Did I miss something?"

"I called her last night when I got in," said Peter. "All marriages have rough patches. We'll work it out."

"Rough patches," repeated Cordelia, eyebrows raised.

"Promise you won't tell Dad," said Peter. "There's no use worrying him."

"Come on, you two," demanded Cordelia. "I need facts. Graphs. Position papers."

Peter scanned the menu. "It's nothing."

Jane didn't believe him, and by the look on Cordelia's face, neither did she.

"Let's order," said Peter. "I had something on the plane, and then I did a little grazing when I got to Cordelia's. . . ."

"You stayed with Cordelia last night?"

"In the Harlow bedroom, lots of pink and fluffy-white fur fabric," said Cordelia. Glancing over at him, she said, "I trust your masculinity is still intact?"

"What time did your plane get in?" asked Jane.

"Must have been around midnight. I took a cab straight to Cordelia's. She was the only one I was sure would be around on New Year's Eve."

Cordelia continued to mutter about being kept in the dark as a waiter appeared to take their order.

"I'd like a Coke," said Peter.

"Hi, David," said Jane, smiling up at him. "Just water for me."

"A White Russian," snapped Cordelia. "Make it a double. Oh, and bring us one of those monster pretzels."

"Would you like to order dinner now?" asked the waiter.

"I need more time," said Peter. "You've added a bunch of new things since I was here last."

"You'll love the pretzel," said Cordelia, flapping her napkin and tucking it into the neck of her fringed flapper dress. The mention of food had deflected her anger and improved her mood. "It's this big, soft, buttery rope of bread, perfectly browned and salted, served with mustard and an onion-bacon marmalade. To die for," she added, kissing her fingers.

Holding the menu to his chest, Peter continued, "We have a lot of catching up to do."

"How long will you be in town?" asked Jane.

"I'm pretty easy about that. The piece I was shooting in Eastern Europe is done. I don't have anything new lined up."

"You'll stay at my place," she said matter-of-factly.

"Nope," said Cordelia. "He's bunking with me."

Jane couldn't hide her disappointment. "Why?"

"I like pink bedrooms?" he offered.

"I'm giving him Octavia's car for the duration." Octavia Thorn-Lester was a stage and screen actor, Hattie's generally missing-in-action mother, and Cordelia's sister. They'd come together to create a playhouse in downtown Minneapolis, for which Octavia had purchased a home to live in when she was in town, which she rarely was. Cordelia had commandeered it and now considered it her own.

"The Maybach?" said Jane. "You think Octavia would want that ungodly expensive thing driven around in the winter with all the salt on the roads?"

Cordelia shrugged. "What's a little salt among friends?"

"Did you ask her?"

"She's at some ashram with her newest husband. No cell phones allowed."

"There's a nuclear war in your future," said Jane.

"Tut," she replied. Fluttering her eyelashes at Peter, she added, "I have a new girlfriend."

"You do?"

Her smile was pregnant with meaning. "She owns an award-winning winery in California. But enough about my sizzling love life. Let's talk some more about what you two have been keeping from me?" She glared.

Peter returned his attention to the menu as their drinks arrived.

Jane figured she'd better 'fess up about Rashad May's brother before Cordelia heard it on the radio or TV. Peter had been tangentially related to the case and had testified at the trial, so he might have an interest in it, too. She briefly explained that Sherwin May believed he'd uncovered new information that would exonerate his brother. She was a little surprised when Peter's posture stiffened.

Hearing the news, Cordelia erupted with joy, nearly leaping out of her chair. "I knew it, I knew it, I knew it. Rashad is innocent. I've said it all along. I still talk to him a few times a month, you know. I thought he'd win the last appeal, but—"

"Remind me how you met him," said Jane.

"Community theater. The NordEast Players. I was asked to direct one of their plays just after the turn of the century, and being the generous person that I am with no free time at all, I said yes. I cast him in the lead. He was a natural. I told him he should quit his day job and come join the repertory troupe at the Allen Grimby. In a moment of sanity, he declined."

"And you?" said Jane, turning to her brother.

"Met him at one of Cordelia's poker nights."

"Ah, I remember those," said Cordelia, her voice growing wistful. She brightened when the pretzel arrived. "Once I left my loft and moved into Thornfield Hall, they became a thing of the past." She pulled off a hunk of bread, slathered it with mustard, and popped it into her mouth. Holding up the White Russian, she said, "My three favorite food groups: Salt, sugar, and alcohol."

"And Dad's taken the case again?" asked Peter.

"If we can verify what Rashad's brother uncovered, then yes, he's on board."

"You had dinner with Rashad that long ago, fateful night," continued Cordelia, pushing the pretzel plate toward him. "I mean, what a freakin' coincidence, right?"

"Yeah. Bizarre."

"Do you remember the dinner?" asked Jane. "What you talked about? What kind of mood he was in?"

Peter shrugged. "He seemed normal. He didn't indicate that he was about to go home and bludgeon his husband to death, if that's what you're asking. The whole thing never made any sense to me."

"Well," said Cordelia, ripping off another hunk of pretzel, "Never fear. I will help you get to the bottom of it, Janey. You tell your dad that the legendary Cordelia M. Thorn is *on the case*."

Jane and her brother exchanged glances.

"He'll be so glad to hear it," said Jane.

"I know," said Cordelia matter-of-factly, closing her eyes and chewing.

11

Peter was glad he'd decided to stay with Cordelia. After his conversation last night with his sister, he realized he had things he needed to do and didn't want Jane pressing him for explanations about how he spent his time. He also didn't want her tagging along.

Rising late on Monday morning, he dressed and found his way downstairs. The house was a hive of activity, with members of the catering crew cleaning up the mess from the New Year's Eve party.

Once in the kitchen, he poured himself a bowl of cereal and milk, grabbed a blueberry yoghurt from the refrigerator, and entered the breakfast room, where he found Hattie halfway through a slice of apple pie as she read from a magazine.

"What's the magazine?" he asked.

"*World Archeology*. It's super interesting."

With her springy blond curls, dimples, and serious brain power, she was a fascinating kid. "Looks like you're having dessert for breakfast," he added, grinning as he sat down across from her.

"Want to compare the amount of sugar in that cereal and yoghurt with my pie? Bet there's not much difference. Most people eat the equivalent of dessert for breakfast. I'm just more honest about it."

"Okay." So, she'd developed a bit of an edge since the last time he'd talked to her. "But . . . I mean . . . they put extra vitamins in the cereal."

"Uh huh." She didn't seem impressed.

"Where's your aunt?"

"Asleep. She's not an early riser."

"No school today?"

"It's Christmas break. I'm off for the rest of the week."

Peter asked what her plans were for the day. She responded that it would probably be a "home day," unless she could convince her aunt to take her somewhere—like the science museum. She said she adored spending time there and asked if he'd like to go. He could see the eagerness in her eyes and felt bad that he couldn't say yes.

"Look," he said, removing the top of the yoghurt carton, "I promise I'll take you before I go back home. Deal?"

"Deal," she said. She chewed her pie and studied him. "You know, what I'd really like is to visit the science museum in Chicago. Don't suppose you're interested in a road trip."

In so many ways, Hattie was nothing like her aunt, and yet she had a similar kind of determination. "Let me give it some thought."

"I also want to join the Planetary Society." She flicked her eyes to him and then back to the pie. "They have this really cool magazine called *The Planetary Report*."

"How much does it cost?"

"Fifty bucks. That's the beginning level."

Fifty dollars was a lot less than it would cost him to take her to Chicago. "I might be able to swing that."

"Really?" Her face brightened. "I'll find the information."

Peter figured he'd better finish his breakfast before she convinced him to buy her a spaceship. Cordelia had left the keys to Octavia's car on the kitchen counter. He ate quickly, kissed Hattie on top of her head, and was out the door.

The three-stall garage was at the rear of the mansion. Seeing the Maybach sitting there, cold and sleek in the dim light, he was of two minds. He was terrified that he was about to scratch the leather interior or put a ding in the perfect white paint. Cordelia's sister wouldn't be happy to learn that her monument to extravagance had been offered up as temporary wheels. If he, or the winter weather, did anything to alter its perfection, he was certain Octavia would chase him across the universe seeking revenge. On the other hand, the idea of driving a Mercedes-Maybach S600 and pretending, at least for a few days, that it was his, was too much to resist.

Driving north on Lyndale Avenue toward downtown Minneapolis, Peter was glad for the sunny morning and the dry streets. Under normal circumstances, he would've had little reason to visit the J.H. Chenoweth Gallery. His problems in London continued to dominate his thoughts. Still, now that he'd learned from his sister that the conviction of Rashad May was in doubt, he had something else to worry about. The names Eli Chenoweth and Kit Lipton conjured up chaotic memories of the months before Peter had packed up his family and fled to South America. That time was all so mixed up, a blur that needed to be brought into focus.

As he turned onto Hennepin Avenue, heading for the North Loop, a new problem presented itself: where to park the Maybach. Leaving it on the street wasn't an option. The gallery was located on the first two floors of an early twentieth-century brownstone warehouse. The first time Peter had visited the place with Eli, the warehouse district had already begun to make a name for itself as Minneapolis's answer to New York's Soho. But at the time, the building had been pretty run down.

An ornate arcade with five deep, rounded bays fronted the street. Somewhere along the line, Eli's dad had added five dome awnings, one over each bay window. Industrial-looking galvanized metal letters above the front door advertised the business name: J.H. Chenoweth. An ancient wooden loading dock ran along the side street. Inside, one larger and two smaller gallery spaces took up the first floor, with the second floor used for office space and framing.

Recalling a private parking area in the back, Peter slowed until he spied a narrow alley, still paved with hundred-year-old bricks, that ran between two buildings. Halfway to the back, the entrance was blocked by a metal barrier arm. Peter used to park in the lot occasionally when he couldn't find a spot on the street. In all those years, the code had never changed: 1977 was the year Eli's father had opened the gallery. Easing the car next to the electronic keypad, Peter punched in the number. Sure enough, the barrier arm rose.

The double-wide doors along the loading dock were locked, so Peter made his way around to the front. Once inside, he was met by a serious-looking middle-aged man in a business suit.

"If you need any assistance, just let me know," said the man quietly. He handed Peter his card. "I'm Mason Arsenault."

"I'm here to see Eli," said Peter.

"Oh, of course. Do you have an appointment?"

"No. Is that a problem?"

"I'm not sure he's here. Let me check."

As Peter waited, staring up at a painting of a beautiful blond girl who reminded him of his daughter, Mia, he heard a familiar voice.

"Peter Lawless? Is that you?"

When he turned, a woman with insanely curly reddish-brown hair walked straight toward him, her high heels clicking against the floor.

He grinned. "Kit."

Her lips parted in a warm, toothy smile as they hugged. "I almost didn't know you."

Peter had always liked her. In fact, once upon a time he'd had a fairly serious crush on her. Kit Lipton was flirty, confident, and a great listener. She had one trait that appealed to him most of all: She didn't do moral outrage. It didn't matter how badly you'd screwed up, Kit would still be your friend.

"What are you doing here?" she asked, linking her arm through his and walking him away from the painting into one of the side galleries.

He liked the feel of her arm. "I came to see Eli. And you, of course."

"Of course," she repeated, stopping and pivoting toward him, picking a piece of lint off his jacket. "He's upstairs." Studying him for a moment more, she added, "You're even more handsome now than you were four years ago."

"Right."

"Still the same old Peter. You don't believe me when I compliment you." She cocked her head. "I like the new look. It suits you."

She wore a chic, gauzy red-print jumpsuit. Maybe it wasn't chic, not by rich people's standards, but Kit made all her clothes seem sophisticated just by the way she wore them. Her shoulders were bare, the jumpsuit held up by thin straps. He didn't know all the words for women's fashion, but figured the outfit had to be more expensive than what she used to wear. Back in the day. Back when she sat behind an elegant antique desk toward the rear of the main gallery in her thrift-store clothing, looking like a bold piece of art herself, the official greeter/receptionist. Kit hadn't known a lot about the art world when Eli had hired her. After a year of steady employment, John Henry—Eli's dad—offered to pay for her to audit art history classes at the university, something she agreed to with enthusiasm.

As they were talking, Peter caught sight of another man coming into the gallery. It took him a moment to realize who it was. Eli had always been thin, but now seemed almost gaunt. Back in college, he'd been a guy who'd managed to look sensitive and bookish even when sweating through a game of pickup football. He wasn't handsome, and yet his dark hair, which always seemed to part in the middle no matter what he did, made him seem younger than he was. His look also suggested a man out of time, one who belonged to the early years of the last century.

Before Eli had a chance to greet Peter, his dad came around the corner into the side gallery. Except for the new wrinkles and a bit more gray hair, John Henry hadn't changed much. Both father and son had long, narrow faces with high foreheads. While Eli had always been searching for a good look, John Henry had found his long ago. He wore his hair long, sometimes in a ponytail, sometimes hanging loose, and he always sported a perfectly clipped beard. In the last few years he'd developed a minor paunch.

"Why, Peter Lawless," said John Henry. "What a surprise." He walked over to pump Peter's hand. "How are you?"

"Still slugging away."

"Good to know. Last I heard, you'd moved your family abroad."

"We're in London," said Peter.

"Really," John Henry said, his smile amping to high beam. "So many terrific art venues. Have you visited the Serpentine Galleries?"

"Once," said Peter. As they continued to talk, Peter took in John Henry's signature pastel suit and striped bow tie. The guy was a real character. He was also passionate about art and, unlike many of the businessmen Peter had known, never seemed to be only about money.

"I'm sorry to interrupt your reunion," said John Henry turning to Kit, "but you need to call Russ Carlson back. He's one of the head cephalopods over at the college of art and design."

Head cephalopods was the way John Henry always referred to people in authority.

"If you'll excuse me," said Kit, glancing at Eli, then Peter.

John Henry walked her out, a hand pressed to her back.

"Interesting," said Peter, watching them walk away. "Kit's talking to head cephalopods these days?"

"Oh, yeah," said Eli. "She's really risen in the ranks." He shoved his hands into his pockets. "So, are you back to stay?"

"Just visiting family for New Year's."

"Ah. Sigrid and Mia with you?"

"No, just me."

He nodded and smiled. "How long will you be in town?"

"Not sure. I was hoping we could all get together for coffee or a meal. You know, catch up."

Eli glanced at his watch. "I wish I had more time. Look, why don't you come over to my place tonight for dinner?"

"You and Kit still living in that old duplex?"

71

The question seemed to unsettle Eli. "You remember where my dad lives? I'm staying in that small house near the pond at the rear of the property, the one my uncle built. You remember it, right? We played strip poker there once, with Tina Langdon and Sara Clark."

"How could I forget?"

"How does six thirty sound?"

"What can I bring?"

"Just yourself. I, ah——" He pulled on his ear. "I don't drink anymore. Or do drugs. I finally got clean."

"Me too," said Peter.

"We've got a lot to talk about. Hope we can figure out a way to tell the truth without getting high."

"Did we ever tell the truth when we were high?"

"Good point, man. See you tonight."

12

Jane left the restaurant around noon and drove downtown. After parking her truck in a ramp, she took the elevator up to the fifteenth floor of the IDS Tower and was ushered into a sleek, modern conference room at the law offices of Cantrell & Diaz. Four years before, "Wise" had been the first name on the masthead. She'd called ahead for an appointment with Andrew Cantrell, a senior partner and one of Gideon Wise's closest friends. She mentioned up front that she was working with her father, Raymond Lawless, on the possibility of reopening the investigation into the Wise murder case, hoping that it might pique Cantrell's interest and get him to agree to the meeting. He had agreed, and so here she was, drumming her fingers on the polished wood table, thinking through the questions she wanted to ask.

Jane's father had driven to Stillwater that morning to visit Rashad at the state prison. She'd been hoping to accompany him, but learned it would take time to jump through all the legal hoops necessary to make that happen. Her dad had called her after the meeting to say that Rashad looked good and was elated at the prospect of getting another chance to prove his innocence.

As the minutes ticked by with no Cantrell, Jane's thoughts turned once again to her brother. After their dinner last night, it seemed clear that he wanted his space while he was in town. Before he'd left the restaurant with Cordelia, she'd made him promise to contact their dad today. She wanted to be there to see the joy on her dad's face when Peter appeared, but decided not to push it. Something she couldn't quite put her finger on still lingered between them. She'd hoped that, in the time they'd been apart, whatever it was would have faded. It hadn't. The ease they'd once shared had been replaced by a kind of tight wariness.

Standing as the door opened, Jane came face-to-face with Andrew Cantrell. She'd searched the internet last night until she found a picture of him. Standing before him now, she realized that the photo was taken years, if not decades, ago. His black hair had turned gray. His standard, totally forgettable, businessman glasses had morphed into an eccentric, round, black-rimmed pair.

They shook hands and sat down. Cantrell exuded a kind of kinetic energy. He peppered Jane with questions, wanting to know what new information had been found, if it really seemed plausible that Rashad May hadn't been Gideon's killer. Once satisfied that the meeting wasn't a complete waste of his time, he sat back and asked how he could help.

"I'm trying to get a handle on what was going on in Gideon's life before he died."

"Looking for other potential suspects," said Cantrell. "I'm not a criminal lawyer, but yeah, I get that. But are you saying you don't think the police did their investigation properly?"

"Did anyone ever come here to talk to you about Gideon's law practice?"

He hesitated. "No."

"Could they have talked to someone other than you?"

"They might have, but I would've heard about it."

Jane felt she'd made her point. Removing a notepad from her pocket, she began with a broad question. "Do you have any thoughts on Gideon's life around that time? Were there any particular issues?"

He pushed his chair back from the table so he could cross his legs. "There were always issues with Gideon. He was a brilliant man, but as with most brilliant men, he could be difficult. He had a temper, and he didn't suffer fools. As I recall, his daughter had been taking a toll on his peace of mind in the months before his death. She was determined to marry a man just a few years younger than Gideon. He opposed it. Got pretty heated, from what he told me. Have you met Marlo?"

Jane shook her head.

A smile played at his lips. "The phrase 'bitch on wheels' comes to mind." He raised his eyes to Jane, trying to gauge her response. "Don't get me wrong. She's incredibly talented and isn't afraid of hard work, as long as it's something that interests her. There were times, mainly when she was in college, when I thought she saw Gideon primarily as a bank. Of course, I could say the same about my two sons. Gideon and Marlo loved each other fiercely. Never any doubt about that. She owns her own business, you know. Quite the entrepreneur." His eyes drifted to the ceiling lights. "A greeting card company, I believe. She wanted Gideon to invest."

"Did he?"

"I don't think so, though I'm not one hundred percent sure. It was moot after Gideon died. She inherited his estate."

Jane scratched a few notes. "Tell me more about Marlo's boyfriend."

"George, yes. Can't recall his last name. I've only met him a couple of times, and it was a few years back, but I have to say he seemed rather lost to me. Didn't have a job. That was a big issue for Gideon. I don't think it was a matter of the two of them not getting along. Gideon simply felt he was unsuitable."

"So there was no bad blood?"

"Not that I'm aware of."

It seemed to Jane that if Marlo was a "bitch on wheels," Gideon had a temper, and the boyfriend was the focus of a serious disagreement between the two, further investigation was warranted. "What about Gideon's relationship with Rashad?"

"It was good, as far as I know. My wife and I would socialize with them occasionally. Dinner parties, that sort of thing. They always seemed happy together."

"What about Gideon's work life here at the firm?"

"Oh, you know. There are always issues when it comes to corporate litigation."

"Did he have any clients who might have had it in for him?"

Cantrell thought about it. "Not that I knew about. If he was being harassed, threatened, or targeted, he would have said something. We have people who handle things like that. I won't say it doesn't happen, but it's rare."

"What about here in the office?"

"Oh," he said with a sigh, "there's always office politics. But Gideon was well-liked. He was a respected leader."

It struck her for the first time that Cantrell might not be telling her everything. "Nobody was angry at him?"

"Nothing that rose to the level you're talking about."

Jane took another tack. "Did anyone get fired around that time?"

His eyes locked on hers as he considered the question. "Now that you mention it, yes, we did have a problem with one man. I don't know the details because Gideon was intent on keeping them private. He let Chuck go a few months before he died."

"Chuck?"

"Charles Atchison. Gideon's nephew. He'd worked here for, oh, maybe five years. Gideon hired him. And he was the one who fired him."

"Must have been some hard feelings about that."

"Yes, I'm sure there were."

"What was the stated reason for his firing?"

Cantrell used his cell to make a call. "Brett, find Chuck Atchison's termination papers and bring them to me in conference room C."

"What did you personally think of Chuck Atchison?" asked Jane. She'd written his name on the notepad and underlined it three times.

He shrugged. "He didn't distinguish himself in any way that I can remember. Other than his ego." He smiled. "A systemic problem with lawyers."

"Was he married? Did he have a family?"

"I have no memory of ever meeting his wife. No idea about children."

Jane asked if Cantrell had talked to Gideon on the day he died.

"I did," he said, gazing out the window. "I was on my way to a meeting, so we walked out together. He'd been to the dentist earlier in the day and his tooth was killing him, which was why he left early. He was aggravated, in pain, but other than that, he seemed normal."

Jane asked a few more questions until the assistant arrived with a file folder.

Cantrell thanked him and, as the young man left the conference room, opened the folder. "Let's see," he said, adjusting his glasses as he ran a finger down the first page. "All it says here is low production. Meaning not enough billable hours."

"That's a reason for termination?"

"Of course. We're not a philanthropy. I will say, when something like this happens, it's often a matter that other lawyers in the firm aren't willing to work with him."

"Because . . . ?"

"Well, all law firms have their little fiefdoms. But generally speaking, it's because the work product is lacking in some way."

"Meaning Chuck wasn't very good at his job?"

"That would be the most likely explanation."

Jane tapped the tip of her pen against the notepad. "Is there anyone else at the firm who might have more details about the firing?"

"Gideon's secretary would be your best bet. Let me speak with her. If she's willing to talk to you, I'll have her call."

"That would be wonderful," said Jane.

Cantrell rose from his chair. Jane assumed the meeting was over.

"One last question," she asked. "Do you know what happened to Chuck Atchison? Where he went after he left your firm?"

"No idea. You might contact Gideon's daughter. She lives in Gideon's midtown condo. I can get you the address if you need it. Since she and Chuck are cousins, she'd likely have more information."

Marlo Wise was already on Jane's list. This was one more reason to contact her.

13

Peter spent a couple hours with his father late in the afternoon. There were so many things he wanted to tell him, but couldn't. He was too ashamed. He steeled himself for his dad's questions, trying his best to make his responses sound casual. Yes, Sigrid was good. Yes, she loved her new job. Mia, his daughter, was deaf, so they spoke at some length about deaf culture in England, eventually moving on to the last documentary Peter had filmed in Poland and Estonia. The conversation was a tightrope walk. When his dad failed to show any signs that he'd caught on, that he understood his son wasn't being completely candid, Peter registered silent relief.

As he stood in his dad's office, putting on his coat, he screwed up his courage and brought up the subject of the money his father had loaned him before he left for Brazil. He wasn't in a position to pay it back and said so, but he also wanted to let his father know that he hadn't forgotten.

"Don't worry about it," his dad had said, giving him a parting hug. "Consider it a gift."

Peter wasn't a weeper, but the comment made tears well in his eyes. He hoped that one day, he could be as generous with his daughter. The truth was, Peter ached to be strong and decent. Like his father. Like his sister. But when it came right down to it, he wasn't sure he had it in him.

As Peter drove down 35W toward Eli's parents' house in Apple Valley, his phone rang. He fished it out of his shirt pocket and saw that it was Sigrid. "Not now," he whispered. "Not yet."

Peter only vaguely remembered the house in question. He knew it was a sixties rambler, one that sat on several acres. There was a small, weedy pond a few hundred feet from the smaller house, the one Eli was living in. That house sat on the far side of a rise, hidden from the view of the main house. Peter was glad he'd jotted down the address before he left the gallery. As he drove along a dark country highway, he searched the reflective numbers on the mailboxes whizzing past, slowing as he reached the one he was looking for.

Turning in on a narrow paved road bordered by landscape lights, he continued to the driveway. The main house—one story, tan-and-brown siding, with a two-stall garage on one end—was as ugly as he remembered it. As he got out of the Maybach, locking the door behind him, he looked around for the graveled road to Eli's place. Thankfully, it had been partially shoveled. He could see tire tracks in the snow, which probably meant Eli had carved out a space to park his truck. As he came over the hill, he stopped for a moment. Even thirty yards away, the small house, blazing with light, looked surprisingly inviting.

It was a one-story wood-frame building that Eli's uncle had built after he lost the job he'd been working at for most of his life. If

Peter recalled correctly, the uncle, Eli's mother's brother, had suffered from depression. Allowing him to live on the property had been a kindness, though one that had been short-lived. The uncle had hanged himself from a tree down by the pond a few years after he'd moved in. Eli confided the story to Peter one night as they killed nearly an entire bottle of rum. At the time, they shared a four bedroom dump near the university with two other students. That had been Peter's junior year. Eli was a year ahead of him, the quiet dude you could always go to when you needed weed.

Back then, Eli had been an enigma to Peter. If left to his own devices, he would happily tinker on a car engine, sweating through a sweltering summer afternoon as he drank his way through a six-pack. Just as easily, he could spend an afternoon with his nose in a book. Sometimes, when the mood struck, he'd dig out his .22 and take off for some gun range. He was definitely a loner, although after he had a few drinks in him, he could become the life of the party. When he had to work at the gallery, he changed —turned into Mr. Sophistication, as Peter called it. His voice would even change, grow quieter and deepen.

Peter remembered the first time he'd seen Eli's bedroom closet. The left half held three perfectly pressed suits and half a dozen dress shirts. The right half was stuffed haphazardly with sweats, shorts, faded jeans, and wrinkled clothes of one form or another. Flip-flops, hiking boots and athletic shoes all tumbled together on the floor underneath the chaos. On the other side was a single pair of perfectly polished wing tips. It was like the guy had two personalities, two warring sides vying for dominance.

With his breath visible in the cold night air, Peter knocked on the front door. Eli appeared a few seconds later, dressed in jeans and a Minnesota Vikings jersey.

"Come in," he said, helping Peter off with his coat. "Did you have a hard time finding Dad's house?"

"GPS app," said Peter, waving his cell phone. Glancing around, he was surprised by what he saw. "This is so much nicer than I remember it." The brown paneling had been painted white, the linoleum flooring replaced by an oatmeal-colored Berber carpet.

Eli stepped behind a counter in the kitchen and returned to cutting up a cucumber. "Look around if you want. I've updated a lot of stuff. Bought new furniture. Fixed the plumbing."

To Peter's right was a remarkably spacious living room, complete with couch, small coffee table, flat-screen TV, and two comfortable-looking chairs.

As he was about to move into a hallway, he noticed something white, gray, and furry wedged behind a couch cushion. "Do you have a cat?"

"Yes and no. I rescued her the other night. She was cold and frightened and very hungry."

"What's her name?"

"She had a tag on her. 'My name is Charlotte.' She answers to it—sort of. When I called her into my bed this morning she actually came. No use changing it. I'm going to put her up for adoption on Craigslist when I get a chance."

"Can't keep her?"

"Well, I could, but I think she could do better than me. I'm not around much."

Peter watched the cat patrol the couch, her white paws looking like socks. "She seems pretty happy here."

"She loves to burrow into blankets. I always have cat litter in my trunk in the winter, in case I get stuck in the snow, so making her a litter box was pretty easy. Had to give her a bath—she was really dirty. She didn't like that much, but I think she's forgiven me because she sat on my chest for a while before I left for work this morning. I have an appointment for her at a vet tomorrow. I just need to know she's okay before she moves on."

The cat regarded Peter with her bright coppery eyes. "I think she may be a British shorthair. If she is, she'll grow to be a lot chunkier." He watched her for a few seconds, then walked over to a small, round table, already set with plates, glasses, and silver-ware. "You don't mind living so close to your dad?"

Eli raised his eyes and looked straight ahead. "Not really."

"That's cool. Hey, it smells wonderful in here. What's for dinner?"

"Stuffed manicotti and a salad."

"Where's your other half?"

Turning his back to Peter, Eli opened the oven door. "Kit and me, we're not together anymore."

"You're not? But I thought . . . she was at the gallery this morning."

"She still works there. I suppose you could say it's complicated." He returned to the cutting board, picking it up and brushing the cucumber slices into a wooden bowl. "I got home kind of late, so it will be a while before we eat. I made a pot of oolong. You okay with that?"

"Sure."

"Go make yourself comfortable and I'll bring it in."

Peter paused for a moment next to a narrow bookshelf. His sister always said that a bookshelf was the first thing she tried to peek at when she entered a new home. She felt it told her more about the person occupying the house than just about anything else. On the top shelf were maybe twelve books in all, extremely well-worn volumes on meditation, spirituality, and Buddhism. He slipped out one entitled *The Wisdom of Insecurity* and opened it, finding a sentence highlighted in yellow: "You do not play a sonata in order to reach the final chord, and if the meanings of things were simply in ends, composers would write nothing but finales."

Peter made a mental note to buy himself a copy.

The middle three shelves all contained paperbacks with mystery titles. *Dead By Sunset. Blood Will Out. Green River, Running Red. Portrait of a Killer.* The only one he recognized was *In Cold Blood* by Truman Capote. If he recalled correctly, the story was true, not fiction. Stepping over to one of the chairs, he sat down. He was still thinking about Kit when he noticed another paperback open on the table next to him. The title, *The Stranger Beside Me*, was familiar. Turning around and glancing into the kitchen, he saw that Eli was finishing up the salad prep but showed no signs of being done. Figuring he had some time, Peter picked up the book and read the back cover. Sure enough, it was another true story, this one about the infamous serial killer Ted Bundy. Eli's tastes in reading matter were certainly varied. No, that wasn't quite correct. He appeared to have only two interests: spirituality and, well, murder.

Eli eventually came into the room carrying a tea tray. When he saw Peter glancing through the book, he set the tray down on the coffee table. "You ever read true crime?"

"Is that what they call it?"

"It's an interest of mine."

"I'll say."

"Ah," he said, pouring tea into two porcelain Chinese teacups. "You saw my collection."

"Buddhism and mayhem?"

"I suppose that's fair, although I prefer to think of it as an exploration of two aspects of the human psyche."

"Your human psyche?"

Eli laughed as he handed Peter a cup. When he sat down, the cat watched him from the other end of the couch. Gradually, she moved closer.

"You haven't changed much," said Peter. "Still the armchair philosopher. But back to this house."

"I like it. It's all I need, all I want."

"You a Buddhist?"

"I try but mostly I fail. It's a hard way to live for someone with my past."

Peter tasted the tea. "How did that happen?"

"The Buddhism? After you left, I crashed and burned. It wasn't pretty. When my dad found out how bad it was, he sent me out to San Diego, to rehab. Paid for the whole thing. My Aunt Vera, my dad's sister, and her husband live there. They promised they'd look after me. I actually stayed for almost a year. They're Buddhists. Wonderful people. I guess I wanted what they had, so I began looking into it. Didn't take long before I was a convert."

"A year," said Peter, musing out loud. "That must have been hard on Kit."

Eli didn't reply. Instead, he dug a pack of cigarettes out of his pocket and lit up. Charlotte seemed a little startled by the flame and began mewing, her tail held high.

"I'm sorry," said Peter. "I know how much you loved her. I'm sure it was painful. You don't need to talk about it."

"No," said Eli, blowing smoke out of the side of his mouth, away from Charlotte. "It's okay. I've made my peace with it. See, Kit and my dad . . . they're married now."

Peter sat up straight, not even trying to hide his shock. "You're not serious. Your *dad?*"

"You have to understand, I was out of the picture. I didn't write because I was . . . well, so screwed up. Kit and my dad kind of . . . you know . . . bonded over their worry about me. One thing led to another and—" He shrugged.

"Jeez, man. I don't know what to say. I mean, it just seems . . . wrong." Eli's dad was nice enough, but he had way too many wrinkles to be married to someone like Kit.

"Water under the bridge," said Eli, sliding an ashtray closer. "After Mom and Dad divorced, he was terribly lonely."

"Sure, I get that, but to go after your girlfriend?"

"It wasn't like that."

"No?"

"It just happened. Nobody was trying to hurt me."

Maybe, thought Peter. Or maybe not. John Henry had never seemed predatory, and yet who knew what made people tick? "But they *live* right over there," he said, jabbing his finger toward the main house. "That's gotta be rough."

"My dad offered this place to me when I came home from rehab because he wanted me close. I appreciated that."

"I know but—"

"Kit wasn't perfect, you know," said Eli.

"I never thought she was."

"Maybe if she'd loved me a little more, she would have waited."

There it was, thought Peter. He wasn't as sanguine as he tried to make out.

"But I have to let go of thinking like that. Attachment is all about the desire to make things the way we think they should be instead of accepting them as they are. I need to develop a more expansive

86

mind." When he cracked his knuckles, the cat seemed fascinated and head-butted his fingers. "Anyway, they were married by the time I came home."

"You didn't know about it until you got back?" This just kept getting worse.

Eli sucked in another lungful of smoke. "Kit said she wanted to tell me, but she didn't know how."

Eli's feeling of betrayal must have risen into the stratosphere. In Peter's opinion, he would have needed to work up an enormous amount of Buddhist detachment to make that turn of events seem okay.

"I had to move on. There was no other choice. It took a while—almost two years—but I did. I really did."

"Meaning?"

"I met someone. Maybe it was a rebound thing. Who knows? I thought I was in love. Her name was Harper. Harper Tillman. She was pretty and smart, and she seemed to really care about me. She wasn't Kit, which was probably good. I wasn't the old Eli anymore, either."

"And?"

"It all happened kind of fast. We met and a few weeks later, she moved in. It felt good. I was beginning to see the light at the end of the tunnel."

"What did Kit think of her?"

"Kit? She liked Harper. They actually became pretty good friends."

"And your dad?"

"Dad likes everyone."

"No, I mean really."

"Well, you know him. He always did these ridiculous interviews with my girlfriends, asking them a bunch of personal questions. Kit thought it was hilarious, played along and gave him outrageous answers. Harper . . . not so much."

"Actually, I don't remember that. What kind of questions?"

"Oh, stuff about sex, about their intentions, about whether or not they were after my money."

"What money?"

Eli tapped ash into the ashtray. "Good point. Kit took the lead in helping Dad and Harper get to know each other. She'd invite us over for a meal every few weeks. Funny how people connect, you know? When the local PBS station came up in conversation one night, both Dad and Harper realized they were big fans. They loved the mysteries and the English dramas. They spent the rest of the evening talking about their favorite shows. Kit and I kept stealing glances at each other. We both thought it was pretty amusing. After that, Dad said he thought Harper was terrific."

"Did the subject of marriage ever come up between you two?" asked Peter.

Eli stubbed out the cigarette. "Yes."

"Didn't work out?"

"She died late last October."

"She . . . died?"

Eli tapped out another cigarette but didn't light it because the cat stretched her neck to sniff it. "One night I came home and she wasn't here. She usually got home before me. I wasn't worried. But then later, when she still hadn't come home or called, I started getting worried. I phoned a few friends. Nobody had seen her. In the middle of the night I started calling hospitals, emergency rooms, and in the morning, I called the police."

Peter just stared at him.

"Sometimes," he said, pressing his palms to his eyes, "I feel like I'm the kiss of death. Everything I touch—"

"What happened?"

Fighting back emotions, Eli said, "Her body was found three days later near a heavily wooded creek up by Taylors Falls. A guy had been out walking his dog. The dog was the one who found her."

"How did she die?"

"Don't ask because I can't talk about it."

"An accident?"

Eli looked away. "No." He wiped tears off his face with the arm of his sweater.

Peter waited, giving him a moment. "Did they ever find out who did it?"

He shook his head. "But I found out later about another woman who died in a similar way up near Duluth. Nobody believes me, but I think it was the work of a serial killer."

Eli's reading interests were beginning to make sense.

"I feel like I've been around a lot of death in my young life. First my uncle. That was when I was in high school, but it really affected me. Then my sister, Tori."

Peter and Eli had lost touch after college. When Peter had seen Tori Chenoweth's obituary in the local paper, he'd come to the funeral, wanting to offer his condolences. It was a heartbreaking loss. From what Peter had been able to piece together, Tori had been on vacation in Switzerland with a girlfriend, hiking up some mountain pass, when her appendix burst. By the time the friend was able help Tori down off the mountain and get her to a hospital miles from the small alpine village where they were staying, it was too late.

"Mom and Dad never recovered from Tori's loss," said Eli. As

Charlotte hunkered down next to him, he touched a match to the tip of the cigarette, inhaled deeply, then blew the match out. "I think it's the main reason they broke up. I mean, I've used since I was sixteen. Weed. Booze. Pills. Depression clearly runs in our family. If Kit hadn't been there for me, who knows? I might have ended up like my uncle."

Peter had some pressing problems of his own right around the time Tori had died, so Eli's offer of coke seemed to be, if not the answer, at least a temporary solution. Thankfully, he'd never moved on to heroin, as Eli had.

"Kit never seemed all that interested in drugs," said Peter.

Eli tipped his head back and closed his eyes, his free hand absently stroking Charlotte. "Oh, we'd smoke a bowl with friends every now and then, but no, she didn't really like drugs. In fact, sometimes I thought she was afraid of them." He tapped ash into the ashtray. "I can't talk about this stuff. It's too hard."

"I'm glad we both were able to ditch that life," said Peter. "We should celebrate it. Every day."

"Yeah," agreed Eli. "Except. Sometimes it feels like I'm holding on to my sobriety by nothing but my fingernails. You ever feel that way?"

"Every waking moment."

"All I know is," Eli continued, leaning over to pick up his teacup, "if I ever start with the heroin again, I'm a dead man."

14

George arrived home that evening with a headache. As he came in the door, he remembered their houseguest. Instantly, his headache grew worse.

Chuck, tying his robe, came out from his bedroom a bit too quickly. "You scared me," he said, smoothing his rumpled pompadour. "I thought you and Marlo were grabbing dinner and a movie tonight."

"Change of plans," said George, hanging up his coat. "Marlo had to work late. She's rolling out a new line of cards next month. A busy time for her."

"Oh, such a shame. Well." Chuck dipped his hands into his pockets. "So."

"Did I wake you?" asked George.

"Me? No. Say, where are you going?" He seemed a little frantic as George made a move toward the first-floor bathroom.

"I'm not sure that's any of your business," said George.

Chuck's smile was more of a simper. "I was just about to run myself a bath."

It didn't take an Einstein to see what was going on. "Think I'll head upstairs to change clothes," George said. "I'll be back down in a few minutes to make a start at dinner."

"You're going to cook? Tonight?"

"I like to eat in the evenings," said George. "A bad habit, I grant you, but one that's deeply ingrained."

"Funny. Yes, ha." Chuck glanced back over his shoulder toward his bedroom. "You go ahead."

"Thank you for your permission," said George. "Means a lot."

"Huh?" said Chuck. "Oh, that's another joke."

George climbed the stairs all the way to the top, counted to thirty, then walked back down, stopping halfway. He began to count again. When he got to forty-two, Chuck reappeared pushing a woman clad in only her slacks, a bra, and a coat, to the front door. He handed her some money and shoved her out.

George waited until the door was closed before he cleared his throat.

Looking up, Chuck said, "Oh, ah . . . . hi. It's you again."

"So it would seem. By the way, Charles, I live here, so you shouldn't be surprised if you catch sight of me every now and again."

"I suppose you're wondering who . . . I mean—"

"Bad boy, Charles. Naughty, naughty boy. Marlo would be so disappointed to learn how you spend your evenings when you're away from your wife."

Chuck seemed shaken by the comment. "You're going to tell her?"

"Well, let's consider that for a moment."

"Come on, George. Be reasonable. You're a man. You understand."

"I expect I do," said George, favoring Chuck with one of his most compassionate smiles. "Let's just say that from this moment on, if I ask you to do something—like, say, leave the room, shine my shoes, agree with my point of view, no matter how outrageous it may seem—you do it. No hesitation. No excuses. Do we understand each other?"

Chuck retied his bathrobe. "We do."

"Good man."

"I'm tired. Think I'll turn in early."

"Of course," said George. "Entertaining can be terribly exhausting. Sweet dreams."

15

Jane was putting away groceries in the kitchen when the teakettle began to whistle. Julia had put it on a few minutes before, saying she'd be right back to make the tea. Wondering if something was wrong, Jane turned off the burner and went upstairs to check. She looked into Julia's makeshift office first, finding it empty before heading down the hall to the bedroom. As she passed the bathroom, she stopped. Julia was standing at the sink, hands propped on either side of the basin, her head bent.

"Are you okay?" asked Jane.

"Fine."

"What are you doing?"

"What do you think? Crying. I thought I should splash some water in my face before I came back down."

Jane moved closer, gingerly placing a hand on Julia's back. "Is it the pain?"

"Someone should just shoot me."

"Stop it."

Julia's head rose until she was looking at herself in the mirror.

She paused for a few seconds, then turned around and pulled Jane into her arms. "I had a good day," she whispered.

Jane was confused. "I'm glad."

"No, you're missing my point. A really good day. Do you realize how rare that's become? I felt almost normal."

"Well, that's—" said Jane, hoping the sentence would find a way to complete itself.

"Sometimes I think I should have the surgery. It's risky, but maybe I should take my chances. If I wait much longer, the cancer will be inoperable. Maybe it already is."

"I didn't know you were reconsidering the surgery."

"I'm not," she said, abruptly letting go. She sidestepped Jane and left the room.

Jane followed her back down into the kitchen. "Could we talk about this? I'm a little confused."

"I don't know what I'm saying half the time. The words just came out." Julia poured the water out of the kettle with a shaky hand, replaced it with fresh water, and set it on the stove to heat.

"You already put the kettle on a few minutes ago. The water was hot."

Julia ignored the comment and instead began opening and closing cupboard doors. "Where's the teapot?"

"On top of the refrigerator, where it always is."

Julia shot Jane an annoyed look. "Lose the snark, okay?" The top of the teapot rattled as she set it on the counter. "And the . . . the tea?"

Jane walked over and opened one of the lower drawers.

Julia sat down at the kitchen table and dropped her head in her hands. "This just isn't working."

"What isn't?"

"*Everything*. My whole damn life."

At the very beginning, when Julia had first moved into Jane's house, she'd discussed the various symptoms associated with her disease, things Jane needed to be prepared for. One of them was heightened anxiety. How could Julia not be anxious?

Jane sat down at the table. "I'm here."

"I know," said Julia after a few moments. "I just get a little agitated sometimes. It's not just in my mind, feels like it's in my body. You probably don't understand that. Hey? What time is it?"

Jane checked her watch. "Five to eight. I thought I'd make us some dinner."

"I have a Skype call at eight."

"You do?"

"It's new. A therapy I just learned about. Wish me luck."

"Of course," said Jane, watching Julia rush out of the room. Mouse got up and trotted after her. He was doing that more and more lately, spending time with Julia when she sequestered herself in her office. When the teakettle whistled again, Jane turned off the burner. Opening the freezer, she took out a bottle of vodka and poured herself a shot. She downed it in one swallow, grimacing at the burn. When she returned to the table, Gimlet hopped into her lap. "Oh, little one," she said, lifting her up to kiss her muzzle. While they were communing, her cell phone rang. Tucking Gimlet against her chest, she answered.

A familiar voice said, "I have an utterly grand idea."

"Cordelia?"

"Let me bring over dinner."

"Aren't you at the theater?"

"I was. Had to take Hattie over to Hazel's house."

"She has a friend named Hazel? One who isn't in her eighties?"

"Don't be ageist. The name's coming back. Hattie and Hazel and Jabril, a boy who lives a couple blocks away, are best buds. They bonded over geology. Can you believe it? Bonding over *dirt*? Don't quote me, but I believe they're the official science mafia at their school."

"That sounds pleasant."

"So what about it? Can I tempt you?"

"With what?" Jane's stomach had been growling for the last hour, and beyond that, she needed to change gears, not spend the rest of evening overanalyzing what had just happened with Julia.

"A surprise. Will the good doctor be joining us?"

"Not right away. She's Skype-ing up in her office."

"More food for us if we eat fast. While we're eating, we can discuss Rashad's case. Peace, Janey. Out." She cut the line.

"Cordelia? Are you there?" She returned her attention to the bottle of vodka, but before she could fill the shot glass a second time, the front bell chimed.

"Food delivery," cried Cordelia as Jane opened the front door. She rattled several white sacks above her head as she swept inside.

"You already bought it? Am I that easy to convince?"

"Who isn't in the mood for the Rainbow's lemongrass meatballs? Just think of me as your personal Grubhub." Instead of her usual fur-lined cap with the requisite ear flaps, she'd donned a man's fedora set at a rakish angle. Reaching the dining room table, she shrugged out of her coat, revealing a vintage maroon-and-gray man's smoking jacket. Very deco. It was an extra-generous size, selected to accentuate her curvaceous girth.

Dropping her coat over the chair, Cordelia eyed Jane. "What's wrong?"

"Huh?"

"You're upset. I can read you like the directions on the back of a frozen pizza. You can talk to me about anything, you know. I am a veritable font of discretion."

Jane was grateful for the concern. "Thanks."

"I am also the reincarnation of Dear Abby, with the soul of Mister Rogers."

"I'm fine, Cordelia. Really."

"All right," she muttered. "Moving on. You have plenty of the elixir of life, I presume. Chilled and ready for *moi*?"

"I have black-cherry soda, no strawberry. You drank it all last time."

"That will do. You go get it, and I'll set up the food display."

Jane released Gimlet from her arms as she crossed back into the kitchen. She pulled the can of pop out of the fridge, grabbed herself a beer, found plates and napkins, and returned to the dining room.

"Honey walnut shrimp," said Cordelia, sweeping her hand over the containers. "Chicken in black bean sauce, a sweet vegetable curry, the egg rolls, chicken-and-chive dumplings, and, of course, the aforementioned meatballs."

They sat down and began to pass the cartons around.

"Before we begin," said Cordelia, removing the paper cover from a pair of plastic chopsticks, "have you heard from Peter today?"

"Not a word."

"Hattie had a brief sighting early this morning. That boy needs to check in once in a while. I'm not his mother, but if he's going to live under my roof, he has to obey the rules."

"Which are?"

"I'll think some up and post them on the refrigerator. Next item

98

on the agenda: Tell me what you know about his marriage. Is something amiss?"

"He hasn't talked to you about it?"

"He clammed up when I asked. Clammed up like a . . . well, like a . . . clam. Sorry, Janey. I can't always be verbally brilliant."

"I think they might be in trouble," said Jane. "I don't have details."

"Well, let's get on the horn after dinner and call Sigrid."

"It's none of our business."

"Of course it's our business. We love them. It's up to us to help."

"I mean it, Cordelia. If one of them decides to open up and tell us what's going on, and if we're *asked* for an opinion, then we give it. Otherwise, we're intruding."

"Horsefeathers. Poppycock. Total and utter baloney."

"Promise me you'll stay out of it."

Cordelia chewed a meatball and refused to commit. "Tell me what you've learned that might help Rashad. Don't leave anything out. Oh, wait." She squeezed her eyes shut and touched the tips of her fingers to her forehead. "Yes, there we are. All my little gray cells are standing at attention. You may begin."

While Jane ate, she went over every significant piece of information her father had given her. She also mentioned that she'd read the police report and was working her way through the trial transcript.

"Been there, done that," Cordelia said.

"It's all new to me," Jane said, finishing up with her visit to Cantrell & Diaz.

"So," said Cordelia, stabbing her chopstick through a chicken-and-chive dumpling, "your dad will deal with all the legal mumbo jumbo while we're supposed to sniff out the real murderer."

Jane stopped chewing.

"Right?"

Swallowing her food, Jane said, "I suppose you could put it that way. Dad seems pretty certain that Gideon knew his murderer."

"Because there was no evidence of a break-in."

"Exactly. Even though the security cameras weren't up and running in the upper stories of the Finnmark, it was still a secure building. You couldn't gain access to the condo tower unless you had a key or knew the key codes."

"And our current suspects are," said Cordelia, checking the names off on her fingers, "Chuck Atchison, Gideon's nephew and the man he fired from his law firm. His daughter, Marlo Wise. And her husband—her fiancé at the time—George Krochak. I'm sure, as I dig further—"

Jane restrained herself from rolling her eyes.

"—into the case, other possibilities will arise."

The doorbell rang.

"Maybe it's Peter," said Cordelia, leaping up.

Before opening the door, Jane checked through the peephole. She didn't recognize the middle-aged woman standing outside. "Can I help you?" she asked, keeping the screen door locked.

"Are you Jane Lawless?" asked the woman.

"Yes."

"My name's Marcia McBride. Andrew Cantrell gave me your information and asked me to contact you. I was Gideon Wise's executive secretary at Cantrell & Diaz. I was out and about tonight and thought . . . I probably should have called first. I hope I'm not coming by too late."

"Not at all," said Jane. She usually had to chase people around to get them to talk to her. This was a pleasant surprise. "Please, come in."

"I don't live far from here," said Marcia, bending and holding her hands out so Gimlet could sniff them.

Cordelia stood by the table, adjusting the belt on her smoking jacket. "I am Cordelia M. Thorn, world-renowned theater impresario." She crossed into the foyer and offered her hand.

"Oh, wow," said Marcia, her eyes growing wide. "I thought you looked familiar. I am *such* a fan. I love your theater. My husband and I have been there many times and never been disappointed."

"You're too kind," said Cordelia, her eyelashes fluttering coyly. Jane helped Marcia off with her coat.

"I'm so sorry if I've interrupted your dinner."

"We were all done," said Cordelia, offering Marcia her arm. "Why don't we adjourn to the living room? Jane, feel free to bring in the after-dinner cordials and cigars."

"She's kidding," said Jane, though Marcia seemed happy to take Cordelia's arm.

Once they were all seated—Jane and Cordelia on the couch, Marcia on the rocking chair by the fireplace—Marcia began, "I guess I was excited by the idea that I would finally get to tell someone about what happened, why Chuck Atchison was fired."

"How long have you worked at the firm?" asked Cordelia, all business now.

Marcia switched her gaze between Cordelia and Jane. "Are you both working on the case?"

"I'm a licensed P.I.," said Jane.

"And I add that extra special zing," said Cordelia. "Every endeavor in life needs that, don't you agree?"

Marcia looked uncertain.

"Another joke," said Jane. "You can speak freely. Cordelia is . . . assisting me."

"Well, cool," said Marcia. "An impresario on the case. You can't beat that."

Cordelia smiled demurely.

"Okay, so I worked for Mr. Wise for nine years. He was the best boss I ever had. Very fair."

"And Chuck Atchison?" asked Jane.

"A horrid man. A month or so before he was fired, Mr. Wise began calling him in for unscheduled meetings, usually late in the day. At the same time, all these female staffers, law clerks, paralegals, and even a few of the new associates began to parade through Mr. Wise's office. Some of them had tears in their eyes when they left. They eventually all came back and handed me a sealed envelope, which I was directed to pass on to Mr. Wise without opening. Perhaps I shouldn't have listened at the door when he finally called Atchison in for the last time, but I couldn't help myself. The conversation got really heated really fast. Mr. Wise said he had seventeen verifiable accusations of sexual harassment against Atchison. They ranged from unwanted touching to, in three instances, attempting to force women to have sex with him by telling them that if they refused, he'd see to it that they lost their jobs."

"Heavens," said Cordelia.

"He denied it, of course. Said the women were out to get him. He demanded to know who'd made the complaints. Mr. Wise refused to tell him. Instead, he fired him, right there on the spot. Said he'd keep the situation private as long as Atchison left quietly. Atchison flat-out refused, said he'd fight it, that he'd sue. It went back and forth like that for a few minutes. Eventually Mr. Wise convinced him to see reason. If the accusations became public, it would end his career."

"It should have ended," said Cordelia, "with him going to prison."

"I couldn't agree more. But it was Mr. Wise's decision. Atchison was his nephew. I'm sure that was why he let the matter go at termination with no letter of recommendation."

"The old boy network is alive and well," snarled Cordelia, "in case anyone was still wondering."

"Mr. Wise told Mr. Atchison that if he ever learned that Atchison was engaging in the same kind of behavior somewhere else, that he would personally see to it that he was disbarred. He insisted that he stay away from his daughter, Marlo. I've never seen a man look as red-faced and furious as Atchison was when he left Mr. Wise's office. A security guard went with him while he cleaned out his office, and then he was walked to his car."

"He must have hated his uncle for talking to him like that," said Jane.

Marcia gave a firm nod. "I've been told that your father is trying to reopen Mr. May's case. I hope he can. The police didn't know anything about what happened between Mr. Wise and Mr. Atchison. I thought about telling them, but in the end, I figured it was best to stay out of it. I mean, the police know what they're doing, right? But I never changed my opinion. If anyone should have been in the hot seat for Mr. Wise's murder, it was Mr. Atchison."

"Just the kind of intelligence we've been looking for," said Cordelia.

Marcia seemed pleased. "Well," she said, "I've said my piece. I should probably get home. You two have a lot of work to do."

"Before you go," said Jane, "will you answer one last question?

You saw Gideon Wise every day. Did anything else happen around that same time that stands out in your memory?"

Marcia fingered a button on her blouse. "Since you bring it up. I don't like to tell tales out of school, but there was this . . . one thing. It had nothing to do with work. I came in one morning and found Mr. Wise's door closed. He almost always kept it open."

"If you listened at the door again," said Cordelia, giving Marcia an encouraging smile, "we promise we won't think badly of you."

"Go on," said Jane.

"Well, I mean, even with the door closed, it was impossible not to hear the shouting. And then, before I knew it, the door flew open, and a man came out. He was a little bit stooped, leaning heavily on a cane. He never looked at me or said a word, just left the office. Once he was gone, Mr. Wise walked into the reception area. He seemed like he was about to say something, perhaps explain what had just happened, but instead he turned and went back into his office."

"Do you know who the man was?" asked Cordelia.

"I didn't at the time. I saw him again at Rashad May's trial. A friend pointed him out to me as George Krochak, the one who'd married Marlo Wise a few months before the trial began."

Jane sat forward. "He was leaning on a cane? Was he ill?"

"No idea."

"Do you remember anything that was said that morning? Any words or scraps of sentences?"

Marcia grew uneasy. "Mr. Wise did a lot of cursing. Name calling. I'd heard him raise his voice before, but never anything like that."

"And Mr. Krochak?" asked Jane.

"If he said anything, I couldn't hear it."

"You have no idea what prompted Mr. Wise's outburst?"

"I assumed he had some sort of business with the man that had soured. The next time I saw Mr. Wise that morning, he was in a good mood, acted as if nothing had happened."

"Is there anything else you remember that might be helpful?"

"Not really. But I'll let you know if I think of something."

"You've been immensely helpful," pronounced Cordelia.

Marcia smiled, still looking a little starstruck. "This is so amazing to meet you like this."

"It was my pleasure."

"I mean, you know so many famous people. And now . . . to learn you're a private eye. You must have an incredibly exciting life."

"I do," said Cordelia. "And wildly glamorous."

Rising from the rocking chair, her eyes still locked on Cordelia, Marcia said, "This is so cool."

Jane helped her on with her coat. Walking her into the front foyer, she said, "I really appreciate how candid you've been with us."

"I'm happy I could help." She snuck one last look at Cordelia, who was standing with her arm resting on the mantel, one hand dipped into the pocket of her smoking jacket. On her way outside, Marcia stopped and turned around. "Before I leave, let me be candid about one last thing. I never felt comfortable with the verdict at Mr. May's trial. I'd seen Mr. Wise and Mr. May together many, many times. They always seemed very much in love to me. I know things aren't always what they seem, but even so, I had a hard time buying the picture the prosecution tried to paint, that it was all an act on Mr. May's part, that his only interest was Mr. Wise's money. I hope you'll be able to get to the bottom of what really happened that night."

"I hope so, too," said Jane.

"Let me know if there's anything else I can do to help."

Cordelia appeared behind Jane, offering Marcia a solemn nod as she wiggled her fingers.

After Marcia had driven away, Jane shut the door and glanced over her shoulder. "You were a big hit."

"One does what one can. Now, Jane, dear. Didn't you forget something? My cigar? My crème de menthe?"

16

The offices, printing and distribution areas for Marlo's greeting card company, SwankyNotes, were located in a single-story warehouse complex in St. Louis Park. Marlo usually arrived by seven each morning and worked late.

As the nine A.M. hour approached, she found herself sitting at her drafting table, staring at nothing in particular. Every few minutes, she would wake out of her reverie and order herself to stop daydreaming. But the problem was, Marlo never liked being ordered around, even when she was the one doing it. She ignored her better self and kept right on thinking about George. He'd been so nice to her lately that she wondered what was going on. Last night, he'd been positively amorous. Had his feelings changed? Was it possible to marry and then fall in love? Nothing about their marriage had been normal, so why change now?

The intercom buzzed. "Marlo?" came a woman's voice. "You got a visitor."

Marlo checked her appointments. She had nothing on the calendar. "Who is it? What's it about?"

"I'm quoting here. 'Something personal.'"

"Oh, all right. Send him in. And hey, find out when I can do that press check. Jason said he'd have it ready by nine."

"Will do."

Margo climbed down off the stool and moved over to her desk. Before she sat down, a woman appeared in the doorway. She was middle-aged and attractive, with short, wavy, brown hair and mirrored aviator shades, dressed in jeans and a navy peacoat. At five two on a tall day, Marlo was shorter than most people, and this woman was no exception. "Can I help you?" Marlo asked, trying her best to sound pleasant.

The woman introduced herself as Jane Lawless.

"Any relation to Raymond Lawless?"

Jane took a few steps into the office. "He's my father. I'm an investigator, working with him on the Rashad May case."

Marlo stopped making any attempt at morning cheer. "Well that's just peachy keen, Ms. Lawless. Turn around and get the hell out of my office."

"We have reason to believe Rashad might be innocent."

"I'm not interested in your *theories*." She sat down with a thud and began rearranging papers on her desk.

"Could I just ask you a couple of questions? Won't take more than a few minutes."

"No," said Marlo.

"It's about your cousin, Chuck Atchison."

Her head jerked up. "What about him?"

"Did you know your father fired him a few weeks before his death?"

"Who told you that?"

"Your father had seventeen written affidavits from women at the law firm accusing Mr. Atchison of sexual harassment. If you don't believe me, you can talk to his secretary, Marcia McBride."

Marlo opened her mouth and was a little nonplussed when nothing came out.

"Do you have any idea how I could get in touch with Mr. Atchison?"

"No. Yes. He's staying with me right now. Are you telling me the truth?"

"I am."

"That pig," Marlo growled under her breath.

The intercom gave another buzz. "Hey, boss, Jason said you can do the press check."

Rocketing out of her chair, Marlo said, "Walk with me." She might be short, but she took long strides. As they came through the door at the end of the hallway, a thought struck her. "Are you saying you think my cousin had something to do with my father's murder?"

"If it turns out that Rashad is innocent—and I believe he is— then the next question is who committed the murder? I'm looking for motive. I believe your cousin might have had one."

"Who else?"

"Excuse me?"

"Who else do you think had a motive? Me?" Marlo felt like she was in an Aaron Sorkin scene, walking and talking.

"I was told you and your father had been quarreling about your upcoming marriage."

Ah, the real point of the interrogation. "Of course we were quarreling. We always quarreled. Come on, you can do better than that."

"I have a few questions about your husband, George Krochak."

Marlo stopped and whirled toward her. "No, no, no. George is off limits. He had nothing to do with it. Neither of us did. Look, if your intent is to smear people just so you can muddy the waters on behalf of Rashad, then get the hell out of my sight."

"That's not my intention."

"Do you consider alibis? I was with George from four o'clock on that day. Neither of us left our townhouse until we received the call from my father's neighbor."

"What I know is that George was your alibi and you were his. Not exactly airtight. There were no security cameras at or around your townhome, so your comings and goings can't be confirmed. Did the police ever check your cell phones to verify your location?"

Marlo felt her face heat up. "It wasn't a *story*, it was the truth."

"Did they ask for your phones?"

"No."

"Did they question you? Or George? Did they ask either of you to take a lie detector test?"

"I did not murder my father, lady. Now, get the hell out of here before I call security." She didn't employ a security guard, but it sounded good.

"I'm sorry to be so direct. I know this is painful for you. If you could just give me a another minute or two—"

"*Leave*," shouted Marlo, pleased when the woman seemed startled. "And don't let the door hit your ass on the way out."

17

The bar and grill just down the street from the gallery seemed empty for a Friday afternoon, with only a few people eating while watching a hockey game on one of the flat screen TVs. Five or six more sat at the bar, content to drink their lunch. Peter had ordered himself a Coke to help kill the time. She was fifteen minutes late, which made him wonder if she'd forgotten or blown him off. Either was possible. And then, there she was, snaking her way through the tables. Kit, as usual, looked wonderful, a fresh, sunny face in the dim bar light, her clothing varying shades of cream and white.

"You didn't wear a coat," he said, standing up as she reached the booth. He gave her a quick kiss.

"The gallery is, like, a stone's throw away. I'm hardly going to freeze."

"Did you have trouble getting free? I know my invitation was kind of last minute." He sat back down, watching her slide in opposite him.

"I'm the owner's wife. If I want to take a long lunch, I take it." She opened the menu and began studying it.

"I'm still having a little trouble getting used to that."

When the waiter arrived, Kit ordered hot tea and Peter ordered another Coke.

"Yes, I hear you had dinner with Eli last night. He told me about your conversation. I'm glad you know what happened."

"It's just . . . I know how much you and Eli cared about each other."

"I did love him," she said, looking wistful, "but we had our problems."

"Oh?"

"Look, Peter." She set the menu down. "Eli is a great guy. I know you two have been friends for years, but to be honest, there were times when he scared me."

"Because of his drug addiction."

She didn't respond.

"Something else?"

"Are you sure you want to talk about this? It's all such ancient history."

"I'd like to understand. If you're willing to tell me."

She glanced at the TV above the bar. "Oh, I suppose. It's not very interesting. See, Eli really changed after his sister died. That was hard on him. And then his parents divorced. He began to use more, which you know, but it went beyond that. He would, like, enter this dark place, sometimes in the blink of an eye. The stuff he'd say when he was in one of his moods—" She shivered. "He started reading all these awful books. Things about serial killers, stalkers. Whatever was happening to him, I couldn't deal with it. I was relieved when he left for rehab in California."

"So he began reading that stuff before he went to rehab?"

"Yeah."

"I didn't know any of that," said Peter.

"Because I never said anything. Except to my dad." She looked down. "I'm lucky. I can always confide in him."

"You two still as close as ever?"

"Always. He's been living in Phoenix for the last couple of years with his second wife."

"And your mother?"

She shrugged. "I can't stand to be around her, haven't seen her in forever."

When the waiter arrived with their drinks, Kit ordered a Greek salad. Peter ordered a cheeseburger and fries.

"That's enough about me," she said, pouring hot water over the teabag. "Tell me about you."

"Talk about a boring topic."

"How's Sigrid?"

He rearranged his silverware. "She's good. Nothing much new to report."

"Eli said you'd done some time in rehab. I was glad to hear it, although it must have been hard on your family."

"It was. Especially Sigrid. But we're as solid as ever." He offered a smile.

She appraised him a bit too intensely for his liking.

"We're a boring old couple," he added, wishing she'd stop staring at him.

"Uh huh. Did you cheat on her or did she cheat on you?"

"What?"

"Tell the truth, Peter. Otherwise your nose will grow."

"I would never cheat on my wife."

"So she cheated on you."

He glanced toward the TV.

She waited until he was looking at her again and then burst out laughing. "I was fishing, turkey. You know me. You're as easy to bait as ever."

"I didn't tell you a thing."

"Sure you did. Does your daughter know?"

"Can we talk about something else?"

"Okay, but before we leave the topic, let me just say this: I've always thought you were a great guy. A real catch. If you hadn't been married back when I first met you, I might have made a play for you myself."

That threw him. "Really?"

"We have bad timing. We're never free at the same time. Beyond that, we both seem to have a knack for getting ourselves into messy relationships."

"Yeah," he said, half smiling. And then it hit him. "You're not talking about you and John Henry."

"Of course not," she said, crossing her arms over her stomach. "He's wonderful. I couldn't be happier."

Peter had invited Kit to lunch because there'd been a question he'd wanted to put to Eli the previous night, but the moment had never seemed right. It was a tricky subject. "Look, there's something I'm hoping you can clear up for me. It's about the night Gideon Wise was murdered."

She took a sip of tea. "You heard Rashad May's brother discovered some new evidence that may exonerate him."

"Actually, both my father and my sister are working on the case."

"Seriously? Have they made any progress?"

"No idea," said Peter. He pressed on. "Look, about the drink I had that night with Rashad. You knew Eli asked me to invite him, to help him out."

"Yeah."

"He wanted a chance to talk to Gideon alone, without Rashad around. He never offered much more than that, even when I pressed him on it. He said it was personal. I mean, I did it. He was a friend and I wanted to help. And then, when I was sitting there with Rashad at the bar, you called and said Eli needed more time, so I asked Rashad to stay and have dinner with me. Now I'm beginning to wonder if I did something wrong."

"Meaning what?"

"I'm not sure," said Peter. He felt both terrible and relieved that he'd finally voiced his concern, fuzzy as it was. "Did Eli have anything to do with Gideon's murder?"

She placed her hands patiently on the table and leaned toward him. "No, Peter. Eli may have a dark mind, but not that dark. The fact is, he never even saw Gideon that night."

Peter was thrown. "He didn't? Then why did he need more time?"

She studied him. "If I tell you, I don't want Eli to know. Do we have a deal?"

"Deal," said Peter.

She took a sip of tea. "Eli was supposed to meet with Gideon that night. He wanted to talk to him privately about a painting that was about to come on the market. The artist was a man Gideon particularly liked. Eli knew Rashad had been after Gideon to stop buying so much art, and because Eli was hoping he could sell the painting to Gideon during the meeting, he didn't want Rashad around. When Eli arrived, he kept calling up on the in-house phone system, but Gideon never answered. He stuck around for a while and then called me and asked what I thought he should do. I told him to give it more time."

"But why meet with Gideon at the condo? Wouldn't it have been easier to meet at the gallery?"

Sighing, she said, "It's all pretty boring. You're sure you want to hear this?"

"Please."

"It's simple: Eli didn't want his dad to know. He'd never done anything like that before—visiting a client in his home. John Henry did it all the time, but because Eli had been screwing up so badly at work, his dad never would have allowed it."

"Why was he screwing up?"

"What do you think? Drugs. He was a mess. He figured if he could broker the deal with Gideon, his dad would be impressed with his hustle, and his growing business chops. The thing is, you know Eli. He overanalyzes everything. While he was waiting for Gideon, he started worrying he couldn't do it. That he'd make a mess. Before I knew it, he was home, walking in the front door. I'm afraid I lost it. I yelled at him, told him he was a weakling, that he needed to grow a pair. He reluctantly agreed to go back. That's when I called you and told you he needed more time."

"What happened?"

"He drove back to the condo, waited around the lobby for another fifteen minutes, but Gideon never picked up the phone. The reason Eli never wanted to talk about it with you was . . . he was totally embarrassed. He assumed Gideon had blown him off. The whole thing was such a fiasco that he just wanted to forget it. He eventually came home, went into the bedroom, and shot up. That was the end of it."

Peter leaned back. "Maybe Gideon was already dead."

"That's what I've always assumed."

"Eli didn't . . . I mean . . . he didn't have any blood on him when he came home, did he?"

"I think I would have noticed something like that, don't you?"

If what Kit said was true, and he had no reason to believe she'd lie to him, he could finally relax. "Boy, that takes a load off."

"Good. Glad I could help."

When the food arrived, Peter tucked enthusiastically into his cheeseburger. He hadn't realized how much that long-ago dinner with Rashad had been weighing on him until the weight was lifted.

Kit pulled the napkin into her lap before picking up her fork. "My dad used to make Greek food. Moussaka. Spanakopita." She pushed the arms of her sweater back.

"What's that?" asked Peter, nodding to a bruise just below her left elbow. "Looks nasty."

She pulled her sleeves back down. "It's nothing. I was carrying a tray the other day and ran into a door."

"That sounds like a made-up story."

"It does?"

"I'm kidding, Kit."

"Oh." She laughed.

"I mean, nobody's hurting you, right?"

"Hurting me?" she repeated, stabbing an olive. "First guy who tries will end up in the emergency ward."

He blinked at her a couple of times and then returned to his burger. She was probably right. Kit had never been anybody's victim.

18

According to a small bronze plaque on the brownstone facade outside the clothing shop, Olsen Mercantile had been opened in 1923 by Olaf P. Olsen. Jane had never been inside, but knew it by reputation as one of the oldest and finest men's clothing stores in the Twin Cities.

Pausing next to a table of cashmere scarves, she waited for George Krochak to finish with a customer. She'd seen a couple pictures of him, though in person he was quite tall, well over six feet, and far better looking. She had a hard time picturing him with Marlo Wise. Marlo seemed like a woman far more interested in comfort than style, someone who ate lesser mortals for breakfast. Jane had no problem with that sort of woman. Perhaps, in the spirit of "opposites attract," George and Marlo were the perfect match.

George handed a sack to his customer and then walked him to the door. Jane took it as her cue to approach.

"May I help you?" he asked, turning toward her.

She hadn't expected the English accent. "You're English," she said.

"Guilty. My father taught at Cambridge. We moved here when I was in high school."

"I grew up in Lyme Regis," said Jane. "My mother was English."

He seemed delighted by the news. "We have much in common." When he saw her admiring his clothing, he leaned close and whispered, "Brunello Cucinelli. Are you in the market for a new tweed jacket?"

She laughed. "Not today." She handed him her card. "I'm an investigator. I'm wondering if you'd be willing to give me a few minutes of your time."

"What are you investigating?"

"The Gideon Wise homicide."

He pursed his lips. After speaking quietly to another salesman, he motioned for her to follow him into a back room. They sat down on folding chairs in what felt like a walk-in closet stuffed with clothing.

"I only have a few minutes," he said, crossing his legs.

She wondered if she was looking into the eyes of a murderer. "Then let me get right to it. We believe Rashad May may have been wrongly convicted. If he was, then Gideon Wise's killer is still walking the streets, a free man. I understand that you had a rather heated early morning meeting with him a couple weeks before his death."

George raised an eyebrow. "That's . . . true. Are you suggesting I had something to do with his death?"

"We're doing our best to eliminate the people around him."

"I see," he said, smiling again. "So this visit is entirely altruistic."

She returned his smile. "Can you tell me about that meeting? Why Mr. Wise was so angry?"

"Well, to be fair, one look at me generally sent him into a paroxysm. But that morning I'd come to confess my sins, to tell him why his daughter and I were getting married. You see, Marlo and I met at a mutual acquaintance's party. We talked. I liked her very much. Over the next few months, we became friends. It eventually came out that I'd lost my job at a clothing store in Edina because I could no longer do the work. I'd been diagnosed with a spine condition several years before. At times, I was in so much pain that I couldn't stand for more than a few minutes. I needed surgery, but I didn't have health insurance. No job meant no insurance. No insurance, no surgery. No surgery, no job. The All-American vicious circle. Marlo was the one who suggested a solution. She had great healthcare. If we married, I could have the surgery and then later, after I was back working, if I wanted out of the marriage, she said she'd agree to a divorce. No strings. I argued against it, but if you know Marlo, you know she doesn't take kindly to the word 'no.' I may be imagining this, but I thought she might be a little bit in love with me. Or maybe not." He ducked his head and looked away. "At any rate, I came to the law office that morning to tell Mr. Wise the real reason for our marriage. He was not, as they say, impressed."

Jane found the story unusual, if not downright odd, and yet she was inclined to believe him. "Did you have the surgery?"

"I did, thank you. It was a success."

"And you and Marlo are still married."

"Going on four years."

"If Gideon had lived, do you think he would have stopped the marriage, forced Marlo to back out?"

He thought about it. "Highly possible. He did threaten five or six times to disinherit her. They both enjoyed making the odd threat. Seemed like part of a long-standing family tradition to me. For her part, Marlo had been against his marriage to Rashad. She blamed Rashad for her parent's divorce. Believe me, there was plenty of fodder for disagreement between the two of them, and yet their love for each other was as solid as any I've ever known. Marlo didn't murder her father, Ms. Lawless. Nor did I."

"I understand Chuck Atchison is staying with you."

He seemed surprised. "Chuck? Yes, that's right."

"I wonder if you have his cell phone number."

He checked his phone. "Sure." He read it to her, and she wrote it down in her notes.

"Is Chuck also someone you're trying to *altruistically* eliminate?"

"I just need to talk to him."

"You don't want to tell me. That's fine."

"Did the police interview you?"

"They talked to Marlo and me at some length the night of the murder. We were separated, put in different squad cars. I can imagine they got an earful about Rashad, about what a gold-digger he was."

"Did you think he was a gold digger?"

"No. Not at all. If anything, he seemed far less interested in the trappings of wealth than Gideon. Marlo has a tendency to believe what she wants to believe, no matter how much evidence there is to the contrary. I'm not saying she's not a good woman, just that she can be a tad"—he searched for a word—"single-minded."

"Did the police ever interrogate either of you again?"

"No. Never. Since you're interested, this is what I told them: Marlo and I had been home watching TV when Gideon's neighbor called. She said she'd heard a commotion in the hall. When she looked out, she saw police coming and going from Gideon's condo.

I offered to drive Marlo over because she was upset. I sat in the living room while—"

"Wait, wait. You're saying you were there? Inside the condo?"

"Yes."

"I read the police report. There's no mention of you."

"Perhaps I'm not very memorable."

"It was a crime scene. No one, including family, is generally allowed in."

He cocked his head. "Yes, now that you mention it, there were some words about whether we should be there. As I recall, there were only two officers inside when we arrived, and both were young. Marlo was not about to be stopped. She pushed past the man at the door and made straight for the other one who was standing just outside the bathroom. He caught her and prevented her from going in, but when she looked inside the room, she screamed. I wasn't about to leave her, so I sat down in the living room. A few minutes later, a group of officers descended, some in uniform, some in plain clothes. A whispered conference ensued under the stairway. I was pointed out a couple of times, but nothing was done about me. Once they started looking around, my presence seemed to be forgotten. Oh . . . except, a plainclothes cop did come over at one point and tell me to get the F up and go stand against the windows."

"Why?"

"They were starting to take photos. They didn't want me in the living room."

"Tell me, do you remember a black-and-white tote sitting under that long gallery wall? There were block letters—JHC—on the front."

"Funny you should mention that. Yes, I do. I stood by the win-

122

dows for a few minutes and then I was ordered to go back to my chair. That's when several men and one woman began their examination of the living room. One of the men was crawling along the floor, looking for, I assume, clues. When he got to me, he told me to move my f-ing bag closer to my chair. He seemed annoyed that it was blocking his path. I don't know why he assumed it was mine, he just did. Believe me, by then, I had no interest in engaging with any of them, so I did what he asked. I moved it in front of me. While nobody was looking, I peeked inside."

"And?"

"Empty. When one of the officers finally led Marlo out of the rear of the condo, he conferred for a few seconds with one of the men doing the search, and then hollered for me to pick up my f-ing bag and follow him outside."

"You took it?"

"I did."

"Nobody ever looked inside?"

"The uniformed cop standing at the door stopped me and made me open it. He was a tad huffy, in my opinion, as if I was trying to smuggle gold bars out of the condo right under his nose. When he saw there was nothing in it, he told me to get lost."

Jane felt as if the sun had finally risen over the mountain. This was why the bag had been visible in one of the photos, but for those taken after George's departure, it was gone. "What happened to the bag?"

He tapped a finger against his chin. "You know, I have no memory of that. I imagine I took it back to our townhouse. We always used totes when we bought groceries. I suppose I put it with the rest of them. It was really quite nice, as I recall."

"And you have no idea where it is now?"

"None. We have our groceries delivered these days."

"Would you be willing to look for it? You might still have it."

"Yes, I could do that."

"You have my card. If you find it, would you call me? This could be a very big piece of evidence."

"Of course." He checked his watch. "I'm afraid—"

"It's fine," said Jane. "I really appreciate your taking the time to talk to me."

"Have you spoken with Marlo?"

"This morning."

"Can I assume she wasn't much help?"

"Not much."

"Well." He pressed his hands together and stood. "Still no interest in that new designer tweed jacket?"

"Let me think about it."

"You do that," he said, grinning.

19

Eli sat at a desk in a large, open room on the second floor of the gallery. He was in the process of googling information on cat behavior when Kit came in. She usually told him when she was going out, but today, she hadn't. Glancing up, he asked, a bit more gruffly than he intended, "Where were you?"

She didn't respond, just got busy at a desk a few feet away. She'd been working on the monthly newsletter most of the morning.

"Not gonna tell me?" he asked.

She shot him a peeved look.

John Henry came out the door of his office carrying a framed print. Walking up to a long, battered work table, he said, "What's this I hear about Gideon Wise? They're reopening his murder case?"

"I don't think it's gone that far," said Eli. "But, yeah. Sounds like Raymond Lawless is pursuing his own investigation."

"That right," said John Henry, staring off into space. "Sad business. Gideon wasn't just a client of mine, he was a friend. Let me know if you hear anything else."

"Will do," said Eli.

"Now, do I have a portfolio review this afternoon?"

"I think so," said Kit. "Anna would know the details."

As if by magic, a plump, bosomy older woman opened the door of her tiny office and stepped out.

For as long as Eli could remember, Anna Morley had handled the daily business of the gallery—cutting checks, banking, quarterly taxes, and generally keeping the lights on. She was also his father's de facto private secretary. Anna and her husband, Lenny, had been good friends with his parents. They often spent their evenings together playing bridge.

"What was the question?" Anna asked, handing a stack of contracts to John Henry.

"Any portfolio reviews for me today?"

"One at four thirty."

"Here or somewhere else?"

"Here," said Anna. "You have another one on Monday morning at a home studio in Woodbury. By the way, I wanted to mention something because I forgot when we were having lunch: I've been thinking it's high time we raised our review fees. I'm going to do some research on what other galleries of our standing charge."

"Have I told you recently how amazing you are?" asked John Henry, gazing warmly at her.

She blushed. Attempting to hide it, she turned and walked briskly back to her office.

John Henry now turned his full attention to Kit. "Where were you for the last hour and a half?"

"Did you miss me?"

Eli loathed it when she flirted with him.

Kit took out her phone. "I had lunch with Peter Lawless. See? I took a couple of selfies."

Eli got up and leaned in close to get a better look. The sight of Peter's arms around her made the anvil in his stomach grow even heavier. What the hell was he thinking, pawing her like that?

"You two seem cozy," said John Henry, crossing the room to a desk pushed up against the far wall. Pulling out a chair, he continued, "Did you have a good time?"

"He's a really sweet guy. I think his marriage is in trouble."

"Oh?" said Eli. Peter hadn't mentioned anything about that last night.

"Kit, honey, come here," said John Henry.

She stuffed her phone back into her purse. "Why?"

"I want to show you something." He searched through an art magazine.

Glancing at Eli, she moved over next to him.

"Bend down," he said.

She seemed to hesitate.

Reaching up to touch her face, John Henry asked, "Do you love me, Kit?"

"Of course I do, silly. With all my heart." She kissed him, long and lingering.

Now Eli's stomach really began to sour. Screw them. He headed for the door. He needed a cigarette.

"I'll come with you," said Kit, rushing to his side and grabbing his arm. "I need to talk to Winslow about the upcoming installation."

"Have fun, you two," said John Henry, waving them off.

When Eli saw Kit leave the gallery earlier than usual that afternoon, he decided to do the same. His dad would be working late tonight. Mason would be on the floor until six, so it wasn't as if he was leaving his dad in the lurch.

Eli ducked out around five, doing errands on the way home. As he came in the front door carrying his dry cleaning, looking forward to spending some time with Charlotte, he was met by a wild sight. Women's clothing had been flung in a zigzag pattern all the way to the door of his bathroom.

"Hello?" he called, looking around. Charlotte was nowhere in sight. He found Kit in the bathtub surrounded by a mass of bubbles.

"Hi, babe," she said, raising a foot and wiggling it at him.

"You shouldn't be here."

"Why not? It's like a tomb over in the main house. I hate being alone. Besides, your place is more cozy. And speaking of cozy, why didn't you mention you adopted a cat?"

"She's a stray. I'm going to put her up on Craigslist when I get a chance."

"She's cute. But not very friendly."

"Where is she?"

"I think I scared her. Last I saw, she was holding court under your bed."

He stepped a little closer. "Kit, come on, you can't be here like this."

"What do you think *this* is? I'm taking a bath."

"If Dad found you in here—"

"He won't. Come sit down on the edge. Talk to me."

She did things like this. She wasn't good at coloring within the lines. Once upon a time he'd found it sexy. Problem was, he still did. He hung the dry cleaning on a hook behind the door. "I should go make sure Charlotte's okay."

"She's fine. Come on, sit with me. I won't bite. Unless you want me to."

This was the last thing he needed. He already had too many

complications in his tangled life. And yet, as hard as he fought it, he felt like an iron filing in the presence of a magnet. "What do you want to talk about?"

"Stuff. I don't care. You start."

He couldn't help himself. The comment made him laugh. She was so unencumbered by rules and social norms. He was a brooder, a man full of shame and regret. She was a free spirit, happy in a way he could never be. When he was with her, he often felt like an anthropologist investigating a new human species. Homo Kit-us.

He sat down on the edge of the tub.

"Your father's a jerk."

"Is he? Why?"

"He thinks I'm messy."

"You are messy."

"And that I don't care about him enough."

"Is that true?"

She played with the bubbles. "What's enough?"

"I suppose you should ask him."

"He's mean."

"Come on, Kit."

"You don't know him the way I do."

That was a reasonable statement. Still, it was the first time she'd ever said anything like it.

Sinking her chin into the bubbles, she continued, "I want to tell you a secret but I can't."

"Tell me anyway."

The comment amused her. "I better not because I hope to live to a ripe old age."

He dipped his hand into the water.

"Nice and warm, huh?"

"Very." Did he have the guts to do what he really wanted? His hand moved slowly up her side until it was only inches from her breast.

"What are you doing?"

All around him was a curious buzzing noise.

"I like it," she said.

"I'm glad."

She lifted her arm out of the bubbles and placed it on his thigh. When he saw the bruise, he said, "That still hurt?"

"It's no big deal."

Inside him a shouting match had begun. When he heard his voice silently plead, "Pull your damn hand out of the damn water," he did. "Why did you let Peter Lawless paw you like that?"

"Paw me? In that selfie? We were just kidding around. If I didn't know better, I'd say you're jealous."

"What if I was?"

"I'm a married woman, Eli. And besides, Peter's a puppy. Adorable in a wholesome sort of way. But, come on. You know me. I don't like my men wholesome."

"Wholesome men don't put their family at risk because they can't stay away from blow."

"Okay, point taken. But I don't want to talk about him. He's nothing. Nobody. Put your hand back in the water."

"No, I should—"

"Do it. For me." She guided his hand toward her, under the water. "Quiet now, baby. Just do what comes naturally."

He closed his eyes. In a life full of bad decisions, this might be one of the worst.

"Yes, right there," she said. "So good. Don't stop."

20

Late that afternoon, Jane met with the investigator Sherwin May had hired. The office was on West Broadway, a little one-story hole-in-the wall that was dwarfed by the brick buildings on either side. The P.I., one Darnell Brown, gave her a box of files he'd gathered, telling her that she should spend some time trying to track down Trevor Loy, Rashad's onetime boyfriend. Brown felt certain that someone had gotten to him, that Loy never would have testified if there hadn't been something in it for him. He told Jane she should also check out a guy named Dean Frick, a beat cop, one of the men who'd responded to the 911 at Rashad and Gideon's condo. According to Brown, Frick had a well-known hatred of "the gays," as Brown put it. He said the guy was nasty, and had been brought up on charges of using excessive force at least three times in his nine-year service.

"You call me, girl," said Brown as Jane stood to leave. "You got all my info. If I can help, I will. Those boys, neither of them deserved what came down. We gotta get Rashad out of that hole."

She thanked him for taking the time to talk to her. He insisted on carrying the box out to her truck. Once he'd gone back inside, Jane opened her phone. She had a bunch of emails, which she clicked through quickly, determining that there was nothing urgent from the restaurant. She then turned her attention to the texts. Most were from Cordelia, who seemed to be having one of her stream-of-consciousness texting days. None of what she'd written made much sense, though Jane was sure it did to Cordelia. Several were from Julia saying she would likely be home late. Her meeting at the Mayo Clinic in Rochester had gone long and because of that, she said, she and her assistant, Carol, would grab some dinner on the way home.

The text Jane was most interested in was from her father. She'd sent him one after meeting with George Krochak, explaining that she'd finally solved the mystery of the tote bag.

He'd texted back:

Great work. But can we prove it?
Maybe press him again to find the tote.

Of course, he was right. He understood the complex legal ramifications far better than she did. Without the bag, it was just an unsubstantiated story, easily explained by another unsubstantiated story. And even with the bag, it would still be problematic. Even so, Jane continued to view it as progress.

After driving home, she carried the P.I.'s box inside and set it down on the dining room table. She took a few minutes to play with the dogs, lying on the rug in the living room as they bounded around and over her, snuggling, snuffling, licking her face while she scratched their backs and gently pulled their ears. She dug out a couple of bully sticks in the kitchen and got them set up on their large, comfy bed in the corner of her study. As they chewed away contentedly, she cleared everything off the bulletin board behind her desk, readying it for a new case. But before she could begin going through the information from Darnell Brown, her cell phone rang.

"Let me in, *let me in*," came an urgent, pleading voice. Cordelia's voice.

"Where are you?"

"On your front steps. I'm freezing out here."

Jane hurried to answer the door. "What's up?" she asked as Cordelia fluttered inside.

"You never answered any of my texts."

"That's because I had no idea what you were talking about. Aardvarks?"

"*The Captive Aardvark*," said Cordelia. "I told you all about it."

Jane had no memory of ever discussing aardvarks with Cordelia.

She whipped off her cape and tossed it over a dining room chair. "The play, Jane, the one I intend to mount in the spring."

Jane shook her head. "Nope. Nothing in my memory banks."

"Piffle," said Cordelia, hand rising to her hip. "It's all about the power of political theater. If we've ever needed that voice, it's now. Like Bertolt Brecht, Arthur Miller, freakin' Shakespeare. A long history. I don't mean something didactic, but a great story. Story always comes first, last, and in-between. That's what *The Captive Aardvark* is. Do you know anything about captive aardvarks?"

"Any reason I should?" Jane grabbed the box from the dining room table and headed back to her study.

Cordelia charged after her. "It's what Peter Hall said."

"Who's Peter Hall?"

"Sir Peter Reginald Frederick Hall was an English director,

probably the most important figure in British theater in the last fifty years. He was a genius, in my never-to-be-humble opinion. He said that if theater doesn't challenge, provoke, or illuminate, it's not fulfilling its mission." She stopped in front of the box that Jane had just placed on her desk. "What's this?" she asked, fingering the cover.

"It's all the info collected by a private investigator on Rashad's case."

Her eyebrow arched. "Really? Can I look?" Without waiting for an answer, she removed the top. "Oh, Janey. You seriously need my help with this."

"Do I?"

She lifted out a folder of photos. Thumbing through them, she said, "I can tell you who these people are."

"Good," said Jane, removing a bunch of pushpins from the top desk drawer.

"Okay. So this is Marlo Wise." She handed a five-by-seven over. "Probably old. She had bangs at the trial."

"She still does. I met her this morning." Jane took a few minutes to give Cordelia the down and dirty on her encounter.

"Doesn't surprise me. At trial, she looked like the sort of woman who ate nails for breakfast. Not that I don't appreciate a good bowl of nails myself on occasion." She pulled out another photo. "And this is Marlo's husband. George something or other."

"Met with him, too."

"Boy, you have been a busy little bee." She handed Jane another picture. "That's Gideon Wise. Not exactly a handsome man, but he had a powerful presence. And he giggled. I like that in a man."

Jane was pretty sure it wasn't a significant detail.

"And here's Rashad. He's about as beautiful as they come. Very introspective, very kind." It took her a full minute before she handed it over.

Jane tacked it up on the board with the others. She put Gideon in the center, with Rashad's photo next to him. Possible suspects, such as Marlo and George, were stacked in a row to the left. Once she found a picture of Chuck Atchison, he would be added to the row.

"Who's this?" asked Cordelia, removing a somewhat damaged five by seven. Oh, I remember now. It's Trevor Loy. The guy who turned the trial upside down. He's younger here, no facial hair. He had a beard four years ago, if I recall correctly, and I'm sure I do. And he sweated a lot."

"Takes a lot of effort to lie on the witness stand," said Jane. "Is that the last photo?"

Cordelia dipped her hand inside the folder and came up with a small snapshot. "Who's this guy?" She held it up.

"No idea."

She flipped it over. "Somebody named Frick."

"Oh, he's the cop Sherwin May's P.I. thought might have pressured Loy into his last-minute testimony. Hand it over." She took a moment to study it. Frick was middle-aged, with close-cropped sandy hair and a round, meaty face. In the picture, he was wearing a tight black T-shirt.

"So who's our primary suspect?" asked Cordelia, carrying the box over to the love seat and making herself comfortable.

Mouse looked up at her, wagged his tail, but kept on chewing.

"I don't have one," said Jane. "I've got a lot more digging to do. What else is in that box?"

Before Cordelia could begin her search, the doorbell chimed. "You expecting someone?"

"Not that know of. Answer it for me, will you? I want to keep working."

"FYI, I am not your butler."

"Pretty please?"

"Oh, all right," Cordelia said, dragging herself out the door.

Sitting down next to the box, Jane pulled out a file labeled CRIME SCENE. She started paging through it, but stopped when Peter walked in.

"I saw your truck in the driveway," he said, hands tucked into the pockets of his leather bomber jacket.

"Peter," said Jane, rising to give him a hug. "I'm so glad you're here."

It seemed that Peter's arrival was of sufficient importance to cause Mouse to stop chewing and come over to greet him. Gimlet looked up, but kept on chewing.

"Good boy," said Peter, leaning over to fondle the lab's ears. "Wow, his muzzle is starting to gray."

"He's still young at heart," said Jane.

"So, my man," said Cordelia, leaning against the doorframe, "you've been MIA for what? Two days?"

"No I haven't. I've been visiting friends, catching up."

"Really? Like who?"

"Well, for one, I had coffee with Ted Rucker this afternoon."

"I always liked Ted," said Jane. "He comes by the pub every now and then."

"He's got a new job at the Met Council. A systems engineer. Said it pays really well. He likes it."

"I'm glad," she said nodding to the desk chair. She returned to the love seat.

"What's that?" asked Peter, pointing to the bulletin board.

Cordelia chewed absently on a toothpick. "In case you forgot, dearheart, we're working on the May case." She said the words with a kind of weary nonchalance. "Those are our prime suspects."

He walked up and took a closer look. "How's that going?"

"Just a matter of time before we nail the perp," said Cordelia.

"The perp?"

"Don't you ever watch *Law & Order* reruns?"

"Not if I can help it. Listen, Janey, I was hoping you could help me with something." He parked himself on the chair. "Do you remember my old buddy Eli Chenoweth? We lived together off campus during my junior year. His father owns an art gallery in the warehouse district."

"Only vaguely," said Jane.

"I don't remember him at all," offered Cordelia.

"I had dinner with him last night. Seems he was involved with a woman for a while, someone he said he loved. She was murdered last October."

"Murdered," repeated Jane. "How awful. Did they ever find out who did it?"

"It's still unsolved. He seemed pretty torn up about it."

"I can imagine."

"Do you think he did it?" asked Cordelia, never one to approach difficult questions with caution.

Peter locked eyes with her. "Why would you ask that?"

"It's often the boyfriend or the husband. Just saying."

"Well, I'm sure the police checked him out. But, I mean, sure, I'll admit it. I did wonder. He's got this extensive library of books about serial killers, stalkers, murderers. Don't you think that's kind of odd?"

"It's called true crime," said Jane. She had more than a few volumes like that herself.

"He thinks a serial killer might have murdered her. A similar murder was committed up near Duluth right around the same time."

"Why are you so interested?" asked Cordelia.

"Because . . . because he's my friend."

"Is that it?"

"Isn't that enough? Look, I know you're busy with that other stuff, Jane, but—" He removed a folded piece of paper from the pocket of his jacket and pushed it across the desk toward her. "I looked it up on the internet to see what I could find out. There wasn't much. But I did find that."

She adjusted her reading glasses. "Where's it from?"

"The *Star Tribune*."

"Read it out loud," said Cordelia, wedging herself into the space next to Jane on the love seat.

"It's dated October nineteenth. The headline is, 'Woman Found Slain Near Taylors Falls.' 'Officers called to the scene on Tuesday afternoon encountered a Franconia man and his dog who led them to a body in a wooded section of Wayside Park on Highway 8. The woman, Harper Elaine Tillman, was pronounced dead at the scene by fire department paramedics. According to a police statement released this morning, the death has been ruled a homicide. Investigators remained at the scene to collect evidence and interview possible witnesses. Ms. Tillman was the daughter of Jim and Karen Tillman of Minot, North Dakota. Suspects are being actively sought.'"

"Doesn't tell us much," said Jane.

"Is there any way you can find out more?" asked Peter.

She watched him pick at a fingernail. He seemed distracted, even a little nervous. "Possibly. Did your friend, Eli, say anything else about it? Did she have enemies? Was it possible she was seeing someone on the side? Did they have a fight? Did she engage in risky behavior?"

"No idea. All I know is he was serious about her and he thought she was serious about him. They were living together, had been for a while. He came home from work one night, expecting her to be there, and she wasn't. He gave her a few hours, then started calling friends, even hospitals. I asked him a few more questions about it before I left his place. He told me the police had interrogated him for several hours before they released him."

"And what was the cause of death?"

"She was knocked unconscious. They think the killer may have used a rock. And then she was stabbed."

"And your friend has a solid alibi?"

"I guess. The police wouldn't have let him go if they thought he was guilty."

That was an assumption Jane wasn't willing to make. There could be many reasons the police had released him, not the least of which was their need to collect more evidence before they made an arrest. Then again, that had been months ago. She wondered if anyone was still working the case. "Honestly, Peter, I don't know how far I can go with this right now, but I'll do what I can."

"Thank you. I'll keep working on it, too."

"You must really care about this guy," said Cordelia.

He seemed uncertain how to respond. "I . . . I don't like to think someone I've known for so many years is capable of . . . you know."

Jane wrote the name Eli Chenoweth at the bottom of the piece of paper, then rose, moved around the desk and pinned it up on the far edge of the board. The information about the murdered woman had no place in her investigation into the Gideon Wise homicide, and yet she left it there to remind her of her promise to Peter. She would do what she could. If nothing else, it would serve as a way to connect with him while he was home.

21

The first floor of Cordelia's house was ablaze with light, and the circular drive was jammed with cars. Peter assumed there was some kind of meeting or party going on inside. With zero desire to get dragged into one of Cordelia's "happenings," he entered the house through the back door and tiptoed up the old servants' stairway to his bedroom. He needed a shower, but there was something he wanted to get out of the way first.

Removing his jacket, he perched on the edge of the bed and tapped in Sigrid's number. It was nine P.M. in Minneapolis, which meant it was three in the morning in London. He waited through four rings until she answered.

"Hello?" came a groggy, whispered voice.

"Hi."

Silence. "Peter?"

"Is he there?"

"What? Do you know what time it is here?"

"Is he in bed with you? Our bed?"

"Wait. Just wait."

He could hear muffled sounds. He felt like throwing up.

"Okay, I can talk now."

"Wouldn't want to wake him, would we?"

"I've texted you dozens of times. You pick the middle of the night to call me back?"

"You said you wanted to talk. Let's talk."

More silence. Then: "How are you?" she asked, her voice tentative.

"Like you care."

"I do care, Peter."

"Just not enough." He could hear her fumbling with the phone. She was probably stepping out onto the balcony, separating herself from the filthy SOB keeping her bed warm.

"Listen."

"No, you listen," said Peter. "I've been thinking about what I should do. Separation? Divorce? Murder? I'll put it to you like this: You can have me or him, but you can't have us both."

"I know that. It's just . . . I never expected to find myself in this kind of predicament."

"So I've moved from husband to predicament." He got up and walked over to the window, drawing back the curtain. "I wrote Mia a long email."

"You did? What did you say to her?"

From the urgency in her voice, he could tell he'd landed a punch. It felt good. "That's between Mia and me."

"Peter, please. Whatever happens between us, we have to protect her."

"I know that."

"When . . . when are you coming home?"

He looked down on the circular drive.

"Peter?"

"Is he there?"

"Why do you keep asking that?"

"Because I want to *know*. Oh, screw it. Of course he is. You have what you want, Sigrid. Now I have to figure out what I want."

"Come home."

"London isn't my home. My home used to be where you and Mia were, but not anymore. I'm hanging up." He waited to see what she'd say. When all that came across the line was silence, he clicked the phone off and tossed it on the bed. Leaning his head against the cold window glass, helpless, angry tears streamed down his face. "Screw you, Siggy," he choked out. "And screw him. I hate you both." He wanted a drink so bad.

His cell rang. He had no intention of answering it, and yet, almost against his will, he threw himself on the bed and pressed the phone to his ear. "What?" he snapped. "Have you figured out some new way to twist the knife?"

"Um, hi?" came a low, female voice, nothing like Sigrid's.

"Who's this?"

"It's Kit."

He sat up. "Oh, hi. Sorry, I thought you were someone else."

"Clearly," she said, her voice full of amusement.

"What's up?"

"Did I catch you at a bad time?"

"No, it's fine."

"Okay, well, here's the deal. I've had kind of a super weird day."

"You mean our lunch?"

"No, no. Stuff that happened after."

"You want to talk about it?"

"I want to forget it. I thought maybe you'd like to get a drink."

143

"Now?"

"Past your bedtime?"

"Funny. What about John Henry? Will he be joining us?"

"He's staying late at the gallery. If it's anything like the last couple of months, he'll probably sleep there, too."

"That sounds pleasant."

"Sometimes I feel like I don't have a friend in the world, Peter. Someone I can really confide in."

She was exaggerating, but then, she often did. "I'm your friend."

"Are you? Can I trust you?"

"Absolutely."

"I phoned my dad before I called you. I knew just hearing his voice would make me feel better, but it went to voice mail. He's in San Francisco, according to his dimwit of a wife. On a business trip."

"Do you want me to pick you up?"

"No. I'll drive and meet you."

"Where?"

"There's a place not far from here. It's called the Lighthouse. Kind of tacky. An old supper club. But it has a wicked cool bar."

"Okay. Maybe we should invite Eli."

"No," she said quickly. "Just us, okay?"

"Sure," said Peter, feeling his mood improve. He would drink Coke and enjoy her company. Why the hell not?

"I need to get away from here. You are seriously saving my life."

"I doubt that. See you in a few."

Candles glowed softly from a corner of the bedroom. The general turmoil of the day was over, and Jane was holding Julia in her arms. "What are you thinking about?" she whispered.

"That there's something I need to tell you."

There it was again, that sudden trapdoor feeling in her stomach. At least Julia had waited until after they'd made love. Health announcements, if that's what this was, weren't exactly aphrodisiacs. "What?" she asked, smoothing back a lock of Julia's hair. "Something to do with your visit to Rochester today?"

"In a way."

Jane wanted to memorize the feel of Julia's body against hers, how purely alive moments like this were. She spent so much of her life focusing on work that she missed a lot. Too much.

"The cancer hasn't grown."

"That's great news."

"The doctors at the Mayo don't recommend surgery at this point. In essence, they're saying it's too late."

"Oh."

"Yeah."

There were times when Jane struggled to make the brutal word "cancer" real in her mind. "But you'll continue with the chemo."

"I don't know."

It wasn't the response Jane had expected. "Why wouldn't you? If the tumor hasn't grown, then it must be working."

"The chemo makes me sick. I'm tired all the time. I hate it."

"But if you don't continue with it, what's the prognosis?"

"You mean how long will I live?" She turned on her side so she could face Jane. "If I were my own doctor, I suppose I'd give myself a few months—a year if I'm lucky."

Julia was an oncologist. If anyone knew the ramifications of her disease and her decisions, she did.

"Contrary to what doctors believe, they're not God. I rarely gave one of my patients a time limit. There's no point. I've seen

145

too much and been surprised, both negatively and positively, way too many times. The truth is, I could die in a month. Or I could be around five years from now. I might outlive you."

Jane was glad that they weren't sitting across a table, or across a room. She needed to be close for a conversation like this. "You know I'll support any decision you make."

"Will you? Are you sure about that?"

"Well, I mean—" Julia was right. It was a big ask. If Julia did decide to go off chemo, could Jane really give up all hope of a cure and simply watch her die?

"There's one other thing I need to tell you. I'm flying to Sault Ste. Marie, Michigan, tomorrow."

"What? Why?"

"There's a woman I need to see. I don't want to say more. Not yet."

"Is it about your illness?"

"Yes. I'll be gone a few days. Three or four at the most. Carol will take me to the airport in the morning."

"No," said Jane. "I'll do it."

"I hate saying goodbye at crowded airport curbsides. I'd rather do it here. Just the way we are right now. Don't be angry."

"I'm not angry," said Jane. "I'm just . . . this is a lot."

Julia kissed her long and slow. And then she kissed her again. "All will be made clear, my love. All I ask is a little patience."

22

"What to do?" George said to himself, drumming his fingers on the arm of a chair. Because he had seniority, when he asked for a Saturday off, he usually got it. He was seated in the den, the morning newspaper open in his lap, a cup of coffee on the table next to him. Marlo didn't always work weekends, but because of the new card line, she needed to be there. Chuck hadn't come home at all last night, which was fine with George.

All morning, he'd been thinking about what Jane the Altruist had said to him yesterday. He had no idea where that tote had gone, but thought he might spend some time today digging around. With that in mind, he'd dressed in a comfortable old pair of jeans and a clean, tight, white T-shirt, a look he'd liked ever since he'd first seen James Dean in *Rebel Without a Cause*. Not that he looked like Dean, but a man could dream, couldn't he?

Pocketing his keys, he left the condo and strolled down the hall to another door. Behind it were the storage units. Because they owned one of the penthouses, their unit was quite large. Pulling up the metal garage-style door, he flipped on the overhead light, a bare sixty-watt bulb. He hadn't been inside in years. Most of the stuff shoved against the far wall was from his apartment. He liked to think of it as "thrift-store chic." He'd used threadbare rugs as wall art, a bass drum as a table in the living room, and his bookshelf was made of old, black, industrial piping screwed into the studs. Marlo was visibly charmed by his place the first time he'd invited her over.

Now, where to look first. He did a thorough search of the kitchen boxes and found nothing. Moving through the room, he pawed through the rest of the boxes, dug into every drawer, every trunk. An hour later, he was done, convinced that he hadn't missed anything.

Before they'd moved into the condo, George had prevailed upon Marlo to toss the worst of her old junk. He owned less junk, but was equally ruthless with his own stuff. It seemed possible that he'd tossed the tote, although that didn't really make sense because they both used them all the time back then, when they shopped for groceries. Now that they had groceries delivered, he wondered where those once-well-used totes had all gone.

Returning to the condo, he searched through the kitchen, finding nothing. In the pantry, he did locate a couple of old Lunds totes, folded and resting on a lower shelf. One was in use as a makeshift shelf liner under a couple bottles of olive oil and a jar of honey. Feeling as if he were on a fool's errand, he took a mug out of the freezer and filled it with root beer. Walking around, he poked through each room, sipping his drink.

As he came into their bedroom a few minutes later, he began humming a song that had been in his head all morning. Embarrassingly, he knew every word of "Wake Me Up Before You Go-Go" by the English pop group Wham! He would never have admitted it in polite society, but here, alone in the bedroom, he could try out his George Michael moves. Setting the mug down on the nightstand, he spun around and grooved his way across the rug, imagining himself as a great-looking young blondish man with insanely white teeth. Flipping open the closet door in time to the music, he was about to do another twirl when the sight of something white-and-black caught his eye.

There it was. On the floor next to the wall. He'd never noticed it before. It was packed with old, rolled-up rock posters—the ones Marlo hadn't quite been able to toss. He scooped it up and dumped the posters onto the bed, and then sat down to examine it. Except there wasn't anything to examine. It was empty, just as he remembered it. There was a small pocket, but again, it was empty. Or—

As he felt around inside, he discovered a business card that had somehow stuck to the side. Removing it, he read out loud, "J.H. Chenoweth Gallery, 104 Barber Street, Minneapolis." At the bottom was a phone number and two names. John Henry Chenoweth on top, and Eli Chenoweth underneath.

"Huh," he said. He vaguely remembered the name as one of the galleries Gideon bought from on occasion. So, if the tote belonged to the gallery, why had it been in the condo the night Gideon was murdered?

George patted the back pocket of his jeans and removed his cell phone. He opened the case flap where he'd stuck the card Jane the Investigator had given him yesterday. Punching in the number, he sent a text:

**Found the tote. Card from the
JH Chenoweth Gallery inside.
Gideon used to buy from them.**

**On my way downtown to check
it out.
George K**

Placing the card back where he'd found it, he left the tote on the bed, trotted downstairs, and grabbed his coat.

The parking in the north loop was as bad as he remembered. Sliding his Volvo into a tight spot on a side street, he got out, checking the distance between his car and the Chevy behind it. Feeling that it should be okay, that there was plenty of room to maneuver—unless the driver of the Chevy was a complete idiot—he headed straight for the gallery.

Taking in the galvanized metal sign above the door, George pushed inside. The interior of the warehouse had been beautifully renovated. The wooden floors were perfectly polished and looked original. The walls were white. Toward the back was an antique desk. The middle-aged man behind it stood and walked toward him.

"May I help you?" he asked.

"Why, yes," said George. For some reason, when he met someone new, his English accent returned with a vengeance. "I'd like to see John Henry or Eli Chenoweth."

"I believe they're both here," said the man. "Do you have a preference?"

"Either is fine," said George with a smile.

"May I ask what this is about?"

"We . . . that is, my wife and I . . . have some artwork we'd like to have appraised. Do you do that?"

"Of course."

"It originally belonged to my father-in-law, Gideon Wise. I believe he bought much of it here."

"Good to know," said the man. "Why don't you look around while you're waiting? If you have any questions, I'd be happy to answer them." He moved back behind the desk, picked up a phone, and punched in a number.

George walked into one of the side galleries. Perhaps he should have talked to Jane Lawless first—leaving it to the professionals as it were—but he was too curious. And besides, he was fully capable of doing a bit of a reconnoiter himself.

Jane had finally been granted access to visit Rashad May at Stillwater state prison. Cordelia was already on his list and begged to come along, so shortly after eight—the middle of the night for her—she arrived at Jane's house just as Julia was leaving, trailing a rolling suitcase behind her. Jane watched from the dining room window as the two most important women in her life passed like two snarling ships in the night. Jane waited until Julia was safely inside Carol's car and then went to open the door for Cordelia.

With rush hour traffic and a stop for a hearty breakfast of chocolate milk and Funyuns for Cordelia, it was ten o'clock before they found themselves inside the grim fortress, being searched and passed through a metal detector. Accompanied by security, they walked down a long hallway as gates clanged shut behind them. By working for her father, Jane had become part of Rashad's legal team. Her dad had arranged for a private room. Cordelia seemed oblivious to her surroundings, likely because she'd visited Rashad many times before, but Jane's reaction wasn't as sanguine. She'd never liked being inside a prison, which, of course, was the point. Nobody did. This morning, however, she felt the claustrophobic sense of separation from the world even more keenly, worried, as she was, about Julia.

"I think I ate too many Funyuns," muttered Cordelia as they were ushered into the room.

A door eventually opened and Rashad, wearing a prison uniform, came in. Cordelia instantly jumped up and gave him a hug and a kiss. This, according to the guard, was the only contact permitted until the end of the meeting, when another short contact was allowed. Rashad beamed his affection at Cordelia, but the guard standing in the doorway cut it short by ordering them both to sit down.

The photo Jane had of Rashad looked nothing like the man sitting across from her. Four years ago, he'd been clean-shaven, open-faced and handsome. Now, except for a slight wariness about the eyes, his face was expressionless. He'd put on weight, too, looking like a man who spent hours each day in the gym. His upper arms were huge, the size of pork roasts. His head was shaved, and he had a scar running from the edge of his right eye to his chin.

"It's so great to see you," enthused Cordelia. "Boy, you're even more pumped than you were last time I saw you."

He seemed embarrassed. "In a place where I have control over virtually nothing, it's something I can control."

"I get it," said Cordelia. She was about to pat his wrist, but pulled her hand back, remembering the rules.

"I've actually met a lot of guys while working out. There are some great people in here. Plenty not so great, but honestly, I'm lucky. I've made some real friends, which makes life a little more bearable." He glanced at Jane almost shyly. "Thanks for coming. Both of you. I talked to your dad, Jane, a few days ago. I guess Sherwin convinced him that I still might have a chance."

"How do you feel about that?" asked Jane.

"Good. Well, yeah, good. Except . . ." He scratched the scruff on his face. "This place . . . it's hard. At first, I lived and breathed my appeals. It was all I thought about. I kept hoping they'd reverse the decision, that they'd see they'd made a mistake. When it didn't happen, I crashed. Over time, I found that the only way to deal with being in here was to forget about hope altogether."

"That sounds awfully bleak," said Jane.

"You can't lose hope," Cordelia chimed in.

He shifted his gaze to his hands. "I read this book once. It was fantasy or science fiction, can't remember which. Don't remember the writer's name either, but there was this passage about Pandora. You know the story: Zeus gives her a box and tells her not to look inside, but she does, and when she opens it, all the evils of the world that were trapped inside fly out. Except for hope. What, the character in the book asks, was hope doing in there in the first place? She thinks about it and eventually concludes that hope was in there because it was as bad as the rest. In fact, it was so bad, so weighed down by evil, it couldn't even struggle out of the goddamn box. I know that's not the way most people read the myth, the allegory, or whatever the hell it is, but I never forgot it. Seems like the truth to me. Maybe I should call it prison truth."

Jane found the comment deeply sad, and yet, from his standpoint, it made a certain sense. "I wish I could promise we'll get you out."

"I'm not asking for that. Truth is, I always figured I was in here because when the cops looked around for the murderer, they took one look at me, the only black man in the room——a gay black man at that——and it was game over."

Jane wasn't about to argue the point.

"They interrogated me that night for nine hours. Then they left me alone in this small room for another few hours, until my lawyer arrived. He was arranging to get me out when they came back in and arrested me. I never even got to go home. Wasn't allowed to go to Gideon's funeral." He shook his head.

"I'd like to fill you in on what we've been able to dig up so far," said Jane.

"Please," he said, though his bitter expression didn't change. "Your father told me a few things, but he said you'd have more details."

She spent the next few minutes going through each new piece of information, ending with the conversation she'd had yesterday with George Krochak. "If he can find the tote, it will be a big step forward. My father said you confirmed that you and Gideon never owned a tote like that."

"It's not the kind of thing Gideon would've wanted around. Pardon me for putting it this way, but it would have been too housewifey for him. Too suburban."

"Any idea what the initials JHC stand for? I looked it up on the web, found a gaming company, a tech company, a firm that does program analysis."

He thought about it. "All I can think of is the J.H. Chenoweth gallery in downtown Minneapolis. Gideon bought fine art from them, though I don't know what the connection would be."

At the sound of the name Chenoweth, Jane's head snapped up. "Any relation to Eli Chenoweth?"

"Yeah, he's the owner's son. You know him?"

"I know the name."

Hesitating, he looked down. "That's weird, you know?"

"What's weird?" asked Cordelia.

"Well, I mean, now that you bring him up, it reminds me of something—nothing I ever thought about before. I was asked who had the security code to our condo. I told the police we'd given it to Marlo, which meant George had it, too. But that was it. We set it ourselves, and we were encouraged to change it often. We'd only been there for a month or so when Gideon died. Except—" He scratched his cheek. "How could I have forgotten this? Gideon *must* have given it to that gallery because while we were at work, they came in and hung all his artwork. It was the first week we were there. Gideon wanted it professionally done and he trusted the gallery because he'd done so much business with them. I may be wrong, but I think Eli was the one he worked with."

Jane and Cordelia exchanged glances.

"And you didn't change the code when the job was complete?" asked Jane.

"I never gave it a thought. Apparently, neither did Gideon. I didn't have any dealings with that gallery or any of Gideon's art buying. I'm not saying the gallery or Eli had anything to do with Gideon's death, but they must have had the key code."

"Eli Chenoweth is a good friend of my brother's," said Jane. "They roomed together in college and stayed friends."

"Peter?" said Rashad, raising his eyebrows. "I went out for a drink with him that night. A drink that turned into dinner."

"What time did Gideon normally get home from work?" asked Jane.

"Seven, sometimes later. Except, that day, he had a dentist's appointment. He texted me from work and said the Novocain was wearing off and his tooth hurt like hell. Said he was going home early."

"Peter was the one who asked you out that night?" asked Jane.

"He wanted to talk about some new documentary he hoped to film. I think he was looking for investment capital."

"And if it had been a normal day, Gideon would have been gone until at least seven. Nobody would have been around?"

"Yeah, that's right."

"What time did you usually get home?"

"I was off at five thirty, so maybe six."

"If Peter hadn't asked you out, you would have gone home that night?"

"Yeah."

"This guy in the hoodie," said Jane. "We have him on the security camera in the parking garage at six twenty-five."

Rashad leaned forward, a deep frown on his face. "What are you suggesting? That your brother invited me out to dinner to make sure I wasn't home so his friend could come in and . . . what? Rob the place?"

Jane felt like a firecracker had just exploded inside her head. She couldn't believe Peter would willingly agree to help a friend illegally enter another friend's condo. And yet as much as she resisted the idea, the facts seemed to point in that direction.

"You're saying that guy in the hoodie came into our condo confident that nobody would be there? Does that mean you think Eli Chenoweth was the one who murdered Gideon?"

"I don't know," said Jane. "But I'm beginning to wonder if his murder was somehow connected to that gallery."

"Jesus," Rashad whispered, his eyes flying around the room. "You gotta talk to that brother of yours. Find out what he knows."

"Believe me, I will."

Before they left, Cordelia tried to lighten Rashad's mood by filling him in on what was going on with their mutual friends.

Mostly it was gossip. Rashad listened, but, as with Jane, his focus was elsewhere.

On the way to the car, Cordelia said, "Peter's got some serious 'splaining to do."

Jane checked her cell phone for messages. One caught her eye. "Just a sec," she said, stopping right in the middle of the parking lot.

"What?" asked Cordelia, now back to digging through the Funyuns bag in her purse.

"George sent me a text. He found the tote."

Cordelia whooped, then covered her mouth. "Probably best not to express unbridled jubilation in a prison parking lot."

Jane felt dizzy as she read his words. "There was a business card inside the tote from the J.H. Chenoweth gallery. It has Eli's name on it."

Cordelia stopped midchew.

"He's headed there right now." She glanced at her watch. "Or he was headed there two hours ago."

"You think—"

"I think he may have walked into a hornet's nest."

"We need to go rescue him."

Cordelia was right. They could hardly call the police because George Krochak found a sack and a business card. "Come on," she said, unlocking her truck. "Let's get out of here."

23

Cordelia loomed in the gallery doorway surveying her surroundings, her dark, smoldering eyes glinting under the track lighting. She was Greta Garbo in *Queen Christina*, standing at the prow of a ship, staring into the wine-dark sea with the rapt gaze of a monk, ready to take on the world for the sake of her beloved Sweden. Except, this wasn't Sweden, it was an art gallery, and Cordelia wasn't a queen, except in her own mind.

Jane was already inside, strolling around, musing over the art on display. Their task: Find out if George had already come and gone. Cordelia saw no blood on the floor, which she took as a good sign. Then again, there were probably lots of back rooms. If she had to rough someone up at sword point to get an answer, she was the person for the job.

As soon as she crossed the threshold, a somewhat gaunt man in a three-piece suit, his floppy brown hair parted in the middle, approached. "I'm Eli Chenoweth," he said, smiling. He'd been looking at his cell phone when she came in. "Can I help you?"

So this was the notorious Eli. He didn't look like a murderer, though that remained to be seen. "Possibly." She stalked up to a painting of two black-and-gray figures hunched together inside a puke-tan barn, or maybe it was a cupboard. One figure appeared to be pounding a large nail through the head of the other.

"What do you think?" asked Eli.

"Well, huh. Hard to find the right word, don't you agree?"

"I'd call it sensitive," he said. "This artist is doing some amazing work." He took another peek at his phone.

"Something interesting?" she asked, nodding to it.

"Oh, nothing really. I found a lost cat the other night. I took some pictures of her this morning."

Cordelia leaned over to see. "She's cute."

"Yeah, I think so, too."

"A nice cat?"

"Oh, yeah. Super friendly. And endlessly entertained by my dripping faucet in the bathroom."

Cordelia moved on to a frenetic orange owl on a messy red, green, and yellow background.

"It's a wonderful example abstract expressionism," offered Eli. "The artist, Mayuri Naidu, is South African. I'd be happy to get you more information on her if you're interested."

The dude was into the hard sell. Not appealing. Examining the note next to the painting and taking in the price, she couldn't help herself. She hooted. The hoot caused Jane to look in her direction. Cordelia tugged on her cape. "Do you have a business card?" she asked.

"Of course." He slipped one out of his breast pocket and handed it to her.

Squinting at the tiny print, she said, "And this John Henry. Who's he?"

"My father."

Jane was being followed around by a different pursuer, a young woman who gave off a decadent Zelda Fitzgerald vibe—curly hair, bright red lips, eccentric clothing.

Following Cordelia's gaze, Eli said, "That's my mother-in-law."

"Sure it is."

"No, I'm not joking. Kit Chenoweth. She's married to my father."

Cordelia repositioned the earflaps on her hunter's cap. "Moving on. A friend of mine, George Krochak, told me about your little operation here. He suggested I come take a look. Do you know him? George?"

"Name doesn't ring a bell."

"He was in today. In fact, I thought I might run into him." She craned her neck and looked around. "Englishman. Looks a bit like Hugh Grant."

"Sorry. Maybe my father or Kit worked with him. Is there something specific you were looking for?"

"Me? No, just, you know, browsing for deals. When do you have your sales? Probably before Christmas, yes? Memorial Day? For instance, if I waited for a sale, how much of a discount could I get on that owl picture?"

"We don't do discounts. Or sales."

"No sales? How do you move your merchandise?"

"So . . . we don't have that sort of business model. We work on a rather small margin—"

"What about haggling? Surely you let customers haggle." She ducked her head into a side gallery that was cordoned off by a red velvet rope. Seeing two men working on an art installation, she wheeled back around. Out of the corner of her eye, she caught sight of a man entering from the rear. Thinking it might be

George, she turned to face him. Sliding closer to Eli, she lowered her voice and said, "Don't look now, but I think Jesus just came in."

He turned to look.

"You might want to alert the media. This could be a huge break for your gallery." Bending closer to his ear, she added, "I have to say, he's really aged. I like the horn-rimmed glasses, but—don't take this the wrong way—the biblical robes were a better look on him than the mauve suite and striped bow tie."

Eli drew away from her. "That's my father."

"Jesus is your father?"

"He's not Jesus. I told you. His name is John Henry Chenoweth."

Cordelia stared at him a moment, then smiled. "Well, you could have fooled me. Does he always look that dour?"

"Dour?"

The Jesus figure pulled out a chair and sat down behind the antique desk, his hands pressed forlornly to the sides of his face.

"Would you like more information on the Naidu?" asked Eli, trying but failing to hide his irritation.

Fluttering her eyelashes coyly, she said, "I'll have to think about it."

"You do that. I should probably let you . . . browse. If you have any questions, just let me know."

"Thank you. You've been most helpful."

"We try," he said snidely, walking away.

Cordelia milled around for the next few minutes, eyeing this painting and that as Jane continued to talk to Zelda Fitzgerald. Because breakfast, such as it was, had been so nutritionally limited, she began to think about restaurants nearby where they could have lunch. By the time her mental list had reached a dozen, Jane was heading for the door. Cordelia followed her out, hoping that Eli's mother-in-law had offered more intriguing tidbits than Eli.

Marlo stood at the top of a remote hillside, staring down the snowy embankment at her husband's Volvo. The police officer next to her appeared to be speaking, though she had to struggle up through her panic to hear him.

"Careened off the road," she heard him say. "Must have rolled over because the top is partially crushed. Good thing it's upright. Will make it easier. Have to hope." Workman down below fought with the twisted metal around the door to remove George from the wreck.

Marlo had spent a good part of the morning in the women's room outside her office. She'd eaten some bad sushi yesterday and was paying the price. By midafternoon she'd recovered sufficiently to sit at her desk and nibble at the ham and Jarlsberg sandwich George had made for her. That's when the call came in. The woman on the other end of the line said she was from the MPD, that they'd traced her through her husband's cell phone. The cell had been thrown from the car and recovered by a teenager. The kid was the one who'd discovered the wreck and called 911. Marlo couldn't recall, but felt pretty certain the word *serious* had been used.

It was all a muddle after that. She'd jumped in her car and raced across town, blowing through stop signs, weaving through traffic. Now, looking down at the smashed Volvo, her entire body clenched and shivering under her coat, she waited to see if he was alive. The cop standing next to her was a talker. He kept saying things about people surviving all kinds of terrible accidents. She closed her eyes, praying that he'd shut up.

George was eventually pulled ever so carefully from the wreckage and strapped to a board. There was no easy way to bring him up to the road, but the paramedics did their best. As he was carried past her, Marlo saw the damage up close. He was unconscious, bleeding from his nose and mouth, both eyes purpled by bruises. The paramedics assured her that he was breathing. "Still alive," she whispered to herself. "Still alive."

Marlo drove to the hospital emergency room in a kind of daze. She squeezed into a spot too narrow for her SUV and rested her forehead against the steering wheel. How could this happen? George was a great driver. She'd overheard one of the paramedics say he didn't have his seat belt on. That was just silly. Of course he had his seat belt on. He always wore a seat belt. He was extremely safety conscious, which was why he'd bought that particular car. It had stellar safety ratings.

The world tilted and blurred as Margo made her way into the hospital. She wasn't allowed to see George because, in the time it had taken her to drive from the scene of the accident to the hospital, he'd already been rushed into surgery. She was informed that a doctor would come talk to her as soon as they had anything to report.

Marlo found a place to sit in the waiting room. An hour went by. Then two. Numbness alternated with sickening adrenaline rushes that felt like panic. She took out George's cell phone, given to her, along with his wallet, by one of the uniforms. The face of the phone was cracked, but it still seemed to work. She scrolled through his calls. Five were from the same number. Why the hell had Jane Lawless called her husband five times within the space of a few hours?

When a man in scrubs finally came to the waiting room to talk to her, she stood. She did her best to force away the crushed feeling in her chest. She had to concentrate, take in every word for later analysis. She dug her fingernails into the palms of her hands to steel against a reality that she knew, without a doubt, would change her life forever.

24

Eli bent his head against the wind as he made his way over the hill and down the gravel road from his house to his father's place, annoyed to find that it was snowing again. His dash over to the main house left his shoes soggy and his clothing damp. He would much rather have stayed in and watched TV with Charlotte tucked in his arms, but this was an invitation he couldn't turn down.

Standing in the shadows just inside the back door, Eli caught his breath as he watched Kit read a magazine at the island. She had her back to him, so he was in no danger of being discovered and accused of voyeurism. That had always been a joke between them. She had no idea how close to the truth it was.

Eli had been invited for dinner. Since he'd eaten his weight in a shrimp stir-fry last week, it was strange that he'd been invited again so soon.

Kit turned around when the floorboards creaked. She had a martini glass in her hand, one that was nearly empty.

"What's for dinner?" he asked, smiling, giving himself a moment to gauge her mood. She'd changed into an ankle-length thing, part dress, part robe, made of some flimsy red fabric. Buttons ran from the top to the hem. The top was so large that it almost fell off her shoulders. He doubted she was wearing a bra underneath.

"Oh, it's you," she said, floating him a disinterested look. "Barbecue."

"Take-out barbecue?"

"John Henry's picking it up on the way home. Sit down and talk to me." She finished her drink and began making another.

"So, we're still speaking to each other after what happened yesterday? You seemed pretty cold all day at the gallery."

"Jeez, keep a lid on that," she muttered.

"Is Dad here?"

"No, but it doesn't matter. The walls have ears."

He pulled out a stool and sat down.

"Do you know who that was who came into the gallery this afternoon?" she asked.

He folded his arms and shrugged.

"Jane freakin' Lawless, Peter's sister."

"Oh?"

"And the fat woman in the stupid hat? That was her friend. The theater director. The one who was friends with Rashad."

That explained her ridiculous questions. "So? You said we have nothing to worry about."

"How come you listen to me, genius? I don't know what I'm talking about." She tossed a grin over her shoulder as she opened the freezer and removed a bottle of vodka.

The grin helped. She wasn't mad. "So are you worried or not worried?"

"I don't worry, Eli. It's a waste of time." Removing a tray of olives, cheese, and cherry tomatoes from the refrigerator, she set

166

it on the island next to a bowl of salted nuts and a sleeve of Ritz crackers. After mixing her drink, she said, "What did the theater director have to say?"

"Nothing much."

"Good evening all," boomed John Henry, coming through the back door. He set several white sacks smelling of barbecue on the island, then removed his coat and scarf tossed them over a kitchen chair.

Eli pulled the bowl of nuts closer and began digging around for pecans.

John Henry patted him on the back on his way to give Kit a kiss. "I have a present for you, my love," he announced, holding up a liquor bottle.

Kit flashed her eyes at Eli. "See how well my husband treats me."

"I've made an important discovery, Eli. My wife likes cordials."

Didn't seem like a much of a revelation. She liked anything sweet.

Kit took the bottle from him and read the name. "Limoncello."

"Add it to that nightly cocktail of yours. It's Italian. A nice, bright lemon flavor."

"Looks like some bad scratches on your hand, Dad," said Eli, nodding to them.

"Yeah, I was helping Mason unpack some crates when I was attacked by the binding wire. Anna put some antibiotic cream on it. Should be fine."

"Is something up?" asked Eli. "You don't usually invite me back so soon."

His father laughed. "I guess the old man is pretty transparent." Scratching the back of his neck, he continued, "I suppose I might as well get this over with before dinner."

"Please do," said Kit. She continued to maintain her bored expression, but Eli thought he saw some real concern.

"The gallery is in a bit of financial trouble. I won't sugarcoat it. It's not good. I took out a loan a few years ago to help us through a rough patch. Borrowed from a friend with deep pockets. I've been paying him back little by little, but apparently he's having a bit of a shortfall himself. He wants his money back."

Eli pushed the bowl of nuts away. "How much?"

"I'd rather not say."

"Okay, then how long do we have to come up with it?"

"Two months."

"What were the terms of the loan?"

"Exorbitant interest, the principal paid back upon demand. Like I said, he was a friend, so I thought he'd carry me as long as I needed."

"What do we do?" asked Kit, swirling the olive in her martini glass.

"I'm talking to a banker on Monday morning. Anna suggested I cancel all my appointments for the day. The fact is, we're in much better shape than we were when I borrowed the money, so I might be able to finesse something. I'll keep you posted. I don't want either of you to worry."

"So Anna knew all about this but we didn't?"

"There was no need to worry you." He popped an almond into his mouth. "I need to make a phone call, and then change into something more comfortable. I won't be long." Before he left the room, he opened the bottle of Limoncello and poured some into Kit's martini. "Enjoy."

Kit stared daggers at his back as he walked out.

"You're pissed?" asked Eli.

"What do you think?"

"Because of Anna?"

"She's a troll. An ugly, aging, fat little woman, and he thinks the sun rises and sets on her."

"They've been friends forever."

"Whoopee."

Eli found her reaction excessive. Surely she wasn't jealous of his dad's friendship with Anna. "I suppose, if he can't raise money any other way, he can always sell this place."

She snorted. After taking several hefty swallows of her drink, she said, "First time I saw this house, I thought it was a palace. It's not. It's old and dumpy and the basement smells like mold." Picking up her drink, she nodded for Eli to follow her.

Once settled on the carpet in front of the fire, she finished off her martini.

"How many of those have you had?"

"Not enough."

"Dad's news isn't worth getting sick over. Why don't we change the subject?"

"Works for me."

He lowered his voice to a whisper. "Are we having an affair? Or was yesterday a one-off?"

"You have a one-track mind, Eli."

"What's that supposed to mean?"

Instead of responding, she began to unbutton her dress.

"Jeez, Kit." Three buttons down, she stopped and pulled it off over her head. Underneath, she was naked.

"I feel like dancing," she said, running her hands through her hair.

"Put your clothes back on. What if Dad comes back?"

"He likes to see me naked."

"What the hell. Are you drunk?"

"He likes that, too. Thinks it makes me more interested in sex."

Eli couldn't breathe.

Kit jumped up. "Come on, genius. Dance with me." She tried to tug him off the floor.

"Put that back on," he said, tossing the dress at her.

"You used to be more fun."

"That was before you married my dad."

She twirled around and around, then began to move more slowly, more seductively.

Eli knew he shouldn't watch, but he couldn't take his eyes off her.

Finally dropping down next to him, she leaned her head against his shoulder. "Your dad is creepy."

"Come on."

"And he has a secret."

"You said that before. Don't keep dangling it in front of my face if you're not going to tell me."

"If I did tell you," she said, slipping back into her dress, "he'd kill me."

"Are you joking?"

"Is she or isn't she?"

He decided to joke back. "You can tell me because I have a cape. I'll protect you."

She turned to look him full in the face. "Will you? You'd really do that?"

John Henry picked that moment to breeze into the room. He was wearing pajamas and a silk bathrobe. "Hey, you two. I do have some good news," he said, warming his hands by the fire.

"Oh?" said Eli, instantly pulling away from Kit.

"I sold one of the Glastons today."

"Wow. Congratulations." Saturdays were always busy at the gallery, though rarely did they ever sell a significant painting on a Saturday. Most people just came to feel artsy.

"Did I miss anything?" asked John Henry, easing down on the floor next to Kit.

"I better go unpack our dinner," she said, jumping up.

Eli listened politely as his father went on and on about the sale. He smiled, nodded, and acted interested, all the while mentally turning down the sound on what felt like a tedious infomercial.

25

As soon as Jane got back to the restaurant that afternoon, she sent several more texts to Peter. The earlier ones hadn't been returned, which might be all for the good. When she'd left Stillwater state prison, she'd been pretty angry. She'd cooled off a little, though she still needed to talk to him. Even more importantly, she needed his cooperation.

Everything she'd learned from today's visit with Rashad pointed directly to the Chenoweth gallery. The timing suggested that both Gideon's and Rashad's routines had been studied. Since their habits were regular, whoever had planned the illegal entrance had probably assumed they'd be safe until at least seven fifteen. What they hadn't counted on was Gideon's dental appointment. So what had actually happened? Was it premeditated murder, a robbery gone wrong, or something else?

While Eli seemed the most likely suspect, since he'd been the one to hang Gideon's artwork, Jane had to look carefully at his father, too. Even Kit, the woman she'd met at the gallery right before lunch, could have been involved. Kit seemed knowledgeable about the art and appeared to have some talent at sales, but she also seemed slick, her nonchalance studied, fake. When Jane introduced herself, Kit appeared surprised. From that moment on, she trained her eyes on Jane and never looked away. Jane could only guess at the reason.

Eventually, Jane brought up the subject of George, describing him and saying she was hoping she might run into him. He was planning to stop by the gallery before lunch. Kit shrugged, saying she'd gone out to do some errands. Perhaps, if he'd arrived during that time, Eli or John Henry had helped him. As they walked around, she said that Peter was a good friend. She talked about him easily, with a kind of casual intimacy, saying how glad she was that he'd come back to town, that she wished he'd stick around, especially now that his marriage was on the rocks. Jane was more than a little miffed that her brother had apparently confided some of the details to Kit when he'd mentioned virtually nothing about his marriage to her. She was left to wonder if her negative reaction to Kit was mostly the result of that omission. Her most important takeaway from the visit was the knowledge that Peter knew these people well, which made his dinner with Rashad on the night of Gideon's murder seem even more ominous.

During the dinner rush, Jane worked for an hour or so as an expediter in the kitchen. The man who usually did the job needed to run to the hospital to bring his mother home. Since they were also short one bus person, Jane spent another hour clearing and resetting tables. She was back in her office by eight, when Nicole Gunness, the ex-police officer Jane had hired to do background work for her, knocked on her door.

"Come in," Jane called, standing to shake her hand. "Great to see you. Have a seat."

Nicole was a heavyset woman in her midfifties, with dyed blond hair and a sober manner. She'd burnt out as a cop and had no desire to jump through all the necessary hoops to become a licensed P.I. in Minnesota, but she loved investigation and wanted to keep her hand in. "Mike's here, too," she said.

Mike Hustvedt was Nicole's partner. They weren't married but had been living together for at least a decade.

"And my cousin Terry came with us. They're in the pub having a beer." Nicole carried a manila folder and an iPad. She handed the folder to Jane, and they both sat down. "Think I've got everything you asked for."

Jane opened the folder and began flipping through the top pages. "Tell me first about Harper Tillman." Because Jane had concluded that Eli might be connected to Gideon's murder, she was even more interested in what had happened to his girlfriend.

"Not much to tell. She was from Minot, North Dakota. She worked as a reception agent at the Hyatt Regency in downtown Minneapolis for a year or so. No arrests. No known mental health or drug problems. Good student in high school. One year of college at the university in Minot before she dropped out. I talked to her parents. They said Harper had always been a good girl. She wasn't a partygoer, didn't engage in risky behavior—to their knowledge, I should add. They'd never met Eli, but confirmed that Harper was head over heels in love."

"What about Eli? He must have been a suspect in her murder."

"In homicide investigations, the police always look at the male relatives in the woman's life, so that would also include J. H. Chenoweth, Eli's father, and all of her old boyfriends. But, yeah, Eli was the prime suspect." Nicole fired up her iPad. "It turned out to be kind of a turf war between the Franconia Township police and the Chisago County sheriff's department. I've got a buddy who works for the sheriff. He said their investigator was sure Eli had done it."

"But not sure enough for an arrest?"

"What you know and what you can prove are two different things. What they found, however, did seem suspicious. Apparently Harper had been crying at work on the day she went missing. A woman coworker said Harper indicated it was about Eli, but didn't elaborate."

"Was this coworker a close friend?"

"More of a work friend. She said Harper hadn't been in the Twin Cities more than a few months when she met Eli. They moved in together almost immediately. The woman didn't think Harper had many friends in town. She said that at least once a week, a bunch of coworkers would get together after work to go out for a drink. At first Harper went with them, but after she met Eli, she was always doing something with him. They eventually stopped asking."

"Where was Eli that day?"

"He left the gallery early. He never mentioned that to the investigator until the guy independently verified it and came back and asked him about it. Eli said he'd been shopping. He couldn't provide any receipts or proof of parking. The investigator figured he was lying. And then there's his weird cell phone behavior."

Jane set the folder on her desk and leaned back in her chair. Once again, Nicole had done great work.

Nicole scrolled through her notes. "Here it is. Eli turned his cell phone off just after four that afternoon. He didn't turn it back on until almost eight that evening. Odd behavior for someone concerned about his girlfriend."

"How did he explain it?"

175

"He said he always meditated when he came home after work. He would turn off his phone because he didn't want to be interrupted. Usually, he said, he would turn it back on right away when he was done, but that night he didn't. He said he forgot."

"Forgot? If he'd really been worried about Harper, he would have been checking his phone constantly."

"And think about this: Turning off his phone gave him a four-hour window during which he could have gone anywhere. If his cell phone wasn't pinging off towers and establishing his location, he was effectively invisible."

"What about Harper's phone?"

"Never found."

"Her car?"

"She didn't own a car. She rode her bike to work if the weather was good, or she took the bus."

"She didn't ride her bike to Taylors Falls," said Jane.

"No one ever determined how she got there." Nicole scrolled a bit more. "Here. The police did a search of Eli's place. He lives on his dad's property, in a small house about a football field away from the main house. They found his calendar—it was the kind that lets you write a little about each day, laid out one month at a time. He always made notes, his appointments, important things he wanted to remember. The day before Harper was murdered, the space was blank. Same for the day of the murder. That's the only time in the entire year that the spaces were empty."

"Interesting, but as you said, not proof."

"Okay, listen to this: During the search, they found a set of steak knives in the kitchen drawer. Twelve serrated knives. Natural rosewood. Full tang. Nice knives. You see them everywhere online, so I'm not saying they were unusual. One of Eli's knives was missing. The murder weapon was eventually found. It matched those knives. It had been wiped clean, but there was still blood evidence."

Jane crossed her arms. "That could be big."

"Damn straight."

"So other than Eli, who had access to his kitchen?"

"His father. His father's wife. Friends?"

Cordelia had passed along an important detail after their trip to the gallery this morning. Kit Lipton was married to John Henry, the owner of the gallery. The age difference was huge.

Nicole returned to scrolling. "I did a little research on Eli's family. His dad—John Henry—is sixty-four. Divorced. Two children, one of whom died in Switzerland years ago while on vacation. He owns the gallery where Eli works. No arrests. He remarried three years ago to Kit Lipton. She was twenty-six at the time."

"Yeah, I met her today. Did you do a background check on her?"

"She moved around a lot when she was a kid, ended up in South Minneapolis. Her mom still lives in the same house. I noted the address in my report. There really isn't a lot to say. No arrests. Attended Washburn High School. Middling student. John Henry is paying for her to get an online degree in art history."

"Did you find any more on the woman who died up near Duluth? The one Eli said was murdered by a serial killer, the same man he maintained murdered Harper?"

Scrolling again, Nicole read for a second and then said, "As it happens, three days ago, the police found the man who committed the murder. Name's Don Gilbert. The woman in question, Tammy Seaton, was in her midfifties, a waitress at a cafe in Bayfield. They'd been dating for a while, and she wanted out. He wasn't having it. It wasn't a serial killing. I figure Eli was just blowing smoke."

Eli seemed to be surrounded by death. First Gideon, and then Harper. Was he the common denominator? Peter might have come home for New Year's Eve to get away from Sigrid and to spend time with his family, but that wasn't the way it was turning out. What was going on with him? The thought that he was somehow involved in Gideon's murder terrified her.

"Want to hear about Marlo and George Krochak?"

"Anything interesting?"

"Not really."

"We should probably go over it."

"Whatever you say, boss." Nicole returned her attention to the iPad.

26

Peter made his way toward the stairway in Cordelia's house while staring at his cell phone. He had a new email from Mia, one he needed to answer before he turned in for the night. Checking his texts, he saw that, over a period of a couple of hours, Jane had sent him three, each one asking him to call as soon as he got it. He assumed it was about Harper Tillman, that she'd found out something she wanted to pass on. He wasn't in the mood to talk to her, so he clicked on the last text, which was from Sigrid.

We can't leave it like we did the other night. I know you need time. I never wanted to hurt you. Please Peter, come home.

Instead of heading up to his bedroom, he sat down on a comfortably padded chair in the great room, gazing up at the triptych of stained glass windows. Who the hell built a place like this, he wondered. Had to have been some wealthy megalomaniac with delusions of grandeur, perfect surroundings for Cordelia and her sister—and their delusions.

An eight-foot-tall Christmas tree still stood in a corner of the room, lit with hundreds of tiny colored lights and groaning under a ton of glittery ornaments. He'd always enjoyed the serene quality of a Christmas tree in a darkened room, the hushed, reverential feel it created inside him. He had so little of that in his life these days. Sitting here, drinking in the quiet, bathed in the soothing light, he felt at peace.

The mood was broken when Cordelia wandered in dressed in a fluffy pink terrycloth robe and matching slippers. She held a glass of milk. "Peter," she said, lifting her chin and staring down at him. "I thought you'd be out carousing with your friends instead of sticking around Chez Thorn."

"Right," he said with a bitter grunt. "I spend all my evenings carousing."

She dragged one of the channel-back chairs closer to him and sat down. "Jane's been texting you all day."

"Yeah, I know," he said, brushing off the question. "I'll get back to her."

"Promise?"

He tried to hide his annoyance. "Sure."

She sat back and studied him. "What's wrong, dearheart? You seem so preoccupied. Even discouraged. You can talk to me, you know. I am, as always, a font of wisdom."

Peter desperately needed a friend. He thought Eli might be that person, but as it turned out, Eli seemed more troubled now than he had years ago. Watching a glass of milk rapidly disappear down Cordelia's throat, he said, "You really like that stuff?"

"Milk? Helps me sleep. Want a glass?"

He shuddered. "No thanks."

"How about a bourbon?"

"I don't drink anymore. I'm an alcoholic." The words just slipped out.

"You're . . . you're . . ." She couldn't seem to finish the sentence.

"I'm also addicted to pain pills and, the cherry on the top of the sundae, cocaine in all its infinite variety."

"Oh, Peter." She slid out of her chair onto her knees, kneed her way over to his chair, and gripped him around the waist, pulling him toward her and pressing her cheek against his chest. "You poor boy. I'm here for you. Anything I can ever do to help you, all you have to do is ask."

As much as he fought his feelings, tears burned his eyes. Her arms felt so good wrapped around him. There'd been little human touch in his life for a very long time. He did believe Cordelia cared about him, and he needed that care. Something unlocked inside him. He wanted to tell her everything.

"How did this happen?" she asked, pulling back and searching his face. "How did I not see?"

"I never let you see," he said, helping her up.

They embraced for a few moments more and then, reluctantly, she resumed her seat.

"I was a mess before we left Minnesota. Sigrid informed me that if things didn't change, if I didn't stop using, we were headed for divorce. I mean, I wanted to change. I hated what my life had become."

"You needed a good rehab."

He lowered his head. "We weren't in Buenos Aires a month before I screwed up the filming one day. The writer and the director were furious. Not only was the footage ruined, but we'd wasted time and money, and it was all my fault. I think the writer, who was a friend, suspected I was using. I know the director wanted to fire me. I got a reprieve that time, and I swore to myself that I'd only use at night. But of course, a couple months later I screwed up again, this time even worse. I begged them to give me one more chance. Mia was in a school she liked. Sigrid finally seemed to be settling in. She even had a job prospect. We were supposed to be in the country for at least nine months. I lasted four. There was no money except for the little I had left from what I'd borrowed from Dad. I called a friend in Seattle. He agreed to loan me enough so I could get the family home and find a rehab. But I couldn't come back to Minneapolis. I was too ashamed. We flew instead to Boston, where one of Siggy's married brothers has a home. He and his wife let Sigrid and Mia stay with them while I was away."

"You could have called me," said Cordelia. "I would have gladly given you the money."

"But then Jane would have found out."

She shot him an indignant look. "I can keep a secret."

Like hell, he thought. She would have been so freaked that the moment she got off the line with him, she would have been on the horn to Jane. He couldn't really blame her, so he never called. "I know you can keep a secret. I just didn't want to put you in that position."

She thought about it. "Well, okay. I guess. Did the rehab help?"

"It was miserable. But, yeah. When I came out, I felt like I had a chance to repair things with Sigrid and Mia. We stayed with Sigrid's brother and his family for the next ten months. Sigrid wanted to return to counseling. She'd been interested in cognitive behavioral therapy for years, particularly as it relates to children. She decided to do some coursework. She found a couple of classes at Boston College that interested her, and because she already has a Masters in psychology, they let her in. That's where she met Dr. Tobias Pool. He was teaching one of the classes. He's South African, has a home there and one in Watford, England, and is well-known and well-respected in the field. He was so impressed by Sigrid that he began taking her under his wing. He even promised her a work visa and a job at one of his clinics in London if she'd consider relocating. He told her she needed to learn from a master."

"He actually said that?"

"Yup."

Cordelia rolled her eyes.

"When she didn't immediately jump at the idea, he sweetened the deal by offering to help her get into the CBT program at King's College in London, another place he teaches. We discussed it. I saw what an incredible opportunity it was for her so, I mean, I agreed. What I didn't know then was that Dr. Tobias Pool, Toby to friends and sycophants, wasn't just interested in Sigrid's brain."

"Heavens," said Cordelia, a hand flying to her chest. "Did she know?"

"She says she didn't. Honestly, the guy's not a looker. He's probably ten years older than Sigrid, but she was charmed by him, by the attention he paid her and all the positive feedback. I finally found a job working for a group doing a documentary on the far-right political shift in Eastern Europe. I was gone for a month at a time. I didn't realize that while I was out of the country, Toby was worming his way into my wife's personal life. When I was home, I sensed that something was off. For one thing, Sigrid seemed happier than she'd been in ages. I told myself that it was because I was out of her life more than I was in it. That kind of self-talk does wonders for a guy's self-esteem."

"Did you ever start . . . using again?"

"It's been a struggle, but no. One day at a time." He could see the relief in her eyes. "Before I flew here a few days ago, Sigrid and I had a fight. A bad one. She admitted that she'd been seeing Toby. That they'd been to bed a few times. She thought she was in love with him, but was confused because she said she loved me, too."

"Oh, Peter," was all Cordelia could squeeze out.

"It's not all her fault. I screwed up. You have no idea what she put up with while I was using. It was a testament to her love for me that she stayed as long as she did."

"Are you saying it's over?"

The last thing he wanted was to break down in front of her. "I think so, yeah." He cleared his throat, clenched his jaw. "I spend every night wondering what to do. I guess I'll give her an easy divorce. The only thing I want is Mia. I want her with me. Sigrid is her mother and I'm not her biological father, but she's always been closer to me. I was the one who found her, the one who brought her home. We have a special bond. Even Sigrid would have to admit that."

"But, if you continue doing documentaries, that means you'll be gone a lot."

"I'll find something else to do. She's only got two years before she goes off to college. I want her to live with me. She loves her school in London, so I'd stay there. I can't stand the thought that Pool might be under the same roof as Mia. Just the idea makes my skin crawl."

"You're not suggesting he has his eye on Mia, too."

"I'm saying," said Peter, "that for a genius psychologist, he doesn't have much understanding of boundaries."

"Have you said any of this to Sigrid?"

"No. Not yet. I need to do it face-to-face."

"So . . . you're leaving?"

"Soon," he said. "It's just . . . I hate to go when a friend of mine seems to be in crisis."

"Eli?"

"No, his old girlfriend. I'd forgotten how much I liked her. She's actually pretty amazing. I knew her as Kit Lipton. That was before she married John Henry."

Cordelia's eyes bugged out. "Kit was *Eli's* girlfriend?"

"Long story."

"You don't say."

"I don't think she's happy. Not sure why. Every time I talk to her, she lets a little more out, but it's like pulling teeth. I guess if I'm being honest, I'd have to admit that I'm attracted to her."

"Listen, Peter, I'm not sure I should say anything, but you know Jane and I have been digging into the Gideon Wise homicide. It seems not only possible but likely that someone at the gallery was involved in his murder."

Peter's world suddenly tilted sideways. "What?"

"Tell me: The night you took Rashad out to eat . . . was that your idea?"

Gripping the arms of his chair, he said, "Partly." He hated lying to her. He hadn't considered his testimony at trial lying, though he had left out certain elements of the story.

"What do you mean, *partly*?"

"Eli asked me if I could keep Rashad away from the condo for a couple hours."

Cordelia eyes widened. Instead of responding, she stood. "Come with me."

"Where are we going?"

"You may not want a drink, but I do."

He followed her into the kitchen, where she opened the refrigerator and removed a can of strawberry soda. Crooking her finger at him, she flipped the light on in the breakfast room and sat down at the long table, nodding for him to do the same. She cracked open the can and took a gulp. "That's better. Now." Pressing her hands on the table, she leaned toward him and asked, "You do realize, Peter, my love, that you perjured yourself at trial."

"No I didn't."

"You were asked if it was your idea."

"It was. Partly."

"Would you have asked him out that *exact* night if Eli hadn't been behind it?"

"Well, I guess . . . no."

She emitted a low, exasperated moan. "Why did Eli need Rashad out of the way?"

"He wanted to talk to Gideon about buying a painting. Rashad thought they spent too much money on fine art, so Eli wanted him out of the way. See, Eli was doing drugs, too. He was my dealer."

Cordelia emitted another low moan, closing her eyes and holding the cold can of pop against her forehead. "This just gets worse and worse."

"No, you need to listen. He was in the dog house at the gallery because . . . well, he was screwing up because of the heroin. When he learned a piece of art from a painter Gideon loved was about to go up for sale, he figured if he could make the sale himself, his dad would see him in a different light. But turns out he never saw Gideon that night. Gideon blew him off."

"That's pretty convenient, don't you think?"

"It's the truth."

"You know that for a fact?"

"Kit told me."

"And Kit has no reason to lie?"

It was Peter's turn to be indignant. "No. Why would she?"

"I can think of a whopper. Eli murdered Gideon and she's trying to protect him."

"No," said Peter flatly. "You're wrong. You don't know her like I do. She's kind of crazy, but . . . no, she'd never do something like that."

"They manipulated you into lying on the stand."

"No, I told you —"

She cut him off. "Peter, this is bad. You were used. By Eli. By Kit. By both of them. And who knows? Maybe old John Henry had a hand in it, too."

"You're way out of line. You say you've found evidence that someone at the gallery killed Gideon. What's your proof? You better have something solid, because this conversation is seriously pissing me off."

"Okay, then listen up: A month or so before his death, Gideon asked the Chenoweth gallery to hang his artwork. This was right after they moved into their new condo. Since both Gideon and Rashad were gone during the day, Gideon gave Eli the code. Eli was the one who took charge of it." She explained about the JHC tote bag and the stranger who approached the elevators that night carrying it. "Come on, Peter. Use your head. Someone from the gallery with access to that key code was in the condo that night. This is serious. Those people you consider your friends are in way over their heads. You need to stay away from them."

He squeezed the bridge of his nose.

"There's more, but I can't get into it. Jane would strangle me. Will you be careful, Peter? Will you find some other friends to play with while you're in town?"

"I'm always careful." As soon as he said the words, he realized how lame they sounded. "I have to go. I promised Mia I'd write her an email tonight."

"Don't do anything stupid."

She had the gall to say that to a drug addict? A guy who rarely did anything else.

"Always remember that I'm here for you, Peter. I love you. So does Jane."

At the sound of his sister's name, he rose. Jane the virtuous. Jane the upstanding. "Thanks," he said. He turned around and walked out, knowing that if he stuck around even for another minute, he'd say something he'd regret.

Eli held Charlotte in his arms as he carried a candle into his bedroom and set it on the dresser. Opening the top drawer, he removed an old cigar box. He flipped back the cover and touched the earring resting inside, caressed the one small, turquoise teardrop. He remembered when he gave the earrings to Harper for her birthday, the dinner he'd made, how pretty she'd looked. And now she was gone.

Tucked under the earring was a piece of paper. He removed and unfolded it. He didn't need the candle to read the words because he'd memorized them long ago.

I'm sorry for how things
turned out last night, but I
had to tell you the truth.
Maybe we can talk later.
What you said about hostages,
it's how I feel.
H.

The filigreed gold at the top of the earring still had mud im-
bedded in it. When he thought about her now, he saw that her death
had been a gift. Harper didn't need to worry anymore about fail-
ures, difficult hurdles, all the myriad tiny struggles that faced him
every day. She didn't need to be sad when she learned that a friend
had received some terrible news. If she did something stupid or
maybe even something really, really bad, she didn't need to feel
guilty or worry about the repercussions that would surely fly at
her. Eli vaguely understood that his views came from his depression and that most people didn't see life that way. Still, it never
ceased to amaze him that when upsetting things happened, Harper
didn't need to be any part of it. Wherever she was, even if it was
nowhere at all, she was at peace.

And he envied that peace.

27

Jane poured her father the last few drops of tea. They were seated at the kitchen table, nibbling on the oatmeal-raisin cookies she'd made last night—in the middle of the night. She often baked when she couldn't sleep. The truth was, she wasn't as "on board" with Julia's potential decision to give up on chemo as she'd let on. She knew it wasn't her decision, but still, it affected her and she would have to say something to Julia when she got home.

Her dad was three days into a new trial, which was taking most of his focus. He'd stopped by after a meeting at his law office that had run late. Now it was going on ten and she could tell he wanted to get home to bed.

"You hear anything back from Chuck Atchison?" he asked.

"Nothing. I've left several messages."

Before he finished off a last bit of cookie, he said, "You seem pretty convinced that the Chenoweth Gallery is where you should put your energy."

"Wouldn't you be?"

"Makes a certain sense. If Eli was the one in there that night, my assumption is that Gideon surprised him. That's why he was murdered. But why was Eli in there in the first place?"

"To rob the place? Do you know if anything was missing?"

"I asked Rashad about that, back before his trial. Since he was never allowed to return to the condo once he was taken into custody for questioning, he had no idea if anything was taken. I would imagine if Marlo Wise had noticed anything missing, she would have said something to the police right away. That never happened. Then again, Marlo wouldn't have been as knowledgeable about what was in the condo as Rashad."

"Can you imagine how that poor man must have felt? Marlo Wise inherits all of it. A woman who thought he was in it for the money, that he never loved her father. She walks away with everything."

Her dad turned the empty mug around in his hand. "Rashad did mention once that he'd given Gideon a small antique coin amulet. It was from Nepal, something Gideon wore around his neck on a thin silver chain. It wasn't worth more than fifty bucks, but Rashad said it was beautiful, a mandala inside an eight-petaled lotus. When the paramedics moved Gideon from the bathroom floor to a gurney, Rashad said he noticed that the silver chain was broken and hanging loose. The amulet was missing."

"He never found it?"

Her father shrugged. "He figured it got trapped inside Gideon's wet clothing. Maybe Marlo has it. Whatever the case, he never saw it again. He regretted that. He did mention it to the police when they interrogated him, mostly because he wanted it back."

"Would it have had any evidentiary value?"

"Probably not," said her father.

Jane watched his expression turn from resignation to puzzlement. "What?" she asked.

"It's probably nothing."

"Tell me."

"Well, I never even considered this before, but if the person who murdered Gideon was into collecting trophies, that could account for it."

"Trophies," repeated Jane.

"It happens," said Ray. "It's twisted, but some murderers want a reminder of the killing, something they can pull out and look at and remember. We should keep it in the backs of our minds. Anyway," he said, rising from the table, "I better hit the road."

With the dogs trailing behind them, Jane walked her father to the front door. "I'll be in touch," she said, giving him a kiss on his cheek.

"You be careful," he said, wrapping his scarf around his neck. "And keep me posted."

When she was back in the kitchen, Jane's cell phone rang. Hoping it was Julia, she answered without looking at the caller ID.

"Janey, you have to hear this." It was Cordelia. Even though she was whispering, she sounded like she was about to explode.

"Hear what?"

"Peter. He's a bigger idiot than I ever realized. Oh, I have so much to tell you. Or, maybe I'm not supposed to. But he didn't swear me to secrecy, so I think it's okay. Oh, hell. Are you sitting down?"

"Just tell me," said Jane, carrying the teapot from the table to the kitchen counter.

"It wasn't his idea to invite Rashad out for a drink that night."

Jane froze. "He actually said that? But . . . at trial—"

"He lied, Janey. On the stand. A few minutes ago he said it was partly his idea, but it wasn't."

"Whose was it?"

"Eli Chenoweth's."

Jane took Cordelia's advice and pulled out a chair. "Why? There has to be a reason." She listened through Cordelia's long, rambling explanation. "Wait, wait, wait," she said at one point. "Eli was Peter's *dealer*? My brother is an addict?" She dropped her head in her hand and listened, growing more concerned with every revelation. "Why did he tell you all this and not me?"

"That's not the point. The point is, he could be in serious trouble if this comes out. Eli Chenoweth is a snake. He manipulated Peter into helping him and then got him to lie."

"Do you think Kit knew?"

"She's the one who told Peter what really happened that night. In fact, he admitted that he likes her."

"Romantically?"

"That was my impression. Apparently her marriage isn't happy. He's staying in town mostly because of her. They're all vipers, in my opinion. Well, maybe not John Henry. I'm not saying he's not viperous in his own inimitable way, but you'd like to think a guy who's the spitting image of Jesus would behave himself. Then again, he married Kit. By the way, did you know she used to be Eli's girlfriend?"

"What?" Jane's mind raced.

"There's more, but those are the headlines."

Massaging her temple, Jane thanked Cordelia and said she needed time to think everything through. "Let's connect tomorrow. Write everything down so you don't forget."

"No worries, Janey. Mind like a steel trap." After a few more inane comments, Cordelia said she needed another stiff strawberry soda. "Later, girlfriend. Out."

Jane set the phone on the table and glanced over at the dogs lying peacefully in their bed by the refrigerator. "This could be seriously bad," she said out loud.

Reacting to the last word, Mouse roused himself and came over, resting his head on her knee.

"Not you," she said, stroking his ears. "You're a *good* boy. A very *good* boy. In fact, I wish all humans had your sense of morality."

He gazed up at her with his serious brown eyes and then gave her hand a lick.

"God, but I love you," she said, lifting his front legs into her lap and hugging him.

Later, as she walked down the hallway to her study, she got a text from Julia.

**Flight was good. I'm at a house
on Lake George. Lots of snow.
Anxious and excited. May not
be in touch for a few days. All is
good. Love you so. J**

It wasn't the call she'd been hoping for, but it was something.

On her way upstairs to take a shower, she texted Nicole Gunness:

**Was anything missing from Harper
Tillman's body?**

If it turned out that something had been removed, it would give credibility to the theory that Eli might be collecting mementos—

if, that is, the murders were connected. That was, in Jane's mind, still a big *if*.

Jane sat behind her desk and wrote Peter an email, detailing the information Nicole Gunness had dug up on Harper's murder. Toward the end, she urged him to give the Chenoweths a wide berth. She didn't mention Kit by name, and she didn't get into any of the other information Cordelia had passed along. It was overwhelming to think Peter had been dealing with an addiction to drugs and nobody in the family had recognized it. The fact that he'd allowed himself to get sucked into Eli's scheme was further proof that he hadn't been thinking clearly before he left for South America. She needed to talk with him, whether he got angry or not. At the end of the email, she asked him to call her tomorrow, told him that she loved him.

She went to bed around midnight. She'd just dozed off when her cell phone rang once again. Fumbling for it on the nightstand, she pressed it on and held it to her ear. "Hello?"

"Is this Jane Lawless?"

She didn't recognize the voice. "Yes?"

"Marlo Wise. Why the hell did you call my husband five times today?"

Jane ran a hand through her hair and cleared her throat. "Because I wanted to talk to him?"

"About what?"

"A tote bag he found in your condo."

"A what? Look, I'm at HCMC. My husband is fighting for his life. If you know anything about—"

"Wait," said Jane. She sat up and swung her legs out of bed. "What happened?"

"His car went over an embankment. He's got a bunch of broken bones, a bruised kidney, a severe concussion, and the poor man has cuts and bruises all over his body. He's in a coma, so I can't exactly ask him why you called."

Jane was so shocked she almost stopped breathing. "When did it happen?"

"The wreck was discovered by a kid around eleven this morning. That's all I know." Marlo began to sob.

"I'm. . . . stunned. I wish I could tell you more," Jane said.

"How could this happen?" Marlo demanded, her voice husky from the tears. "They said he didn't have his seat belt on. He *always* wore his seatbelt."

George had texted that he was headed to the gallery. It had to be the Chenoweths'. A gust of panic blew through her as she thought of Peter and his potential feelings for Kit. Her brother was vulnerable right now, though he probably didn't see it that way. "I'm so sorry."

"I don't need your sympathy. I need my husband back the way he was this morning." Marlo paused. "Oh, go to hell." She ended the call.

28

The following morning, Peter carried coffee and peanut butter toast into the breakfast room. Hattie, once again, was seated at the table, reading.

"No apple pie today?" he asked, pulling out a chair.

She raised her eyes. "Are we gonna do this again?"

"Ice cream?" he said, not even trying to hide his amusement.

She shrugged. "I finished off the chicken tikka masala and wanted dessert."

"You had chicken masala for breakfast?"

"Leftovers? Bolger's boyfriend came over last night and stayed for dinner. I made the rice." She paused. "In a rice cooker. It's not hard."

"Is it all gone?"

"Yup." She smiled down at her book. "In case you were wondering, it was *delicious*."

Bolger Aspenwall III had been employed as Hattie's nanny for several years while he was getting his MFA in directing at the University of Minnesota. He'd spent another year in film school while living in Los Angeles. He'd come back, partly to resume his position, this time as part-time nanny, but also because he needed somewhere cheap to live so he could work on a screenplay. For his service, Cordelia had given him free room and board. He'd commandeered a couple of the old servants' rooms on the third floor.

Without looking up, Hattie continued, "Bolger's writing a screenplay, you know."

"I heard."

She turned a page. "By the way, I filled out that form for *The Planetary Report*. You can make the fifty-dollar check out to The Planetary Society."

He'd completely forgotten. "Sure. I'll get it to you later today."

"The check's in the mail," she said, again with a smile. Closing the book, she pushed her chair back.

"Big plans today?" he asked.

"It's Sunday. Auntie Cordelia is taking Hazel and me to a movie."

"Sounds like fun."

"And then we're going out for dinner with Jane. Probably Italian. Auntie Cordelia says that Jane needs us right now."

"Really? Why's that?"

"Not entirely sure, but Julia's gone for a few nights and my aunt says Jane's really worried about her. Julia's sick, you know."

Peter didn't have all the details. Last he'd heard, she was having some problems with her eyesight.

"It's cancer," said Hattie.

"Oh. Wow."

"My aunt thinks Jane should be around family. To cheer her up."

He wondered why Jane hadn't said anything to him. Then again, he'd never asked. Cancer was a terrible blow, though it hardly altered his opinion of his sister's enchanted life. Jane Lawless, woman of steel. Successful at everything she touched. Still, he did feel a slight pang of guilt at his lack of compassion.

Hattie walked around to the other side of the table, gave Peter a hug, and then shuffled out, saying, "Later, dude."

"Yeah, later," he said.

Sitting alone, looking through the multipaned windows at the rose garden covered in snow, he brushed his thoughts of Jane away and turned to the conversation he'd had the previous night with Cordelia. He assumed that by now, she'd broadcast his sad tale to everyone in the family and was vying to make it the lead story on the evening news. Peter Lawless is a screwup. Maybe it was easier that way. He wouldn't need to explain it himself. Cordelia's biggest reaction had come when he acknowledged that Eli had been the one behind Peter's invitation to Rashad May. Now that the gallery was considered the epicenter of his sister's investigation into Gideon Wise's murder, he was once again unsure about what he'd gotten himself into.

Taking out his cell phone, he tapped in Kit's number. He waited through half a dozen rings and was about to hang up when she answered.

"Hey. I was just thinking about you," she said, a smile in her voice.

"You were? I mean, that's nice to hear."

"I had a great time at the bar the other night."

"Yeah, me too. Listen, I was wondering if we could get together for lunch today."

"Are you flirting with me, Peter Lawless?"

"What? No, no—"

"Can't," she said. "It's my day off. I need to study."

"Oh. Bummer."

"What about tonight?"

"Can you get away?"

"I'll figure it out. How about the Lighthouse again. Say around eight?"

"Perfect."

"Can't wait. Gotta run, baby. Bye."

Jane stood in front of the first-floor reception desk at the Hennepin County Medical Center and waited for a woman to locate George's room number. If he was in intensive care, she doubted she would be allowed to see him. She hadn't been able to get any information over the phone.

"6244," said the woman.

"Is he in the ICU?"

"No, it's a private room," the receptionist said before explaining where to find the elevators.

On six, Jane walked through a maze of hallways until she finally found the room and, since nobody was around to prevent her, went in. George was lying in the bed, hooked up to various machines, his eyes closed, one arm in a cast, and one leg in a brace. He bore little resemblance to the man she'd met on Friday. There was really no point in coming, she supposed, except that she wanted to see him. If—and when—he woke up, she hoped he'd be able to remember what happened, who'd done this to him. Jane felt guilty because if she hadn't asked him to look for the tote bag, none of this would have happened.

Stepping up to the bed, she whispered, "Hi, George. It's Jane Lawless. I want you to know how sorry I am that I got you involved. I've been thinking about you, pulling for you. I hope we can talk sometime soon." Turning at the sound of footsteps, she backed away as a nurse came in. "Hi," said Jane. "How's George doing this morning?"

"Are you a relative?"

"Friend."

The nurse took a moment to reset one of the machines. "His condition has been upgraded from critical to serious. His vital signs are stable."

"Has he been awake?"

"Not yet." She checked the drip on a fluid bag.

"Where's Marlo?"

"I encouraged her to go home, take a shower, and put on some clean clothes. I don't think she got much sleep last night."

"Has anyone else been up to see him today?" Jane wasn't sure how worried she should be that one of the Chenoweths might try to finish the job they started.

"No, I don't believe so. A number of people have called about him. His cousin in Montana called two or three times."

"Male or female cousin?"

"No idea. I didn't take the calls." The nurse stepped up to a whiteboard on the wall across from the bed, erased the previous day's date and wrote the current day's.

With nothing left to do, Jane whispered goodbye to George and headed back to the elevators, glad, at least, that she hadn't run into Marlo.

In the report Nicole Gunness had compiled, Jane learned that Trevor Loy, the man who'd dropped the bombshell at Rashad's trial, was living in supportive housing for people with mental health issues. At the time of the trial, her father's conclusion was that his hyperverbal behavior when he'd met with Rashad at the condo was most likely due to his being high on drugs or alcohol. His mental health issues seemed to be the actual reason.

Jane didn't hold out a lot of hope that Trevor would talk to her. Still, it was important for her to give it a shot.

The small, one-and-a-half-story house was close to Minnehaha Creek, and also close to bus lines and light rail. Jane stood on the front steps and rang the bell, hoping Loy would be around. She didn't have his phone number, so there was no other way to contact him. She spent a few seconds flipping through her phone to see if Cordelia had responded to a text from earlier that morning. Jane needed to tell her about George's accident, if that's what it was. Since it was going on eleven, Cordelia was likely in the midst of her Sunday morning routine: Rising late, a leisurely bath, and breakfast as she scoured the *Star Tribune* and the *Twin Cities Pioneer Press*, occasionally augmented by the *New York Times* if Bolger happened to be out and about and picked one up.

As Jane brought up her personal calendar, a short, compactly built black man drew back the door.

"Help you?" he asked.

"I hope so. I'm looking for Trevor Loy."

"Yeah? How come?"

"Are you Trevor?"

"Maybe."

She handed him a card. "My name's Jane Lawless."

"Lawless," he repeated, sticking an unlit cigar into the side of his mouth. "You any relation to—"

"He's my father. I'm an investigator. I'm looking into some issues surrounding the Gideon Wise murder."

"That case was already solved, lady."

"May I come in?"

He hesitated. "I guess."

As she crossed in front of the man, she noticed that he had a heavy hand with cologne. The living room was homey: brown carpet, a small TV in the corner, some comfortable-looking furniture. Magazines. Everything was neat.

Trevor dumped himself onto the couch. "Make it quick, okay? I gotta get ready for work."

"I really only have one question," she began. "Did anyone pressure you to testify at Rashad May's trial?"

"What? No," he said, bouncing his leg. "No way."

"Everything you said was true?"

"You saying I lied?"

"Do you know a cop named Dean Frick?"

He appeared to think it over, but he wasn't much of an actor. Dropping the unlit cigar into the pocket of his shirt, he said, "Yeah, I may have met the man."

"I hear he's not a fan of the LGBT community."

Trevor shrugged.

"He never pressured you in any way?"

"Tell me, lady: You ever see Rashad?"

"Yesterday."

"How's he doing?"

"How do you think? He's in prison. For something he didn't do."

Trevor grabbed a throw pillow and hugged it.

"You could help get him out, if you wanted."

"How? You asking me to name names? Screw that. I tell you what you want to know and I can kiss my freedom goodbye. Maybe even my life."

"You really believe that?"

"Frick, he don't play games. And anyway, who'd believe a guy who's spent the last two years in and out of mental health lock-ups? I'm crazy, don't you know that?" He flashed his eyes at her. "Look, I did what I did because I had no choice. It was me or Rashad. I picked me."

"What did Frick have on you?"

"Nothing. Not a goddamn thing." He stood, shoved his hands in his pockets. "That's all I gotta say."

As she reached the door, he gripped her arm and spun her around.

"You tell anyone about this conversation and I promise, you'll regret it."

She studied him. All these years later and the guy was still terrified. "Thanks for your time, Trevor."

29

Marlo dragged herself up the stairs to her bedroom. As she removed her coat, she noticed a tote bag with the letters JHC resting on the bed. Scattered around it were all the rock posters she'd collected in college, most of them creased or ripped beyond repair. Picking up the tote, she glanced inside, vaguely remembering that Jane Lawless had mentioned a tote last night on the phone. Marlo couldn't even begin to imagine that there was a connection between the tote and George's accident, so she set it aside and began to undress. Before she entered the bathroom, her cell phone rang.

"Hello," she said, opening the closet door to grab some clean clothes.

"Marlo?"

"Yes?"

"This is Amy Atchison, Chuck's wife?"

"Oh. Hi."

"I hope I'm not catching you at a bad time."

"Well—"

"It's about Chuck. I got a voice mail from him last night saying he's coming home. I tried calling him, but he doesn't answer. I want you to tell that bastard that if he thinks he's coming back here, he's got another think coming. I threw him out weeks ago. Contacted a lawyer. The divorce is already in the works."

"I had no idea," said Marlo, sitting down on the bed.

"Isn't he staying with you?"

"Yeah, for the last few days. But he said nothing about any problems."

"He's a *walking* problem. He was fired from this job, too, in case he didn't tell you that. I talked to the wife of one of the other lawyers and finally found out what was going on. He'd been trying to bed half a dozen women at the law firm, threatening to get each one fired if she didn't play ball. The firm found out. That's why he left so fast."

"When did that happen? When did he leave?"

"Almost three weeks ago. He's a disgusting little turd, pardon my language. I hope he goes to jail. Be careful around him. He fooled me for years."

Marlo didn't know what to say. "I thought he was doing great in Florida, but he told me you wanted to move back here."

"Another one of his self-serving lies."

"He also said he had this fabulous new boat—"

"A *boat*? In his dreams. Don't believe anything that man says to you. Look, just tell him to stay the hell away from me. Tell him that if he comes back here I'll make sure the police know about it. If he wants to see his little girl, he can hire a lawyer. Just between us, I don't think he's got enough money left to hire a cab."

After ending the call, Marlo put her clothes back on and trotted down the steps to the first floor, heading straight for Chuck's room. The door was closed. She didn't knock. She found him lying on his back, mouth flapping open, the covers pulled up to his neck.

Throwing open the shades, Marlo whirled around.

He didn't move.

The idea of touching him disgusted her. Noticing a half-empty bottle of beer on the nightstand, she tossed what was left over his face.

He sputtered and opened his eyes. "Wha . . . Marlo? What the hell?"

She smiled. "Not going to church this morning, Chuckie?"

He sat up, wiping his face. "Did you just pour beer on me?"

She held her palms up, eyes rising to the ceiling. "Must be raining." She stomped over to the closet and pulled out one of his suitcases. Tossing it on the bed, she went back to the closet and began yanking clothes off hangers.

"What are you doing?"

"Helping you pack. You're leaving."

"I am?"

"Your wife called. Said you were planning to head home to Florida. She wanted me to give you a message."

He drew back the covers and sat gingerly at the edge of the mattress. "Oh?"

"For the sake of time, I'll paraphrase: Go to hell, Chuck. Eat dirt and die."

Whatever his reaction, he processed it silently. "Did she say anything else?"

"About you being fired? About the sexual harassment? About the police wanting to talk to you? And oh my gosh, there's no luxury cabin cruiser. Who knew?"

When he stood, Marlo ordered him to sit back down. She wasn't about to have a conversation with a man wearing nothing but tighty-whities.

"Amy's angry at me."

"You think?"

"Please don't believe her lies, Marlo."

"You'd prefer me to believe yours?" She opened one of the bureau drawers and started pelting him with rolled-up socks.

"Stop," he said, batting them away.

"If you're not out of here in ten minutes, I'm calling the police."

"But . . . I have nowhere to go."

"Try a street corner," she said. One of her all-time favorite pastimes was telling assholes where to go. This time it was particularly heartwarming. "Ten minutes, Chuck. Not one second more."

30

Charlotte rested on her side on the kitchen table across from Eli, licking and biting at her paw. She wasn't looking at him, but he knew she was listening. "You don't know what any of this is," he said, pulling a pack of shoelaces and a syringe out of a brown paper sack.

He'd been talking to her a lot since she'd come home with him. She seemed to like the sound of his voice and sometimes purred when he spoke. He'd taken her to a vet on Friday to get her checked out. The vet thought she was less than a year old and, eventually, after poking and prodding, pronounced her healthy. A tech had located a microchip under her skin and had called the owner, only to learn that the number was no longer in service. On Charlotte's behalf, Eli was furious. How anyone could throw her away was beyond him.

Charlotte didn't much like riding in the car, unless she could be inside his coat. She seemed relieved when they got home. She dove immediately for one of her favorite blankets and slept for several hours.

"Don't be frightened," he said to her. "The syringe is kind of pokey, but it won't hurt you." If only he could promise that nothing would ever hurt her again.

Eli already had a spoon and a lighter. The only piece of the puzzle he was missing was the heroin. He could get that anywhere, anytime. Was he really going to do it? Looking at Charlotte, he felt less certain than he had before. If he went through with it, he assumed it would come down to an emotional decision in the middle of the night, probably after he'd had too much to drink. But since he wasn't drinking, maybe it was something he could continue to fight off.

"I don't want that kind of life ever again," he told Charlotte. What he might want, however, was a quick death. He remembered Woody Allen once saying that he wasn't afraid of dying, he just didn't want to be around when it happened.

"If I ever did decide . . . I'd find you a good home before I . . . you know," he said, his finger scratching the side of Charlotte's head.

She stood up, arched her back, stretched her front paws, and then came over and rubbed her head against his chest. Eli had been looking stuff up on cat behavior on the internet. The more he read, the more he realized that cats were nothing like dogs.

Scraping the partial rig back into the sack, he hid it under the sink next to his revolver and then got up and grabbed his coat. Sundays had become empty days for him. Less so now that Charlotte was here, but still, his loneliness never seemed to go away.

In the last three months, except for his work at the gallery, he'd become a recluse. Things he used to be interested in no longer seemed to matter. Except for Kit. Sometimes he felt like she was the only thing tethering him to the earth. His love for Kit had kept him alive. For months now, heroin and Kit were all he thought about. He wondered sometimes if they were the same thing.

Eli waded through the previous night's three-inch snowfall to the main house. The morning had dawned sunny and cold. After brushing off his jeans and kicking the snow from his boots, he entered the back door. "Hello?" he called. "Anybody home?"

He found Kit in his dad's den, working at the desktop computer.

"I'm studying," she said as he came into the room.

"Can't you take a break?"

"No." She kept her eyes on the screen.

"Where's Dad?"

"No idea."

Eli curled himself into an overstuffed chair. "Have dinner with me tonight."

"Can't."

"Sure you can."

"I'm meeting Peter."

His jaw tightened. "You two getting it on?"

"Of course not," she snapped, shooting him an angry look. "Grow the hell up. He's a friend."

"Uh huh."

"He's also our only conduit to what's happening in the Wise investigation. Would you rather not know?"

He studied his hands.

"Thought so."

"Oh, bite me," he said, angry that she'd found a reasonable excuse for her behavior.

The comment prompted a smile. "You really want me to?"

"More than you know."

She leaned back and scrutinized him. "I'm a married woman, Eli."

"So I keep hearing."

"You push too hard."

"You're a married woman, and I'm a desperate man."

"Are you? I probably shouldn't say this, but I'm not a terribly happily married woman."

"Leave him. Come back to me." It was an awful thing to say, and yet he didn't care. His dad had crossed a line. Now he was crossing one, too. Then, afraid that Kit might order him to leave, he said the first thing to come into his head. "You said Dad had a secret."

"Did I?" She wheeled her chair out from behind the desk. "Don't we all?"

"I suppose. But you keep dangling it in front of me like you want to tell me what it is."

Stretching her arms above her head, she said, "Look, baby, your father has lots of secrets. I will say, one of them is totally driving me insane."

He waited, assuming it was best not to press for details.

"I think he's seeing someone behind my back."

Eli couldn't help himself. He burst out laughing. "So?"

"He promised me before we got married that he'd always be faithful."

"Oh, please. You haven't been exactly faithful yourself. Seems I remember a bubble bath a few days ago—"

She glared. "I knew you'd bring that up. You have my permission to shove off, genius. I've got work to do."

"I'm sorry."

"No you're not."

"Tell me why you think he's cheating."

"Because he's been staying overnight at the gallery a lot lately."

Long ago, Eli's father had fixed up one of the small second-floor offices with bunk beds, a TV, and a mini fridge, for nights when someone needed to work late or didn't want to fight the winter weather.

"Maybe he doesn't like making the long drive home late at night."

"Nope."

"You have proof of an affair?"

She lowered her voice. "A couple of weeks ago, he called me and said he was bunking at the gallery. I don't remember the excuse he gave. It doesn't matter. I decided to see if he was lying, so I drove back up to Minneapolis and checked behind the gallery to see if his car was in the lot. It wasn't."

"Maybe he went out for something to eat."

"At two in the morning?"

Okay. She had a point. "Track him."

"What?"

"There are lots of ways to do it. You could put a GPS tracker on his car."

That got her attention.

"I'll install one for you and show you how to monitor him. You can do it from your cell phone. It's not hard. I guarantee you'll know where he is every minute of the day."

The glint in her eye told him she was hooked. "Is it expensive?"

"Consider it a gift."

"Thank you, Eli." Her voice softened. "You're still my sweet baby, aren't you?"

He liked the sound of that.

"When could we do it?"

The fact that he already owned one made his answer easy. "Come to my place after you get back from your date with Peter."

She threw a magazine at him. "It's not a date."

"I'll be up. Just knock." He figured the offer had scored him a few points. And later tonight, he hoped to collect.

31

Peter arrived at the Lighthouse before Kit did. He ordered himself a nonalcoholic beer so he wouldn't look out of place.

Kit came in a while later wearing all black—an off-the-shoulder dress with a sort of flouncy ruffled thing at the top and thin straps crisscrossing her neck. As she walked up to the booth, Peter saw every guy in the place watching her.

He scolded her once again for not wearing a coat.

"What's up with you and coats?" she asked, sliding into the booth across from him. "It's in the car. I think I can walk ten feet without risking hypothermia."

She ordered a Tom Collins, kind of a silly drink in Peter's opinion, but it suited her as everything she chose seemed to, the frosted glass looking long and elegant in her hand.

"So why did you want to get together again?" he asked.

"I missed you."

"Come on."

"You don't believe me? We had such a great time the other night. I like you, Peter. A bit more than I should."

Was she flirting, telling him the truth, or just playing? When it came to Kit, he could never tell. The bruise on her arm had faded a little, but it was still visible, more green and gray now than black and blue.

She saw him looking at it. "Doesn't hurt anymore."

"Good. That's . . . good." His thoughts went immediately to John Henry. "Where's your husband tonight?"

"The gallery. We've got a new show coming up." She sipped her drink. "I just learned that the gallery's in financial trouble."

"Serious trouble?"

"Could be. I don't have the details. But Eli and I could be out of a job if my darling husband can't raise a significant amount of cash."

His eyes widened. "That's awful."

"Yeah, pretty much."

"Listen, Kit. I don't mean to change the subject, but there's something I really need to ask you about. You know my sister's investigating the Wise murder."

She nodded, looking concerned.

"Well, it turns out that a tote bag from your gallery was found at the scene. You don't know anything about it, do you?"

"No," she said, looking puzzled.

"My sister thinks it's possible that someone at the gallery may be responsible for Gideon's murder."

"Are you kidding me? Why would she think that?"

"I don't have all the details."

"Boy," said Kit, crossing her arms, "I know she's your sister, but that sure sounds like a leap in the dark to me."

"Apparently Eli installed some artwork at the condo a few weeks before Gideon's murder. He was given the key code to get into the unit because Gideon and Rashad were at work, which means he

216

had access—and continued to have access. Gideon never changed the code. The condo showed no signs of breaking and entering. Think about it, Kit. There are way too many coincidences here. Gideon's schedule wasn't a problem because he was never home until after seven at night, but Rashad's was. The solution? Ask a credulous friend to invite Rashad out for a drink and then dinner."

Kit didn't even try to hide her shock. "You're saying it was Eli? No way, Peter. That never happened. He never even talked to Gideon that night. Remember, Gideon blew him off."

"That was Eli's story."

"It was."

"Maybe he lied."

Her eyes fastened on him. "You're not hearing me. I saw with my own two eyes how frustrated he was when he got home. I know he felt humiliated. If he'd just murdered a man, do you think he could hide it? Eli? Remember, I was the one who forced him to go back and try again. You asked if he had any blood on his clothes when he came back the second time. The answer is no, Peter. Don't you think I'd remember something like that? It wasn't there."

Peter's mind hurt. He didn't know what to believe.

Kit continued. "I'd say that Gideon never answered any of Eli's calls that night because he was already dead."

"I . . . suppose that's possible."

"Not just possible, likely."

"Are you saying you don't believe Eli is capable of murder?"

This time, she hesitated. "Who can say what another person is capable of."

It wasn't an answer. "Did you know his girlfriend, Harper Tillman?"

She seemed a bit thrown by the change in subject. "Yeah."

"Did they seem happy?"

"I guess."

"There weren't any major problems?"

"Not that I knew about. How come you're so interested in Harper?"

"Eli thinks she was the victim of a serial killer. He even has a theory about another killing up near Duluth, that they were connected. It was a woman. Did he tell you about that?"

"No," she said, looking bewildered.

"The police found the woman's killer. He was an ex-boyfriend."

She raised an eyebrow. "Well, that doesn't surprise me. Ex-boyfriends are the gifts that keep on giving."

"Did you know the police thought Eli had done it? Murdered Harper?"

"This is just crazy, Peter. Who told you that?"

"He had a set of kitchen knives. One was missing. The police believe it was the same knife used to murder Harper."

She didn't move.

"I asked my sister to do a little digging into the murder."

"Wait, wait, wait," she said, drawing her cell phone out of her purse and clicking it on. "It's my dad. I have to take it."

Peter felt like he'd been stuffed into a washing machine set to the spin cycle. He took a couple of swallows of his fake beer and tried to catch his breath. Everything he'd said to Kit about Harper seemed to come as a complete shock to her.

"Hey, Daddy, thanks for calling back." She listened. "No, that's cool. Where are you?" She lowered her eyes. "Uh huh. But you said—" She pressed her lips together. "Okay." She listened again, longer this time. "No, I get it. I do. Next time, yeah." She looked up at Peter. "Me? I'm good. I'm having dinner with a very handsome man. And no, he's not my husband." She laughed, pulling her drink closer. "I will. I love you, too. Bye." Clicking off the phone, she returned it to her purse. "Just nice to hear his voice, you know? I thought he might be coming here, but I guess not."

A waiter came up and asked if they wanted another drink.

"I think we're good," said Peter.

"I need french fries," said Kit, smiling up at the guy. "A double order. And lots of ketchup. We'll share."

"Of course," said the waiter.

As he walked away, Peter said, "Can I ask one more question about Gideon's murder and then we can change the subject?"

"Okay, I guess."

"What about John Henry?"

"What about him?"

"Do you think he could be the one who was in the condo that night?"

She shook her head, looked exasperated. "Okay, I grant you, he may be creepy as hell, but he's not a murderer. He's way too old."

Not exactly a glowing testimonial. "What do you mean by 'creepy'?"

"Look, did it ever occur to you that your sister's barking up the wrong tree? She's not infallible, you know. The police must have investigated all this. They indicted Rashad. I'd trust their conclusions before I'd trust hers."

For the first time Peter had the sense that she was protesting too much.

"Come on. New topic: Tell me how things are going with your wife."

It was his turn to grimace.

"That bad?"

He wanted to dig deeper into Eli. Every instinct he had told him his troubled old friend was responsible for two murders. But he'd made a promise. "I'm not talking about my marriage."

"Fair enough." She reached for his hand. "Let's regroup, okay? How about this: I want to know all about the UK, what it's like to live there. What your apartment is like. Come to think of it, maybe you should take me with you when you go back." She laughed. Giving his hand a playful tug, she added, "I've always wanted to travel. Wouldn't that be a hoot if we went together?"

"What about John Henry?"

"To hell with John Henry. He can stay home and watch PBS. Or do some of his other, shall we say, less-savory activities."

Once again, Peter didn't know what to make of her. Was she really asking to fly back with him? Taking her to London was hardly an option, though he did like the sound of it—walking into the apartment he shared with Sigrid with Kit on his arm. The look on Sigrid's face might be well worth the price of the ticket.

32

Waiting for Cordelia and Hattie to join her for dinner at the restaurant that night, Jane walked into the pub and found Ted Rucker, Peter's old friend, sitting at the bar, nursing a beer. Stepping up next to him, she said, "Hey, Ted, good to see you."

He turned and smiled. He was a stocky man with a decidedly uncool mullet and a horseshoe mustache. "You, too. I wanted one of your famous pub burgers, but—" He patted his stomach. "—my girlfriend tells me I'm getting fat."

"I hear congratulations are in order. Your new job?"

"Oh, yeah, right. You must have talked to Peter. I'm pretty stoked about it. Pays really well, and I like the work."

"Let me ask you a question," she said, pulling out a stool. "Do you happen to know Eli Chenoweth or Kit Lipton?"

He seemed a bit thrown by the question. "Sure. Both of them."

"I don't suppose you'd have a minute to talk?"

Still looking puzzled, he said, "Okay."

"I'm just trying to get some background on them. I was hoping you could help."

"For an investigation? This P.I. stuff you do?"

"Something like that."

"Well, I mean, I'm not sure what I can tell you. I haven't seen either of them in years."

"How did you meet Eli?"

"Through Peter. And then later we joined the same bowling team." He held up his hand. "I know, I know. He doesn't seem like the bowling type, but once he had a few beers in him and relaxed, it was all good."

"What did you think of him?"

"Eli?" He shrugged. "I'll grant he's kind of odd, but underneath, I think he's a decent guy."

"You knew about his drug addiction?"

"Hard to miss it. I hear he got clean. Probably why I don't see him anymore. He's stopped going to bars and I haven't. I will say, he was always trying to hit up friends for 'a loan,' as he called it. I assumed it was to pay for drugs. Got kind of old, you know? I never had anything to give him. There were times when he really seemed desperate. I mean, I would have felt sorry for the guy if he hadn't been so annoying, so pushy."

If Eli needed money that badly back before he got clean, maybe burglarizing Gideon and Rashad's condo had seemed like a good idea. It would certainly have been a compelling motive.

"What about Kit?"

He smiled at the mention of her name. "I dated her for a few months. In fact, I was the one who told her about the job opening at the gallery."

"What was she like?"

"Crazy. Fun. Unpredictable. I will say she had a rather fast and loose relationship with the truth sometimes. I figured it was

222

always best not to take what she said too literally. Even so, I could have fallen hard for her. But then she started dating Eli, and that was the end of me."

"Did she do drugs with him?"

"I don't know for sure, but I doubt it. She was never very interested in drugs. She liked cocktails. I never saw her drink more than three over the course of an evening. Hated wine. She had sort of blue collar tastes, but she had aspirations. And, if you don't mind my saying so, she was hot and knew it. She wasn't above using that. But—" He looked down at his glass.

"But?"

"There were times when she got super nasty, especially with other women. She had very few female friends, as far as I could tell."

"Not as easy to manipulate as men?"

"Huh?" The comment seemed to catch him off guard. "I suppose that's one way to look at it."

"Can you give me an example of her nastiness?"

"Well, I mean, there was one time when this girl, her name was Stacy, was sitting next to Eli. There were about a dozen of us at the bar that night. We all knew each other. Some people were dating, some were just there to hang out. Anyway, Stacy seemed really into Eli, laughing at all his lame jokes, the kind the rest of us would groan at. When Stacy got up to go to the women's room, Kit followed her. And then, when they came back, Kit sat down next to Eli and Stacy grabbed her coat and left. If you want to know the truth, she seemed kind of scared to me, so I asked her about it later. She said, in no uncertain terms, that Kit was a psycho bitch and that someone should tell Eli to be careful."

"What did you think of that?"

"Probably just a catfight. I can't see Kit actually hurting her. Although—"

Jane waited.

"That woman could turn on a dime. You did something she didn't like, and you better watch out. When she was angry, she'd get this stone-cold look in her eyes. Always made me want to run for the hills."

"You knew she married Eli's father?"

"What? Seriously? John Henry?"

"Peter didn't say anything to you?"

"No. Wow. That is seriously . . . wrong. He must be thirty years older than her."

"Did you know John Henry well?"

"Not well, and I never liked him. Back then, I'd throw a party every few months. I'd buy a keg and some munchies and others would bring the harder stuff. If I invited Eli, John Henry would show up too, totally uninvited. Usually late in the evening. Always alone. He'd have a few beers or a few hits of weed, start dancing around, kind of in his own world. Sometimes he'd grab one of the girls and spin her around. I know most of them thought he was fun, eccentric, a real free spirit. I thought he was old, and strange— way stranger than Eli." Ted tipped his glass back and finished the beer.

Jane could tell he wanted to get going. "One last question: Can you see any of them being violent?"

He considered it. "Nah. Not really."

"This has been helpful."

"Good, I'm glad. But, you know, I gotta get home."

She stood and walked him out, glad that he'd been able to provide her with some much-needed perspective. Most importantly, he'd given her a possible motive for Eli being in the condo that night. She had a lot more work to do to figure out what had actually gone down, but it was Kit, once again, who continued to dominate her thoughts. Even if she didn't have anything to do with Gideon's death, Jane feared she had her sights set on Peter. Gideon's murder was part of an investigation, but with Peter, it was far more personal.

Charlotte was curled into a ball on the couch, snoozing. Eli had spent the last half hour playing with her, dragging a feather on a string around his bed as she tried to grab it. She seemed to love these little games. When they were done, she'd butted her head against his legs again and again, sliding her body along his shins. They were learning about each other. He'd spent a great part of the afternoon watching YouTube videos on cat behavior.

Standing at the kitchen counter, Eli was almost finished with a bowl of cereal when the doorbell rang. Charlotte woke instantly and stood, her tail swishing. When he answered the door, Eli found Kit outside, wearing a black dress he'd never seen before. So she's dressing sexy for Peter now, he thought acidly. The idea launched him into an instant bad mood.

"Are you alone?" she asked.

"Am I ever not alone?" He stepped back so she could enter. Out of the corner of his eye he saw Charlotte make a mad dash for the bedroom. "You're early."

"I am?" she said, setting her purse on the kitchen table.

"Figured you and Lawless would rent yourselves a no-tell motel room for a few of hours of hot sex."

"Just shut up," she said sharply, parking herself at the table. "I told you: He's a friend. That's it." She pulled on a strand of her hair, "I will say, I don't like lying to him."

"Oh, come on."

"That story you thought up about selling Gideon a painting? It was such a godawful mishmash, I can't believe he bought any of it. Now I'm not so sure he did."

"We had to tell him something. Like you said, we couldn't tell him the truth."

"You mean the fact that you couldn't keep your pants zipped?"

He needed a drink. "You still hold that against me, don't you?"

"Nailing your dealer's girlfriend wasn't exactly the action of a playboy genius. And beyond that, how on earth could you be into him for so much money?"

"We've had this conversation a thousand times. I used the product instead of selling it."

"If he hadn't been so pissed off at you about his girlfriend—"

"But he was. And when he demanded the money I owed him, what could I do? Gideon's condo was a freakin' treasure trove, Kit. The guy was a jewelry magnet. He had so much bling that there was no way he could keep track of it all."

"Have you ever thought that if it hadn't been for your poor execution that night, we might still be together?"

"Sure, I'm always the one to blame." He threw himself down on a chair.

His father had forced him into rehab when he'd found out that a drug dealer wanted to break his son's legs. Moving to California had seemed like a pretty good idea. "You still blame me for sleeping with her, don't you? That's why you broke up with me."

"I broke up with you because you're an idiot," said Kit. "Sex is an itch. It's like eating a sandwich. Why would I assign moral weight to something like that?"

He wasn't sure he liked that. "What did Peter say about his sister's investigation?"

"There's no real evidence that links the gallery to Gideon's murder, just a bunch of theories she can't prove. Even so, she thinks you did it, that you murdered Gideon."

He closed his eyes "I should go to the police, talk to them."

"Eli, no. Just think about it. Why give them the opportunity to trip you up? You think you could handle a police interrogation?"

"It wouldn't be like that. I'd just *talk* to them."

"You're not thinking clearly." Hesitating, she asked, "You're not using again, are you?"

"No. Relax. I'm just saying, with my luck, Rashad will get a new trial, be acquitted, and I'll end up in prison."

She searched his face. "Can we be honest for once? Really, truly honest? I wasn't there with you that night. Did you actually make it up to his condo? You can tell me. You know I'd never judge you."

"No, Kit. The part about getting cold feet, that was true. I never saw Gideon."

"Okay."

"You believe me?"

"Of course. I just needed to ask."

"I could ask the same thing of you," said Eli. "Did you lie to me about what you did?"

"Do we have to rehash this all over again? Aren't you sick of it? I sure as hell am."

"Except I can't shake the thought that someone recognized you."

"Listen carefully. This is the last time I'm going to say it: I got off the elevator on the ninth floor and found police crawling all

227

over it. I had no idea what was going on. One of the uniforms asked me what I was doing and I said I was there to see Bree Mitchell."

"That was smart of you, looking at the names over the mailboxes in the lobby." Kit had been so disgusted with him when he'd returned home empty-handed, shooting up before she could get the full story out of him, that she'd driven back to the condo to get the job done herself. "You're absolutely positive that the cop who stopped you didn't think something was fishy?"

"No, baby. There was so much going on that he barely looked at me. He just told me it was a crime scene and I had to leave."

Eli leaned his head back and closed his eyes. "This is such a mess."

"It's *not*. You were never inside the condo, and neither was I."

"Right," he whispered, feeling like a man buried alive under an avalanche of lies.

"Are you ready for my second news flash?"

"Oh God," he whispered.

"Peter asked his sister to look into Harper's homicide."

"What?"

"Apparently you told him she was a victim of a serial killer. Is that why you're reading all those kinky books?"

"She *was* murdered by a serial killer, the same one who killed a woman up north."

"Afraid not, baby. They caught that woman's murderer a couple of days ago. He was an ex-boyfriend."

Eli wiped a shaky hand across his mouth. Removing a pack of cigarettes from his shirt pocket, he lit up.

"Eli, what's going on?"

"For all I know you did it."

"Killed Harper?"

When the weight of her eyes on him was too much to bear he said, "If Peter's sister is right about the gallery and Gideon, then I'd say her suspects are me, you, and Dad."

"Your dad had nothing to do with it."

"He's human, Kit, which means he's capable of doing bad things."

"No disagreement there."

Something in her tone caused the hairs on the back of his neck to stand up.

"He's weak, Eli. If I've learned anything about him in the last few years, it's that. He could never pull something like that off. Besides, his closet is already crammed to the rafters with secrets."

"Are you ever going to tell me about any of them?"

She shrugged. "Maybe."

"Do I have to beat it out of you?"

The comment elicited a smile.

"Come on. I can take it." He took another drag, then stubbed the cigarette out on a dirty plate.

"If I do tell you, it will come as a shock."

"Stop stalling."

She tugged her chair closer to the table. "I'm royally sick of keeping this to myself. Next time you're over at our house, check out his computer in the den. Look for file 3113. Write the number down or you'll forget."

"I can remember."

"No you can't, genius. Write it down."

He scooped a pen off the table and wrote it on his arm.

"If, after you've looked at the file, you should decide to drop a bomb and let your dad know you found out, don't mention me."

"Because? Are you afraid of him?"

"Absolutely not."

"Methinks the lady doth protest too much?"

"Huh? Look, I don't want our marriage to blow up before I'm ready. That's all I'm saying."

That could be the reason, but Eli wasn't so sure. There were times when he actually did think she was afraid of his dad. "What qualifies as 'ready'?"

"None of your business." She made a bridge of her fingers and rested her chin on top. "Now. Did you buy me that tracking device like you promised?"

"It's already installed on Dad's car."

Her face brightened. "Perfect."

He took a few minutes to install an app on her phone and walk her through how to use it.

"So," said Kit, dropping the phone back in her purse, "better head home."

He didn't want her to go. "Stay. We can watch a movie."

"It's late. You seriously want to watch TV?"

"No, I *seriously* want to have sex with you."

She groaned. "You're a broken record."

He tapped out another cigarette. "You too tied up with Lawless these days to give me a chance? You loved me once, Kit. It can be like that again."

She pushed her chair back and stood up.

Before she reached the door, Eli darted in front of her, blocking her path.

"Get out of my way."

"I will, but first I need a goodbye hug."

She studied him, then, grudgingly, put her arms around him. "There. We good?"

Feeling for the zipper on the back of her dress, he began to draw it down.

She shoved him away, but he held on to her arms.

"You're hurting me."

"Don't you love me just a little?"

"Sometimes I do, sometimes I don't."

"What about now? This moment."

"You're an asshole."

"But I'm your asshole, if you want me."

She stared at him a moment, then said, "Oh, crap," and began unbuckling his belt.

"You're everything to me, Kit." He pulled her down to the floor. "I'll never disappoint you again, I promise."

"Shut up. And take your hands off me or I'm out of here."

"Sure, whatever you say." Okay, so this wasn't the way he'd imagined it, but she wouldn't have stayed if she didn't care a little. He would hold on to that for dear life.

33

It seemed like an eternity since Marlo had visited that awful psychic. As she stood at George's bedside, stroking his hair, listening to the beeps from various machines, she continued to resist the notion that the woman really had paranormal powers. What had happened to George was a coincidence, pure and simple.

"I love you, sweetheart," she said, leaning over to kiss his forehead. "Love" was such an overused word that it struck her as trite. But what other words were there? "Adore"? "Worship"? "I hold you in high esteem. I, like, revere you." After another few seconds of deep consideration, she came up with something she could live with. "I'm crazy about you, George," she said.

Leaning on the rail, hunkering down closer to his ear, she continued, "I want everything to be the way it was, except . . . well, it would be nice if—now don't get upset—if we could . . . you know, have a baby. I realize I don't project an ideal motherly image, but there are lots of motherly types, wouldn't you agree? In fact, you could do the dress-up part with the kid, and I could teach her how to throw a ball and ride a motorcycle. It's a workable plan.

While you're recuperating, give it some thought." He was still unconscious, and she didn't know for sure if he would recuperate, but she was making every effort to stay positive.

The nurses had encouraged her talk to him, even play music for him. Her words didn't have to be anything deep or philosophical, just ordinary stuff, they'd said. Something about the intimate act of conversing, even if it was only one-sided, made her feel less alone. He probably couldn't hear her, but she decided to operate on the notion that he could. "Like I said, don't get all hot and bothered about the baby thing. I just wanted to chuck that into the conversational pool. Wouldn't it be incredible to have a little George or a little Marlo running around our condo? We'd have to make a pact not to spoil her."

She pulled a chair over close to the bed and sat down. Holding his hand, she said, "News flash: I kicked Chuck out. The guy's a sexual predator and a liar. I never liked him, now I have an actual reason. I feel so bad for his poor wife and daughter. But they're better off without him. I assume we only know a tiny fraction of what he's done. Let's hope he spends the rest of his miserable life fighting off perverts behind bars."

She thrashed around inside her mind for a new topic. "I talked to Jane Lawless last night. That woman called you five times yesterday. *Five times*. Something about a tote bag. I found it on the bed when I went back home this morning to take a shower and change clothes. What the hell is going on, George?" She realized she was squeezing his hand way too hard. "Sorry," she said quickly, easing up. "I'm just frustrated."

She attempted to regroup. "What about this? Do you remember when we told each other what our dream jobs would be? I've been thinking about that. I said I wanted to be the commissioner of baseball and you said you wanted to be a tailor. You said you'd mentioned it to your dad once and he'd laughed, figured you were kidding. I checked it out on the internet. Setting aside the fact that tailoring pays less than an entry-level bank teller, there are some classes you could take at Hennepin Technical College. Maybe we should look into it when you're feeling better."

A nurse came in and began checking George's vitals.

"How's he doing?" asked Marlo.

"About the same." When the woman leaned over to look at him more closely, she jumped. "Did you see that?"

"See what?"

"His eyes fluttered. There it is again. Say his name."

Standing and clearing her throat, Marlo said, "George? Marlo here. Time to wake up and talk to me. I didn't mean to squeeze your fingers so hard before."

"Squeeze them again," ordered the nurse.

A few moments after Marlo took his hand again, George's eyes opened. And stayed open.

"I need to get a doctor," said the nurse, rushing out.

"Oh, George," said Marlo, stroking the side of his face. "Stay with me. We can talk about anything you like, even . . . even men's fashion." She gritted her teeth. "Or we could talk about cars. I saw this rocket in a showroom a few weeks ago."

He closed his eyes.

Wrong topic. "What about our baby? Have you thought at all about that?"

His eyes opened and angled ever so slightly toward her.

She wasn't sure if that was a good sign or a bad one. But before she could make another conversational stab, the doctor arrived and said he needed her to leave for a few minutes.

234

"I'll be back, George," she called to him from the doorway. "If it's a girl, I think we should name her Camilla or Penelope, or maybe even—" The nurse closed the door. "—Anastasia," Marlo said, to no one in particular.

34

It was a nasty morning, with freezing drizzle making the streets slick. Jane could feel her truck fishtail as she turned off Nicollet and headed into the heart of the Windom neighborhood. She rolled slowly up to the curb a few minutes later, squinting at the number above the door to make sure she had the right place. Most of the homes in south Minneapolis faced the avenues. This one faced a side street and was apparently zoned as a business. It looked as if it might once have been a regular family home. The back half of the house still was. Somewhere along the line, the front section had become The Happy Curl Beauty Shop.

A bell jingled above her head as she pushed her way inside. Even though the sign in the window said the business was open, nobody was around. The room seemed cheerful enough, painted a soft yellow with blue gingham curtains, and smelling of old-fashioned permanent wave solution. Did people still get those? Two styling chairs faced a long mirror. There was the requisite washing station, hair dryers, and a manicure table. Yellowed posters advertising various hairstyles hung on the walls.

"Can I help you?" asked a chunky, sandy-haired woman, emerging through a door in the back. She had on a bright red track suit and white cross-trainers.

"I hope so," said Jane. She introduced herself and handed the woman a card.

"Wow, I've never met a real-life P.I. before." The woman adjusted her glasses as she examined Jane from head to toe. "What's this about?"

"I'd like to ask you a couple of questions about your daughter."

"Kit? Why?"

"I'm working for an attorney who's trying to find evidence to reopen an old homicide case. The lawyer believes the man in prison for the murder is innocent."

"Okay, but what's my daughter got to do with it?"

"She knows some of the people involved."

"Then why don't you talk to her?"

"I have."

She narrowed one eye. "Are you suggesting my daughter had something to do with it?"

"No, not at all," said Jane, trying to sound reassuring. "I promise, I'll only take a few minutes of your time. I just need to get a little background."

"Background," repeated the woman, inspecting the word for possible meanings. "Well, I guess. Sure. I like to be helpful. But there's really no place to sit in here. Why don't we go back to the living room? By the way, I'm Denise."

"Jane."

"I should warn you," she added, tossing a smile over her shoulder, "I'm a talker."

The first thing Jane saw when she entered the living room was a framed photo of Denise and her daughter. Kit was wearing a flowing white dress and holding a rose-and-baby's-breath nosegay. Denise was decked out in a bright pink suit with a white gardenia corsage on her right shoulder.

"That was taken at her wedding to John Henry," said Denise. "Such a beautiful day. I have an entire album, if you'd like to see it."

Jane sat down on a couch covered in a loud floral print. She judged the living room to be about the same size as her kitchen, the kitchen alcove about the size of her foyer.

"Do you mind if I take notes?" asked Jane.

"Whatever you need to do." Denise pushed a bowl of peppermint candies on the coffee table closer to Jane.

"So," Jane began, clicking her pen open, "how long have you lived here?"

"Oh, gosh, let me think. Kitten was thirteen when we moved in, so maybe sixteen years. The place was up for sale but as you can imagine, it wasn't the kind of house most people wanted. The first time I walked in, I knew it would be perfect for me. The price was right. So was the location. I heard that years ago, the salon was a mom-and-pop grocery store. That was back in the fifties. After that closed, it was a yarn shop for a while, and then later a little gift boutique. When I bought it, there was a bunch of hair salon stuff in the front room, but the business had closed the year before. I'd worked at a beauty shop once, so I thought, hell, I'll resurrect it. Turns out, there are lots of old ladies around who still want a wash, a set, and a comb-out."

Jane couldn't imagine two people, one of them a teenager, living in a place this small. Maybe there were two bedrooms, but if there were, they had to be no more than large closets. "Where did Kit go to high school?"

"Washburn. Her grades weren't good, but they were okay enough to graduate. As good as mine were. Neither of us were great students."

"Do you get together often?"

She shrugged. "Yeah, I see her. She used to come by on Sunday nights for supper. That's spaghetti night around here. She always liked my spaghetti. Now that she's married, I don't see her as much."

"Are you still married?"

She snorted. "I never been married. Of course, I been with Karl, my boyfriend, for going on eight years now. He's a trucker, so he's not home a lot. Maybe that's the secret to a lasting romance. Together we make ends meet. He's a sweet guy. Believe me, I deserved to get lucky after every frog I kissed hoping he'd turn into a handsome prince." She laughed.

"I hear you," said Jane, smiling. "What was Kit like as a teenager?"

"Feisty. Allergic to rules. Sneaky as hell. Liked parties and chasing boys. And she lied. Oh, mother, could that kid lie. She was always trying to get stuff past me. I'm sure she stole cash out of my purse more than once. She was incorrigible, really. I guess I was a lot like that at her age, so the apple doesn't fall far from the tree. There were times when it got pretty heated around here. I will say though, I never sassed *my* mom back."

"What about her dad?"

"Never had a dad. Like I said, I was a wild one. I'm not sure who the father is. Coulda been a couple of guys. I had boyfriends when she was growing up, but nobody we ever lived with. She didn't seem to mind not having a father around. She always said most of her friends' dads were total assholes."

"Really," said Jane. The more she learned about Kit, the worse her brother's judgment seemed to be. "Did she ever get into any major trouble?"

"Like with the police? Nah."

"Drugs?"

"That's one thing she was never into, thank God. She drank some when she was out with her friends. We never had any liquor in the house. As for sex, I made sure she had contraception. Didn't want her getting pregnant like I did."

"Do any of her friends still live around here?"

"Sure, her best friend does. Name's Brittany Daniels—used to be Brittany Miller. She brings her grandmother by twice a month for a wash and a set. Nice girl. Married with a couple of kids."

"Do you have her phone number?"

"Let me look. I'm sure I do." Denise rose from the couch and went back to the salon. She returned a few minutes later with an appointment book. Perching on the arm of a recliner, she read out both a phone number and an address.

"After high school what did your daughter do?" asked Jane.

"For a living? Oh, this and that. Wasn't interested in college. That didn't come as a surprise. Once she got married—"

"You mean to John Henry?"

"No, before that. She married a guy the year after she graduated. There was no father of the bride to pay for a fancy wedding, but Kitten spent a good month planning it anyway. I remember they got lots of great wedding presents, but in the end, they eloped. I was sorry I couldn't be there. Davey was a real loser. Lazy. Had the personality of a houseplant. All he had going for him was his looks and a nice car." She lowered her voice before adding, "I don't know this for a fact, but I'll bet he knocked her around some. It wasn't eight months before she was back here, begging me to let her move back in."

"They divorced?"

"Yeah, she couldn't stand the sight of him. Thank God she never got pregnant."

"Do you remember his full name?"

"David Allen Stokes."

"Where is he now?"

"No idea."

Closing her notebook and slipping it back into her pocket, Jane said, "This has been helpful."

For the first time, Denise seemed to grow uncertain. "Look, I may have painted too dark a picture of my daughter. Sure, she was tough to raise, but we got through it. I love her and she loves me. There were times when she was just golden, you know what I mean? Sweet. Happy. Carefree. Young in a good way. And artistic. People never give her credit for how artistic she is."

"I appreciate that," said Jane.

"And one last thing. She never hurt anyone. Oh, she could be sarcastic and snappy, and her judgment wasn't always the best, but down deep, she was a good kid. Remember that. Nobody knows a child better than a mother."

35

While Jane had been inside talking to Denise, the temperature had risen into the mid-thirties. The freezing drizzle was gone, replaced by a thin, misty rain. Jane sat in the front seat of her truck and scrolled through her emails, finally finding the one she'd been waiting for. It was from Nicole Gunness—an answer to her question about any items missing from Harper Tillman's body.

J—Hi. Checked on it. Not sure if this qualifies.
Harper had on earrings—turquoise teardrop with
gold at the top. One was still attached.
Looked like the other had been ripped off. Cops
said it happened in a struggle, but I saw no
evidence of one in the photos. Once she was
hit on the back of the head, she went down, so
it could have been ripped off on purpose. No
real way of telling, though. Hope that helps.
NG.

Jane wasn't sure what to make of this. She tucked the information away inside her mind as she drove north along Nicollet Avenue, heading to another interview, this one with the woman who lived across the hall from Gideon and Rashad—the same woman who'd alerted Marlo that the police were coming in and out of her dad's apartment on the night he died. Jane wasn't sure Bree Mitchell had anything important to tell her. Everything, she'd learned, felt like a hundred-to-one shot when she couldn't bring the entire picture into focus.

When Jane called from the house phone in the lobby, Bree gave her a code that would allow access to the ninth floor. Bree met her at the doors to the elevator and led the way back to her penthouse.

Jane didn't really know what to expect. She'd read about the condos at the Finnmark, heard that they were some of the loveliest in the city. The hallway was more utilitarian than anything else. Cement floors. White walls. Lightbulbs with a metal grid around them. But once inside, Jane could see what all the fuss was about.

"This is amazing," she said, taking a seat in the living room. "It's so bright and airy."

"I love it," said Bree, tucking herself into a corner of the couch. She was a trim woman, probably in her late fifties or early sixties, dressed in gray linen slacks and a white wool tunic. The silver lanyard around her neck kept her reading glasses close. She wore no makeup and still managed to look elegant.

"I've always been troubled by what happened to Gideon."

"Did you know him? Or Rashad?"

"I'd moved into my unit about a month before they arrived. I was so happy when they moved in across the hall. They were a wonderful couple. Very friendly. They invited me in for a glass of wine as soon as they were settled. I reciprocated. I felt lucky, I guess. I could just tell that we'd be great friends."

"Did they seem happy together?"

"Yes, very. I never understood what happened there."

"Did you see anyone go in or out of their condo on the night Gideon died?"

She shook her head. "But when I heard these heavy, clomping footsteps out in the hall, and then a couple deep male voices, I opened my door. Salsa music was coming from inside Gideon and Rashad's place. There was a uniformed police officer inside the unit and another standing by the door. The one by the door told me to shut mine and not to come out again. He didn't seem very friendly."

"What did you do?" asked Jane.

"I closed the door. I immediately phoned Marlo. Gideon had introduced me to her—and to George—one Sunday afternoon, a few weeks before his death. We exchanged phone numbers, you know, for safety. When I called her that night, I told her I thought she should come over right away, that the police were in her father's condo."

"What happened next?"

"I watched everything through the peephole. When Marlo arrived, she charged right in, followed by George. The cop at the door tried to stop her, but she just pushed past him. A few seconds later, I heard her scream. That's when I knew it was bad. Quite honestly, I thought Marlo's appearance threw the police into a real tizzy. That's a term my mother used to use, but in this situation, I think it's appropriate. One of the officers slammed the door, so I couldn't see what was happening for a few minutes, but then this man in a suit and tie arrived, looking like he was in charge, followed by a whole group of people. I later learned they were the crime-scene unit. They kept the door open after that. It was hours before Gideon was wheeled out on a gurney. I didn't keep watch the entire time, but I did see them lead Marlo and George out separately."

"Were either of them carrying anything on their way in?"

"No, not that I recall."

"What about on their way out?"

She thought about it. "You know, I think George might have had a sack or—something he carried by the handles."

"Do you remember the color?"

"Sorry."

Removing several photos from the pocket of her peacoat, Jane handed one to Bree. "Do you recognize him?"

Slipping her reading glasses on, she studied the face. "No."

Jane handed her the second photo. "What about her?"

She shook her head. "Sorry. I've never seen either of them before."

Handing over the last photo, Jane waited.

"Oh, my, yes. He was here. Not a face you'd forget."

"By here, you mean—"

"I was coming home one night after work and I saw him leaving Gideon and Rashad's condo. I nodded and smiled, and he did the same. Who is he?"

"His name is John Henry Chenoweth. Did Gideon or Rashad ever mention him to you?"

"No," she said, handing the photos back. "Not that I recall."

They spoke for a few more minutes. Bree was curious as to why Jane was looking into a murder case that had already been solved. Jane gave a very brief explanation and was glad when Bree seemed satisfied.

On her way back down in the elevator, Jane made a quick decision. She had one more stop before she was done with the day's interviews.

Jane sat across the desk from John Henry, waiting for him to finish signing some papers for his secretary, a woman he introduced as Anna Morley. He'd been gracious when she'd come to the gallery and asked to speak with him. Eli gave her a sidelong glance as she and John Henry took the stairs up to the second floor. Kit was nowhere to be seen.

His office was strangely devoid of artwork. When he was done and Anna had left, Jane asked him about it.

"I need someplace to cleanse my palette, so to speak. Do you see?"

"I do," said Jane.

"I'm around works of fine art all the time. It's good to have a break." After moving some papers to a credenza behind his desk, he said, "So, what can I do for you, Ms. Lawless?"

"I have a couple of questions about Gideon Wise."

"I assumed that was it. I'm told your father is opening an investigation into the matter. Does he really think he can challenge a case that was successfully litigated?"

"That's what I'm trying to determine."

"And you think I can help?"

Jane wasn't sure she needed her notes, but decided to take out the notebook anyway. "In talking to Gideon's neighbor, I learned that you visited him at his condo a few weeks before his murder. Do you remember that?"

He smoothed the front of his shirt. "Yes, I do."

"May I ask why you were there?"

"I'm not sure that's any of your business."

She didn't respond.

"I have a question myself," said John Henry, shifting in his chair. "My son tells me you think someone at the gallery might be involved. Is that true?"

She nodded.

"Because we had the key code for his unit."

"That's right."

He scratched his beard, giving himself a moment to think. "You're speaking about me, my son, and my wife."

"Yes."

"Not that it's any of your business, but I'll tell you why I went to see Gideon that night. I needed money—or rather, the gallery did. I'd worked with him for a good ten years, considered him not just a customer, but a friend."

"And did he give you the money?"

"He did not. Rashad was there as well that night. I knew he wasn't all that keen on Gideon's penchant for collecting. The fact was, they were thinking of buying a chalet-style home just outside of Breckenridge, Colorado. They both loved to ski and liked the town. They'd even gone out to inspect a place and were in negotiations to purchase it."

Jane made a couple of notes. "So no money."

"No money. Nothing nefarious. Let me ask another question: What would my motive be for murdering Gideon? Did I decide to bludgeon a friend because he refused to float me a loan? I would think even you would find that idea has no relationship with reality."

"Did you have any other dealings with him around that time?"

"You're fishing, Ms. Lawless, and I'm not biting." Folding his hands in his lap, he continued, "What, may I ask, was Eli's motive? Or Kit's?"

Jane admitted that she only had theories, none of which she wanted to share.

"Then I'm not sure there's anything else to say."

She was being dismissed. Standing, she thanked him for his time.

"Give my best to Peter," he called as she was on her way out.

36

Jane had tried not to dwell on what Julia was doing or why she hadn't texted or called. Sometimes Julia was simply like that. Reserved. Silent. It wasn't a personality trait Jane would ever get used to, and yet Julia did have a right to her privacy, even in a committed relationship, and even if it was difficult at times for Jane to live with. The thought that Julia would be home soon, that they would be back in each other's arms, was more than enough to keep her spirits high.

Nursing a brandy as she sat in her den, gazing up at the bulletin board with all the notes and photos she'd tacked up in the last few days, it occurred to her that when she'd first put Eli's name up there, it had been as a favor to her brother, not because she thought he had anything to do with Gideon's murder. "Odd," she whispered. Mouse raised his head and looked at her. Gimlet, with her hearing impairment, continued to snore.

As she was walking through the foyer a while later, an idea she'd been nursing finally came into focus. The sound of loud banging on the door stopped her. "Who the hell?" she whispered as Mouse charged in from the living room, followed by Gimlet. She looked through the peephole. "It's Peter," she said, smiling down at the pups.

As soon as Peter came in, he was engulfed by wagging tails and hello kisses, but instead of engaging with them, as he usually did, he brushed them away.

"What the hell do you think you're doing?" he demanded, his face flushed with rage.

She'd expected a hug. "What are you talking about?"

"Kit. You went to see her mother to get the dirt on her. That is so low."

Jane had rarely seen him this angry. "It's part of the investigation."

"Kit's mother called her, told her everything you said. Why did you tell that awful woman Kit was a murderer?"

"Excuse me? I never said anything like that."

"So everyone lies but you, huh? Jane, the purveyor of all truth."

"I'm telling you I never said that. You really believe I go around announcing someone's guilt before I have the actual proof?"

"So you admit it. You have no proof." He stomped into the living room, then whirled around. "Kit is really fragile right now. Her husband is abusing her. The gallery he owns has serious financial problems. And you pile on. I came here to tell you to stop. No more harassment."

"I'm not harassing anyone," said Jane. "Kit's mother agreed to a short interview. I asked some general questions. I wanted to get a feel for what Kit was like when she was younger. Did you know she got married shortly after high school?"

That stopped him. "What?" He turned away, threw himself down on the couch. "Why can't you leave it alone?"

Jane sat down on the rocking chair and began to rock. "I ended up feeling kind of sorry for her. If you've never seen that house, it's tiny. And growing up without a father—"

"You've got everything so mixed up. Her parents are divorced, but her dad has always been a big part of her life. Still is."

Jane was confused. "Her mother said she didn't know who the father was. That it could have been a couple of guys. If *she* didn't know, how could Kit?"

"That's absurd. I'm telling you she talks about him all the time. In fact, while we were out last night, he called."

Something was off. "You . . . went out with her last night?"

"She's a friend. Yeah. Friends do that."

Not what she wanted to hear. "And you heard them talking?"

"I wasn't more than a few feet away. For your information, he lives in Arizona. He's remarried. She was hoping he'd stop here on his way to New York. Jane, Kit's mother is full of it. Always has been. That's why Kit cut her off years ago, why she never sees her."

"But she does see her," said Jane. "Not as often as she used to, but they're in touch. Her mom had a framed photo of herself and Kit at Kit's wedding to John Henry. In fact, she had an entire album of wedding photos."

Peter's glower said it all. It was finally beginning to penetrate, possibly for the first time, that Kit might have lied to him. If she'd lied about her mother, and lied about a nonexistent father, what else had she lied about?

Looking uncertain, Peter said, "I'm sure there's an explanation."

"Did she send you over here to tell me to back off?"

"No," he said, though his voice was less firm. For a long moment, he seemed to turn inward, his eyes lowered.

"I'm not your enemy," she said softly, hoping he was still listening. "I want the same thing you do. We both want the truth."

He offered a somewhat robotic nod.

"Will you look at me?"

Reluctantly, his eyes rose to hers.

"I want you to listen and not react, okay? I need to tell you something. The information I've been gathering on the Chenoweths suggests that Gideon's murder may be part of a larger pattern. I texted you about Harper's homicide, that the police believed strongly that Eli—or someone in his family—was responsible."

"Yes, but—"

She held up her hand. "You remember George Krochak, right? Marlo Wise's husband? I talked to him a couple of days ago. Turns out, he knew about the tote bag in Gideon's condo. I know you know about that because Cordelia told you. It's a long story, but the bottom line is, he was finally able to locate it. And because he was curious and didn't realize who he was dealing with, he drove to the gallery on Saturday morning. I know this because he texted me his destination. What I don't know is who he met with. His car was found a few hours later at the bottom of a steep hill. He was severely injured, but thankfully, he's alive. He's unconscious, so I have no idea if he has any memory of what happened to him. What I'm telling you is: Someone at the gallery is responsible. For Gideon. For George. Possibly even for Harper. I can't prove it. Not yet. But I'm close. Will you help me understand all this, Peter? You've talked to Kit a lot since you've been back. You know things

I don't, specifically about the night Gideon died. Would you be willing to take a few minutes and go through it with me?" Cordelia had already debriefed her on what Peter had told her. Now she needed to hear it from him.

"I suppose," he said gruffly.

She ran to her study and grabbed her notebook and a pen. Once back in the living room, she asked her brother to go through his understanding of what happened that night, giving, as accurately as possible, the time when things occurred. As he began to speak, she only took notes when he said something she hadn't heard before.

Gideon, The day of:
Eli drove to condo after gallery meeting,
which ended around five.
Used lobby phone to call Gideon.
Waited in lobby, but came home in 45.
Kit told him to go back.
Kit called Peter/ask Rashad for dinner
Needed more time.
Eli returned to condo, but more cold
feet. Left. Home. Heroin.
No time on this.
Kit saw no blood on his clothing.
Eli said Gideon had blown him off.
Was embarrassed so didn't want to talk
about it.
***Peter admitted he wouldn't have been
with Rashad that night if Eli hadn't asked.
(Seems worried about that.)

"Great," said Jane, scratching her last note. "Okay, now tell me what time you and Rashad called it a night?"

"Around eight. Can't be more specific. How come you're so interested in the timing?"

"Because it tells us something important."

"Like what?"

"I was reading over Rashad's testimony at the trial again last night. He said that he was done with work at five thirty and usually got home around six. Gideon had what he called golden hours. He left around six in the morning, made it to work by six thirty. The hours between six thirty and nine in the morning and between five thirty and seven in the evening were the most productive times of his day because fewer people were around to interrupt him. He protected those hours, Peter. Rashad said that in the years they were together, the only instance he remembered of Gideon getting home early was when he had the flu. He had a temperature and came home, stayed out for three days."

"So?"

"Why would Eli say he'd scheduled a meeting with Gideon that night at five thirty? Gideon was never home then. If he wanted to see Gideon at that time of day, he would have gone to his law office. And that way he wouldn't have needed you to keep Rashad away from the condo."

"What are you getting at?"

"None of this was about a meeting with Gideon, Peter. It was all about Rashad, getting him out of the way so Eli could enter the condo without anyone being around."

Peter's expression darkened. "Why would he do that?"

"I'm not sure. My guess is he was planning to rob them. Did he have financial problems?"

"He always had financial problems."

She let her theory sit between them, without saying more. She could tell her words had penetrated, but she could also see that he was fighting them. Taking a different tack, she asked, "Does Kit have any theories on who might have murdered Gideon?"

"Sure, Rashad," said Peter. "But," he added, "in kicking it around, she said Eli might be a possibility. She thought John Henry was too old."

"What about Kit herself? Is she off the table for some reason?"

"She realizes that if you're right and the gallery is at the center of it, that she would be one of the logical suspects. She just thinks you're wrong."

"I'm sure she does," said Jane, closing her notebook.

"Look, when it comes to Kit, you're way off base to think she was part of it. If Eli was Gideon's killer, she knows nothing. Only what Eli told her."

He was beginning to get angry again.

"Peter, *please*. I realize there's been some friction between us. If it's something I've done, then tell me what it is and let me make amends. But for now, I hope you'll allow me to ask a favor. These friends of yours—Eli, Kit, John Henry—they could be dangerous. If there's any way you can limit your time with them, or end it all together—"

"Not happening," he said coldly.

"Okay." She placed a hand on top of the notebook. "Then, all I can do is ask you to be careful."

He looked up, squinted at her. "You and Cordelia don't have much confidence in me, do you?"

"That's not true."

"Really?" He pushed off the couch and stomped back into the front hall.

"Peter," she called. "Let's not leave it like this. How much longer will you be in town?"

He slammed the door on his way out.

37

The following morning, Jane was at the Lyme House talking to her executive chef when Cordelia barged into the kitchen. Excusing herself, Jane nodded for Cordelia to follow her down the back stairs. She passed her office and headed for the pub, where she knew a fresh pot of coffee was on the warming plate behind the bar. "Want a cup?" she asked, ducking under the bar flap. She grabbed a couple of mugs.

"I could use a hit," said Cordelia, dithering over which table suited her mood.

"You're up kind of early," said Jane, setting the mugs on a table and then pulling out a chair. The pub didn't open until eleven, so they had the entire place to themselves for the next twenty minutes.

"I've been on a mission. I came to make my official report." She opened her extra-large sack purse and removed a tablet. Switching it on, she brought up a photo and handed it to Jane. "I googled the gallery last night and found a bunch of images. See anything interesting in that one?"

Jane sipped her coffee as she examined the picture. "What am I supposed to see?"

Cordelia offered her best Cheshire cat smile. "Look up at the corners of the room. I saw them right away."

Jane didn't have her reading glasses with her, so she enlarged the photo and squinted.

"The security cameras," said Cordelia, too impatient to wait. "The gallery has a security system. Which means they have a record of who comes and goes. George would be on last Saturday's recording."

"Why didn't I think of that?"

Cordelia tapped her head. "Creative types have lots more gray cells."

"Do they?" Jane handed the tablet back. "Only problem is, we have no access to their hard drive and no way to get it. We don't even know where the server is. It could be off-site."

"Don't they use tapes anymore?"

"Maybe a few gas stations still do."

Cordelia harrumphed. "Back to my mission. I went to the gallery this morning to see how many cameras there are and where they're placed."

"You did what? Did anyone see you?"

"Some woman named Anna."

"Did she think you were casing the place?"

"Oh, I suppose," said Cordelia, patting her finger waves. "But I gave her a story, told her I was opening a business myself and needed some ideas on security."

"Uh huh," said Jane, groaning internally. "Were any of the Chenoweths around?"

"John Henry flitted through. I don't think he saw me. But even if he did, he doesn't know me from Jay Gatsby."

"In keeping with your flapper idiom."

"Exactly."

"So, where were the cameras?"

"Four in each of the showroom corners, one pointed at the front door and one pointed at the reception desk. Fourteen in all. You'd think it was Fort Knox."

"Cameras aren't that expensive." And then it hit her. "Cameras," she whispered.

"You're beginning to repeat yourself, dearheart. Not a good sign."

"No, not the cameras at the gallery. I'm talking about the security cameras in the lobby of the Finnmark building. Peter said Eli waited around the lobby for forty-five minutes. If he was really there, the cameras would show it. And that's something we might actually have access to. Since it was a crime scene, it's possible they were handed over to my father during discovery."

"Then get on the horn and call him," said Cordelia, her eyes lighting up.

Jane checked her watch. "He's in court. I'll text him." She opened the cover on her cell phone and tapped a quick message. "You up for a little security camera sleuthing with me? Four eyes would be better than two."

"I'm your woman." She sniffed the air. "Do I smell baking pretzels?"

"They're making them ahead for when the pub opens."

"I don't suppose there's an extra one lying around somewhere, lonely and unloved?"

Jane called up to the kitchen and asked for a runner to bring one down. It was the least she could do after Cordelia had sparked a new lead.

"They won't forget the mustard, will they? Or the onion-bacon marmalade?"

Jane assured her they wouldn't. "You know, Cordelia, you really are kind of amazing."

Cordelia fluttered her eyes. "I know."

Jane felt her phone vibrate in her back pocket. "This should be Julia with information on her flight."

"When is she coming home?"

"Today, I hope," said Jane. She would have preferred a phone call, but this was a text. Reading through it quickly, her heart sank.

"What?" said Cordelia.

"She's flying to Chicago."

"Do you have a welcome-home party planned?"

"Champagne. And I had one of the pastry chefs make a small version of the apricot cake she loves so much."

"You're a good girlfriend." Cordelia kept looking over at the doorway, eager for the pretzel to arrive. "Did she say what's going on in Chicago?"

"No."

"Not a great communicator. Maybe you should buy her some Ronald Reagan tapes to go with the cake and champagne."

"What a stellar idea." She was surprised by how upset she was.

"I mean, if the cake will spoil before she gets back, Janey, I could always come over and help you eat it—and drink the champagne. And then, when Julia gets back, you could have, oh I don't know, something like Jiffy Pop popcorn and beer?"

260

Jane didn't want to talk about it. She was glad when the pretzel arrived and the subject was dropped.

Eli felt like a man staring into a void. Except the void, in this instance, was his father's computer.

His eyes darted away from the screen when he heard the back door open. He'd been sitting in his dad's den for the past few minutes. There were hundreds of files on his system, most of them filled with photos of artwork and gallery projects. Number 3113 was a file inside another file inside a third. It was well-hidden. He never would have found it if Kit hadn't tipped him off.

Eli assumed he could take an early lunch and nobody would be the wiser. What he hadn't counted on was that his father or Kit would do the same. He leaned back in the chair and waited to see who would appear. When his dad walked past the door, Eli tensed.

Backing up, his dad asked, "What are you doing here?"

"I need to talk to you."

"I just came home to change my shirt, Eli. I don't have much time. I'm meeting with Mark Gaither at one, and I need to grab some lunch first."

"This won't take long."

Pulling off his bow tie and unbuttoning his top button, John Henry stood by the door and waited.

"Come over here," said Eli, rolling his chair to the side. "I want to show you something."

"Oh, all right. But we have to make this quick." John Henry continued unbuttoning his shirt as he crossed to the desk. Staring at the screen, he said, "What the—"

"Maybe you'd like to explain about that."

John Henry's gaze traveled from the screen to Eli. "I have no idea how—" He scrolled through more of the photos. "Lord in heaven. You can't think—"

"That you're a pedophile? That you're sexually attracted to little girls?"

"Eli, no, that's—" He sputtered, not quite able to finish the sentence.

"Are you upset because you're a piece of slime, or because I found out?"

John Henry's eyes blazed with anger. "How dare you talk to me that way? I have never, *ever*, been attracted to children."

Eli wanted so badly to believe him. "Then how do you explain all these images? If I turned this over to the police, you'd be arrested, prosecuted. You'd probably spend the rest of your life in jail."

Now horror filled his father's eyes. "You know me, Eli. You know I'm not like that."

"What I know is that you were never faithful to my mother. You cheated on her the entire time you were married."

"That's . . . absolute nonsense," John Henry stammered.

"You think she didn't know? She hid it, but she knew, and it nearly killed her."

That silenced his father. After a visible struggle, he said, "I don't believe you."

Eli backed the rolling chair away from his dad. He needed to put some distance between them. "I remember once, I was probably eleven or twelve, I saw Mom watching you as you came into the kitchen for breakfast. You were always so perfectly dressed. A while later, as I was getting ready to leave for school, I found her watching me with the exact same look of revulsion on her face. In that moment, I finally grasped the reason for the most painful part of my young life. Mom was always so close, so physically affectionate with Tori, but she was never like that with me. I wanted her to love me so bad. I spent my childhood thinking I wasn't good enough, that there must be something about me that was fundamentally unlovable. At times, I figured if I just tried harder, got better grades, did more chores, that she'd change. She never did, Dad, because . . . when she looked at me, she saw you."

His father's mouth dropped open.

"I think it's why I've always had such a terrible time with women. Maybe I want them to fill a hole that can't be filled. When I first met Harper, I warned her. I said that I didn't do relationships, I took hostages. She laughed, thought it was hilarious. It wasn't."

"But Harper adored you."

Eli swallowed a couple of times. He hadn't planned on getting into any of this, but now that it was all coming out, he figured he would tell his dad the truth. "She had a bad scare. For a week or so, she thought she was pregnant. When she finally said something to me, I was elated. I'd been hoping she'd get pregnant. I thought that if we had a child together, it would bind her to me. That she'd never leave. But when she found out she wasn't pregnant, she told me it was over. She wasn't happy and planned to move out. She told me she'd realized I was too much for her. Too needy. Too controlling. Too pushy. Too desperate."

"I had no idea."

"Just something more to toss on Eli's pile of shame."

Initially, his father had seemed shaken. Now, as he moved over to a chair and sat down, his face hardened. "You blame me for your romantic problems? Believe me, son, you're capable of ruining relationships all by yourself. You're an adult, Eli. You can't blame

263

Mommy and Daddy anymore. And in case you're interested, my marriage to your mother wasn't exactly a bed of roses."

Eli felt they were spinning their wheels. He'd attacked his father and his father had fought back. The main issue was still on the table: John Henry's porn stash. "I took some screen shots of your online photo album."

That sobered his father again. "You don't actually believe that toxic sludge belongs to me."

"How else did it get there?"

John Henry moved to the edge of his seat. "I don't know. But it's *not* mine. I swear on everything I hold dear."

"The police may have a different take."

The words startled John Henry. "You'd really turn me in? I'm your father, Eli. I love you."

"Do you?"

"Look at everything I've done to help you. When I learned you were dealing drugs—on Facebook, no less—I was the one who had the page scrubbed. I made sure you got out of town before that thug dealer of yours could hurt you. I sent you to rehab, paid for it and then for you to stay in Glendale. I brought you home, set you up in that house. I gave you your job back."

It was all true. Eli felt his resolve begin to falter.

"It's not *mine*," his dad all but screamed. "I'm not that kind of man. You know that. Have you ever seen me behave inappropriately with a little girl? I was unfaithful, yes. Uncaring at times. Selfish. But I'm human, Eli, not a monster."

In Eli's opinion, people called each other monsters when they wanted to distance themselves from a bad behavior. The truth was, monsters were all too human. They lived inside business suits, overalls, and pretty dresses. They were the quiet boy next door.

The friendly neighbor who attended church every Sunday. If only people came with warnings: *Monster inside. Keep away.*

"What are you going to do with that file, Eli?" asked his dad.

Rising and tapping out a cigarette from a pack of Camels, Eli lit up, taking a deep drag. He thought for a long moment, blowing smoke into the air, then said, "Afraid I'll have to get back to you on that one, Dad."

38

Peter entered the gallery that afternoon, looking for Eli. He milled around with the other customers for a few minutes, hoping he would appear. When he did, coming through the double doors from the warehouse, Peter tried to catch his attention, but Eli never looked his way. Instead, he headed for the rear door into the stairwell. Charging past the reception desk, Peter caught him on the landing between the first and second floors, grabbing his lapels and shoving him against the wall.

"What the hell?" said Eli, pushing him away.

Peter came at him again. "You're guilty, man. You murdered Gideon. And you made *me* an accomplice by getting me to ask Rashad out for a drink. You knew I wouldn't refuse my dealer, the keeper of all blow."

Eli tried to push him away, but Peter was bigger and far more aggressive.

"Now I find out you might be mixed up in another murder. Your ex. Harper."

"You're crazy, man. Get the hell away from me."

"And then there's George Krochak."

This time, Eli was able to fight Peter off. Breathing hard, he bent over and wiped a hand across his mouth. "Who the hell is George Krochak?"

"Don't play dumb. You're good at that, but it doesn't work with me anymore. George is Marlo Wise's husband. He found that tote bag you brought with you to Gideon's condo the night you were supposed to meet with him. Except there never was a meeting, was there?"

As Eli straightened up, a glimmer of fear flashed across his face. "You're crazy, man."

"You planned to rob him. Problem was, you never counted on him being home. You murdered him in cold blood because he saw your face, knew what you were up to. It's not a theory anymore, man. It's the truth."

"I don't know what the hell you're talking about." Eli yanked his suit back into place.

"How do you explain the bag? It was there in the living room with JHC on the front, your card in the inner pocket. It was photographed. You can't deny it away."

As Eli raked has hands through his hair, his expression changed from anger to puzzlement.

"George is in the hospital fighting for his life. That's right. He's still alive. He came to the gallery last Saturday morning. You met him, you got scared."

"You're full of it."

Peter pushed him against the wall again. This time Eli didn't fight back. "If you even think about hurting Kit, I'll—"

"You'll what?" said Eli through gritted teeth. "Go home. You're in way over your head. Go back to England and leave us the hell alone."

"I might just do that," said Peter, bringing his face close to Eli's. "But before I do, I might have to talk to the police, tell them what I know."

"You perjured yourself, asshole. I'm sure they'd love to hear all about it."

"Yeah? Maybe I can get myself a deal. After all, my dad's a famous defense attorney. I would think he could figure out a way to buy me a little immunity." Peter let go of Eli. "You stay away from Kit or I will personally throw you to the wolves."

By six, that evening, Jane and Cordelia were halfway through the security footage from the Finnmark's lobby. Jane's father had tasked one of his paralegals to find it and set it up for them on a computer in one of the cubicles at the law office. Jane and Cordelia sat hunched together, close to the screen. Jane refused to fast forward. She wanted to see every second of the video.

"This is like watching paint dry," mumbled Cordelia.

"If Eli's going to appear, it better be soon," said Jane. "Peter said he waited there for forty-five minutes. That he'd used the lobby phone next to the elevators several times to call up to Gideon." This security footage had begun taping at four thirty PM and ran for three hours. "Eli should be there by now."

Cordelia snapped her bubble gum. She was about to blow a bubble when she pointed and said, "Is that him?"

"Too tall," said Jane. "And his hair's too light."

A lot of people had walked through the lobby, but few were sitting on benches or seemed to be standing around, waiting. And nobody had used the phone.

"He's got to be there," said Cordelia. "Unless he has a secret cloak of invisibility."

"Or unless he lied about the whole thing." Jane kept watching. Another ten minutes went by. Then another.

When the time stamp turned to six, Cordelia sat back and tossed her gum wrapper at the screen. "Didn't Peter say Eli was home by six fifteen?"

"Nobody had a stopwatch."

At a quarter to seven, Jane admitted defeat and turned off the footage. Cordelia had already called it and was doodling on an envelope while energetically humming the national anthem. "He never appeared," said Jane. If Eli was the man on the security video in the parking garage, he wouldn't have any need to sit around the lobby, as Peter had been told, because there was nothing he needed to wait for.

"Kinda figured out it was a dead end half an hour ago. Like I said before, Kit and Eli used Peter. He was their patsy . . . or, in the modern Russian espionage terms all the rage these days, he was a useful idiot."

Jane thought about that. "I have another interview tonight. This one's with Brittany Daniels, Kit's best friend from high school. Want to come along?"

"Sure," said Cordelia. "But I can't. I have to be at the theater by seven. You think this friend will have anything important to tell you?"

As Jane rose and lifted her coat off the back of the chair, she said, "You never know unless you try."

"Always the optimist."

"Not always."

Brittany, a petite woman with straight blond hair, invited Jane into her kitchen, where she was folding clothes. The remnants of the evening meal, a half-eaten pan of lasagna, sat on the counter. "I have two kids," she offered, resuming her seat at the table. She nodded for Jane to take the one opposite her.

"How old are they?"

"Chapman's six. Dakota's three. They're amazing. Sweet. Silly. Constantly on the go. I'm busy every minute of the day. When Larry gets home from work—he's my husband—he plays with them, gives them their baths, and gets them ready for bed while I pick up the living room, finish the day's laundry, and start dinner. He's a good father. I'm lucky."

Jane took out her pad and pen.

"Are you going to record what I say?"

"I usually take a few notes. Is that a problem?"

"No, it's okay. You said you wanted to talk about Kit."

When Jane had called Brittany to schedule the meeting, she gave the usual explanation.

"First, tell me something," said Brittany. "Do you think Kit had anything to do with that poor man's murder?"

"We're looking at a number of people who knew him."

Brittany took a minute to digest the comment. "I haven't seen her in years, but I'll tell you what I can."

Jane had been under the impression that Kit and Brittany were still close. "When was the last time you saw her?"

"Oh, gosh. Maybe five years ago. We ran into each other at Southdale."

270

"Were you still friends at that time?"

"Sort of. Like, we weren't enemies, but we didn't see each other all that much. We stayed fairly close for a few years after high school, but by then I knew she wasn't the kind of person I wanted in my life."

"Because?"

"I don't know how to say this. There's something wrong with her. I've seen her do things that scared the bejesus out of me."

"Such as?"

"You really want to hear this? I've never told anyone before."

"I do," said Jane. "I'd like to get a better picture of who she is."

"Okay. You asked for it." She put the folded kids' clothes into the empty laundry basket, set it on the floor, then lifted a basket of towels onto the table and began to fold them. "So, in high school, Kit liked to shoplift. I guess her mom didn't make a lot of money from that hair salon, so she'd steal things like makeup, cheap jewelry, candy bars, whatever she felt like. She even stole a Cross pen once from a stationery shop."

"She never got caught?"

"Never, which both surprised me and didn't, you know? She was really good at it. I think she saw it as entertainment. A game. I'd see stuff in her purse, and I just knew she'd stolen it. Beyond that, she'd, like, form these opinions of people that didn't have much relation to the truth. If she liked you, all was great. If she didn't, watch out."

"Can you give me an example?" asked Jane.

"The big one our senior year was Keri Patterson. Jeez, I'll never forget that day. Kit was dating Conor Beck. He was on the golf team, not a jock, but nice looking. Athletic. Kit saw Keri with him one day after school and decided that Keri was trying to put the moves on him. I'd seen them together a couple times, but they just seemed like friends to me. One afternoon, toward the end of the school year, Kit and I and a few others were on our way up the stairs when a bunch of people were coming down, Keri among them. If I hadn't been looking down at just the right moment, I never would have known what happened. Kit stuck out her foot, like, really quick and tripped Keri. She went tumbling, hit her head hard and broke her nose. I think she had a pretty bad concussion because she was out of school for almost a week. People assumed she'd tripped. I think Keri thought that, too."

"Did you ever say anything?"

"And risk Kit's fury? No way."

"Did you ever see her hurt anyone else?"

"Not then."

"Later?"

"Well, the guy she said she married? Dave Stokes?"

"She didn't marry him?"

"She just wanted the wedding presents. I mean, she was sleeping with him. I think she convinced him that they could pull it off—get all these gifts and then tell everyone they'd eloped. But they never did. They drove down to Rochester for a night and then came back. She had a ring that looked really impressive. When I asked her about it, she grinned and said, 'Target. Nineteen ninety-five.' And then she took it off and threw it at me."

"Did something happen to Dave?"

"I'm not sure. I don't have any proof. I remember Kit would tell him to jump and he'd ask how high. The poor guy was totally whipped. They were together for less than a year, but during that time I'd stop by their house sometimes. One day, maybe, oh, seven months after the pretend wedding, I remember I asked her how things were going, if Dave had found a job. She said she hadn't seen him in a couple of weeks. She figured he'd left her, taken off for greener pastures. She didn't seem all that sad about it. She'd just started waitressing at a new place. Mostly she wanted to talk about that. Only thing was, when I went to the bathroom, I noticed Dave's shaving kit was still there, shoved over to the side. On the way back to the kitchen I walked past an open plastic storage box. His pocketknife, his worn brown-leather cowboy boots with the squared-off toes, and some of his clothes were all jumbled together inside it. Why would he leave all that behind?"

"Do you have a theory?" asked Jane.

She hesitated. "This is hard to say, but yes. Kit often bragged that she was a great problem solver. In this case, Dave was the problem. She never wanted anyone to know they weren't married. And I think she was royally sick of him. He spent most of the day lying on the couch, watching TV and drinking beer. I don't know how he managed to pay half the rent, but he did. The only time I ever remember hearing about him standing up to her was when he told her the apartment was half his. I assumed she'd asked him to leave and he'd refused."

"You're saying——"

"That she got rid of him. I don't know how. I don't know where or when. I'd occasionally see his brother at the coffee shop where I worked. He always acted really puzzled when I'd ask about Dave. He confided that he and Kit had divorced quietly. Said his mother would get a postcard from Dave every now and then from different parts of the country. Apparently, one time Dave said he was on his way back to Minnesota, but if he was, he never got here."

"Nobody's seen him? For how many years?"

Brittany looked up, doing the math in her head. "Eight. I mean, it's not like he was close to his family. Kit always seemed to be attracted to loners. But if he's still alive, you'd think someone would have heard from him."

The story left Jane with the sickening sense that her gut reaction to Kit was accurate: She was dangerous. Peter had no idea who she was or the depth of the pit he'd fallen into.

39

After her meeting with Brittany, Jane drove slowly through the dark side streets back to her restaurant. She needed time to think. Once back behind her desk, she attempted to get some work done, but was too keyed up, too worried about her brother. After doing a walk-through of the main dining room, the kitchen, and the downstairs pub, she opened the door to the Lakeside room and flipped on the light. Before she gave up and went home, depressed that it would be another night without Julia, she had one last thing to do. She called Marlo Wise.

"What do you want?" came Marlo's hushed voice.

"Are you at the hospital?"

"No, I'm in outer space. Of course I'm at the hospital. Where the hell else would I be?"

"I have an important question I need to ask you, but first, please tell me how George is."

"Why should I? You're not exactly a friend."

"I've been very concerned about him."

"Just gimme a minute."

Jane could hear noise in the background. And then all was quiet. "He's awake. He's in pain, but the meds seem to help—though in my opinion, not nearly enough. The doctors are most worried about the concussion. He's going to be at greater risk for CTE— you know, what football players get."

"I'm so sorry to hear that. What about his memory? Does he remember what happened to him?"

"Nothing," said Marlo. "It's all blank."

Jane had been afraid of that.

"On the positive side, he knows me and remembers our life to- gether."

"Has his sense of humor returned?"

"Huh," said Marlo, sounding impressed. "I guess maybe you do know him a little. Yes, his sense of irony is remarkably intact."

"I'm glad."

"I need to get back in the room. What's your urgent question?"

"Have you had a chance to go through his things, what he was wearing when they brought him to the hospital?"

"Maybe," Marlo said, her voice a study in suspicion.

"Was anything missing? A piece of jewelry, for instance?"

Silence. Then, "Actually, there was. I figured it got lost in the wreck. It's a small gold pocket watch, belonged to his grandmother back in Kharkov, in the Ukraine. Her name was Yana Krochak. Her initials were in the upper part of the inside cover. You won't be able to read them because they're in Cyrillic. George always kept it in his pocket."

"You looked everywhere?"

"Well, I mean, it could be in the car, but that's basically just a wreck now. Maybe I'll get a chance to look around inside, but more likely I won't. It could have fallen out when he was lifted onto the gurney."

"Okay," said Jane. "That's helpful."

"Why? What's going on? What are you after?" More suspicion.

Jane decided to tell her the truth. "I don't think an accident sent George off that hill."

"What's that supposed to mean? If it wasn't an accident, what was it?" Lowering her voice, she asked, "Are you seriously suggesting someone intentionally tried to hurt him?"

"As soon as I find a few more answers, I promise I'll give you a call and tell you everything."

"Is this related to my father's murder?"

"I'm afraid so."

More silence. "Okay. George and I aren't going anywhere. Hey," she said. "If it turns out you're not a nutcase and what you're telling me is true, is my husband still in danger?"

Jane thought of the calls the nurse had mentioned. "Let me ask a question: Does George have a cousin in Montana?"

"What? No, of course not."

"Then honestly, Marlo, I think it's possible. But I can't go to the police with a theory. Neither can you."

"Then make it quick, Lawless. Figure it out."

"I'm trying."

"Try harder." She disconnected the call.

Peter sat on the bed in the Harlow bedroom, propped against a ridiculous array of furry pink and white pillows, thinking how glad he'd be to put these colors in his rearview mirror. He'd spent the last half hour browsing various cheap-ticket sites, figuring out how much it would cost him to hop a plane back to London. He wasn't ready to leave just yet, though he couldn't stay much longer. Jane was annoying the hell out of him, mostly because she was making points about the Chenoweths and his relationship to them that made him doubt Kit. He found that intolerable. His father's texts had piled up without Peter making any attempt to answer them. Sigrid had texted him several times right after he'd talked to her, though she seemed to have given up. Good for her. She *should* give up on him. It would make things easier when he asked for a divorce.

Flopping onto his stomach, he was about to bring up a favorite video game when he heard loud thumping on his door. "Just a second," he called, crossing the room to open it.

"Hey, man," said Bolger, stuffing the last bite of a Rice Krispies bar into his mouth. "You got a visitor downstairs."

"Man or woman?"

"Woman."

"My sister?"

"Nope. Never seen her before."

"Did you just make those?" he asked, pointing to Bolger's mouth. "Hattie did."

"I didn't know she cooked."

"It isn't cooking, man; it's mostly melting and stirring."

"Is Cordelia here?"

"At the theater until late. I told your visitor to wait in the great hall."

"Thanks."

"Yeah, no problem. Night." He walked off toward the servant's stairway.

Peter checked his look in the mirror above the dresser and then trotted downstairs. Kit was standing by the Christmas tree, staring up at the lights. She looked beautiful, dressed in black

278

leather ankle boots and a party dress made of an odd, abstract, red webbing with a tight red slip underneath. When she heard the floor creak, she turned and ran to him, pressing her body against his.

Hesitantly, he put his arms around her. "You're shivering. Are you cold?"

"I'm scared."

"Of what?"

"Everything. My whole life."

He held her for a few seconds, then walked her over to one of the couches. Drawing her down next to him, he held her hands. "You can tell me anything, Kit." Her fingers were like ice. He tried his best to warm them.

"My life is coming apart." She pulled her hands away, wiped her cheeks, crossed and uncrossed her arms. "I've tried *so* hard to keep Eli happy, to just be friends, but he never—ever—stops pushing. I don't want to be with him ever again, but when I pull away, he gets all agitated and clingy. And *so* angry. He wants me to leave John Henry." She rubbed the fading bruise on her arm. "You thought my husband did that to me, but he didn't. It was Eli."

Peter clenched his jaw.

"I have to get away from him, Peter. And . . . my husband."

"What's up with your husband?"

She turned away. "This is all so awful."

He waited. She seemed to need some time.

Facing him again, she said, "I use his computer for my coursework—you know, for my degree? One night, a few months ago, I found this file. I was just kind of noodling around and there it was. Child porn. Little girls. Tons of it. So disgusting that I ran to the bathroom and threw up. He's a pedophile, Peter. Ever since that night, I can't stand to be in the same room with him. But if I leave him, where would I go?"

"You must have money. You have your salary."

She shook her head. "Because we're married and because he's paying for me to go to school, he said I shouldn't take a salary. Not until I graduate. He's very generous. He gives me an allowance, and beyond that, if I say I need—or want—something, he buys it."

"Without money of your own, you're his prisoner."

Her eyes searched the room. "My life is imploding, Peter, and I don't know what to do. How to fix it."

"I'm glad you came here."

"Are you?"

The conversation they'd had the other night about traveling to England together had stuck with him. In fact, he'd thought about it a lot. "Maybe I can help."

"How?"

"Come to London with me."

"I can't afford that."

"I'll buy the tickets. Friends help friends, Kit. You're my friend."

As the idea sank in, her eyes took on a glow. "You'd do that for me?"

"Do you have a passport?"

She nodded. "But where would I stay when we get there? I can't exactly move in with you and Sigrid."

"I'll rent a flat. We can stay together. No strings, Kit."

She touched his face. "What if I want strings?"

Her touch felt like silk.

"When could we go?" she asked.

"I'll buy the tickets tonight. There's a flight that leaves around two tomorrow afternoon. We'd have to get to the airport by twelve or twelve thirty. I suppose you could stay here for the night."

"I have to pack. I can't just leave with nothing."

"What about John Henry?"

"We had that art opening tonight. It's why I'm dressed up. John Henry said he's staying at the gallery because there's so much to do, which is a lie. He'll either drink too much, bunk there, and not get up until noon, or he'll spend the evening with a woman. Either way, Eli's supposed to open up in the morning."

"John Henry has a girlfriend?"

"She has a house in Bloomington. He's been cheating on me for months—or maybe years. I can't live like this."

"You shouldn't have to. Here's what we do." He put his arm around her as they stood up, and he walked her to the door, explaining how tomorrow would work. He told her to call in sick in the morning. That would buy her some time. He'd leave Octavia's Maybach in the garage and take an Uber down to her house. They would go to the airport together. "You'll have a lot of things to iron out when you get there, but at least you'll be safe."

Looking up into his eyes, she said, "I don't know what I did to deserve you."

As he stammered around inside his mind for a way to respond that didn't make him sound like a total dweeb, she pressed a finger to his lips. And then she kissed him. "See you in the morning, baby."

40

"I'm about to do something unethical," said Jane, still in bed, under the covers. She'd called Cordelia, knowing her friend considered noon the break of day. Jane had slept in, so it was just after eight thirty.

"Can't you be unethical a little later in the day?" came Cordelia's groggy response.

"But you're awake now, right?"

"Officially, no."

"Come on. You want to save Peter from Kit's clutches, don't you? Just haul yourself into the bathroom, turn on the water in the shower, and stand under it for a few minutes."

"Be a good girl and check back after lunch."

Sitting up in bed, Jane said, "Don't hang up. This is important. You have to help me."

"All right, all right. You don't have to shout."

Jane heard a loud thump.

"I am now up. Teetering badly, but up. What's the plan?"

"Get over to my house as fast as possible. I'll explain on the way."

"The way? If I don't know where I'm going, however shall I know what to wear?"

"Wear *clothes,* Cordelia. And bring your binoculars."

An hour later, they were speeding south on I-35W. Cordelia was at the helm of her shiny new Subaru, while Jane tapped an address into her Waze app.

"Listen," said Cordelia, glancing over her shoulder. "I put my purse behind your seat. There's a paper plate covered with aluminum foil inside it. Get it for us."

Jane reached around. "What's in it?"

"Hattie made some Rice Krispies bars last night. I may be wrong, but I think a couple of little mouse banditos, one named Bolger and one named Peter, snuck in and made off with a few. Want one?"

"No thanks."

"Okay, so while I enjoy my breakfast, fill me in on your ethical crisis."

"Breakfast?"

"Rice Krispies? Duh."

What Jane hoped to do wasn't just unethical, it was illegal. "I need to get inside the Chenoweths' house."

Cordelia turned to her, one eyebrow raised.

"I spent some time last night looking at the security footage from the parking garage in Gideon's building. The person in the hoodie, the one you see walking up to the elevators, could easily be a woman."

"Kit?"

"I think so."

"And you need to get into the house . . . why?"

"We've talked about trophies, right? I spoke to Marlo last night.

283

She said George always carried his grandmother's pocket watch with him. After the car crash, it was missing."

"You think you're going to walk in there and, poof, find all these murderous mementos? Where, Janey? If they do exist, they could be anywhere. And what happens if it's not Kit? Maybe the man in the hoodie was Eli."

"Then I'll have to get into his place, too. It's somewhere on the same property."

"What if you find someone home?"

"They all work at the gallery, which opens at ten. Nobody should be around. If someone is, we call it off." She looked over at the plate of Rice Krispies bars. "Maybe I will have one."

"Help yourself." Cordelia fiddled with the heat. "Okay, so back to Kit. I have a question. She's not tiny, but I doubt she weighs more than one thirty. How did she drag a guy like Gideon into the bathroom?"

Chewing for a few seconds, Jane said, "Let me paint a scenario for you. It might not be accurate in every detail, but in the main, I think it's what happened. Kit—"

"Or Eli."

"Let's concentrate on Kit for the moment. She lets herself into the condo with the key code, not expecting to find anyone there. Gideon was probably upstairs. I bet she thought the whole thing was a lark. Maybe, after she set the tote bag in the living room, she went into the kitchen in search of something to snack on."

"I can see her doing that."

"So she walks around, enjoying the relative splendor. Maybe she envisions herself living in a place like that one day. She figures she has at least half an hour, so she's not in any hurry. I think she may even be the one who turned on the music. And that's what alerted

Gideon. Rashad wouldn't be home for at least another hour. I'll bet he came downstairs to see what was up. Maybe they both saw each other at the same time, but more likely she could see his legs on the open stairway before he could see her. I think she picked up something heavy, something she could use to defend herself, and hid in the downstairs bathroom, hoping he'd leave."

"The bronze figure."

"Exactly," said Jane. "Gideon must have started looking around. She may have been hiding behind the door in the bathroom, or perhaps in the tub itself, behind the shower curtain. When he came in, she brought the sculpture down hard on the back of his head. It might be too much to think he fell directly into the bathtub, but it is possible. Whatever the case, her adrenaline was really pumping by then. If she had to lift him into the tub, in that moment, I believe she found the strength to do it. There would have been a fair amount of blood. If she looked in the medicine cabinet, she would have found razors. Maybe she thought that when his body was finally discovered, if the police saw the cut marks on his wrists, they would see it as a suicide attempt. Because of the blow to the back of his head, she probably hoped they'd think Gideon changed his mind and tried to get up, fell back, and that's how the injury happened. It was quick thinking on her part. She had no way of knowing that his head wound couldn't be explained that way. So she waits for the bathtub to fill. She cleans the blood off the statue with toilet paper and then flushes it away. As soon as she shuts off the bathwater, she hightails it out of there. She never thinks about the tote bag again. Blood wouldn't be visible on black clothing. When she gets home, with Eli in heroin-induced la-la land, she could take all the time she needed to get rid of the bloody clothes. In the end, she got away with it."

285

"Until now. You should have told me we were going to do a little breaking and entering. I would have worn black."

"I'm the one who's going in. You're my lookout. I need you to park somewhere along the highway where you can see in both directions. If you see someone pull into the Chenoweths' drive, you call me, and I'll get the hell out. There's a patio off the back, so there must be another door."

"I don't like it," said Cordelia. "You shouldn't go in alone."

Jane checked the time. It was going on ten. "I'll look around first. Make sure nobody's inside. Maybe I'll even ring the doorbell."

When Jane saw the sign for the county highway off ramp, she pointed. Her hands were beginning to sweat. As they approached the Chenoweths' mailbox, Jane asked Cordelia to pull over so she could get out. "Your phone's turned on, right?"

"Yes, Janey. It's on."

Jane pointed to another spot farther up, on the other side of the road. "Why don't you back in there?"

"Wait, wait. I just thought of something."

"What?"

"It's so Edgar Allan Poe. Where do you hide something when you want to keep it secret?"

"I give up. Where?"

"In plain sight, Janey. If I were you, I'd look for her jewelry box."

It was a thought. Jane slammed the car door and headed up the narrow road toward the house. Walking up to the garage, she peered through one of the high windows. Seeing a car inside, her spirits sank. Someone was home. Looking a moment more, she saw that the car was a silver Dodge Charger with white racing stripes.

Could it be the same one that had been parked outside her house on New Year's Eve? It seemed like too much of a coincidence to think it wasn't. The next question was, who did it belong to—John Henry, Eli, or Kit? She was pretty sure Eli had a truck. So, was John Henry home, or Kit?

Stepping over to the front door, Jane rang the bell. She was determined to get inside, even if she had to make up a story. As she waited, she gazed up at the pine trees. It was a lovely spot for a home, even if the house didn't match its surroundings. This far from the city, the wind had picked up. She stuffed her hands into the pockets of her peacoat, her right hand cupping the set of lock picks she carried with her. When no one answered, she pressed the bell again, this time three rings in quick succession. If nothing else, it would annoy the hell out of whoever was inside. Finally, opening the screen door to peer through a window, she noticed that the door was slightly ajar. She looked around, then pushed it open. Walking in, she surveyed the living room, thinking someone would appear at any second and demand to know what she was doing.

But no one came. Standing in the living room, gazing up at the beamed ceiling, she called, "Hello? Anybody home?"

No response.

"Hi, I'm Jane Lawless." She began to move farther into the house. "Is anyone here?"

Finding a hallway to her left, she headed down it. "Hello?" she called. She passed a couple of small bedrooms and a den before she came to the master. Pausing in the doorway, she noticed that a partially packed suitcase lay open on the bed. "Anybody here?" she asked, slipping on a pair of latex gloves. Moving closer to the

287

bed, she could see that the clothes inside the suitcase belonged to a woman. Was Kit planning on leaving? It must have been her car in the garage. But if it was, where had she gone?

Scanning the room for a jewelry box, Jane spied one on top of a tall chest. When she checked inside, she discovered that it was all men's stuff—cufflinks, tie clasps, watches, a blue ribbon given by Southwest High School for winning the hundred-yard dash.

She spent a couple minutes opening and closing dresser drawers, pawing through clothing, then turned her attention to the suitcase. If it was Kit who was leaving, she would undoubtedly take items that were important to her. Jane's eyes opened wide when she found a beautiful inlaid-wood box. Could it be that simple? She opened the top. Inside were earrings, necklaces, rings, bracelets. Nothing that looked all that expensive, though every piece was unusual. Sitting down on the bed, she took everything out. None of the trophies were there. But then an idea occurred to her.

She picked up the box and shook it. Sure enough, she heard the sound of shifting metal. Looking more closely, she found that the red velvet base was false. Lifting it out, her eyes widened. It was all there. Gideon's coin medallion. George's gold pocket watch. And a single turquoise teardrop earring with gold filigree at the top.

But there was more. Things Jane didn't recognize. Were these trophies from others who'd had the misfortune of knowing Kit? Of caring about her? Her pretend husband, Dave, for instance?

Jane used her phone to take a bunch of photos. She backed up and took one of the bed with the suitcase. None of the shots would be admissible. What she needed was to somehow get the police in here. Have them find what she just had.

Her phone rang. She answered immediately.

"A car. It's slowing down, like it's looking for something. OMG, it's turning into the Chenoweths' drive. Janey, get out. Now."

In her haste to see if someone was in the house, Jane had forgotten to look for the door to the patio. She raced back down the hall. Looking around frantically, she finally found sliding glass doors in the study. She burst outside, closing the doors behind her.

Now what? Before she could scramble up a hill to the road, she heard a car's motor, and then a familiar voice call, "Wait for me." Coming around the side of the house, she found Peter on his way to the front door.

"If you're looking for Kit, she's not here."

He stopped dead in his tracks. "What the hell are you doing here?"

"I could ask you the same thing."

"Did you break into that house?"

"The door was open."

"Oh, sure. Right."

"See for yourself. It's warped. Unless you actually pull it shut, it doesn't close. I came to see Kit. There's a suitcase on the bed, but she's nowhere around."

"Of course she's here." He trotted to the door and disappeared inside. When he came out, he seemed worried. "She was supposed to be packed and waiting for me."

"Why?"

"None of your business."

It wasn't hard to figure out. They were leaving together. For Jane, it was the worst possible news.

"What do I do?" asked Peter, running his hands through his hair. "Janey, you may not understand, but you've got to help me. Kit's in danger."

"I want to help you, Peter."

They stood looking at each other from opposite sides of an impossibly difficult divide. When Cordelia's Subaru roared in off the street, they both turned to look.

"The cavalry has arrived," said Peter under his breath.

"Why don't we get out of the cold, maybe go sit with Cordelia and try to figure this out."

It was all there, written on his face. Agitation. Bewilderment. Even anger. He paid the Uber driver, lifted his suitcase out of the trunk, and sent the car away.

41

At the same moment, Eli was inside his house, staring out the window at the gray, depressing day outside. Two weeks ago, he would never have considered anything like this, but he was at the end of his rope. He had to know the truth. Turning around, he walked past Kit, a half-filled pint of bourbon dangling from his fingers. He resumed his position on the couch.

"Can't you at least untie my ankles?" she whined. "You made the tape too tight. It's cutting off my circulation."

"Aw," he said, tossing the bottle cap away. "Poor Kit." She sat awkwardly on one of his living room chairs, her wrists duct-taped behind her back and her ankles bound. Charlotte, who'd come out of the bedroom to watch, was now curled up in the other chair, fast asleep.

"How long have you been——" She nodded at the bottle.

"Since I found out you lied to me."

"You keep saying that, but I don't know what you're talking about. I may tell a few white lies every now and then, but who doesn't?"

"That's why I've called this meeting," he said, amused by his little witticism. "Why were you packing that suitcase?"

"I told you. Because I'm leaving your father. I can't live with him, now that I know who he really is. Come on, Eli. Be a man. Are you going to call the police on him, or do I have to?"

"I'm not calling anyone."

"Why?"

"Because it's what you want. The courts will be less likely to tie the 'shocking revelation' to *your* upcoming divorce if it comes from me."

"Oh, come on. You think I'm that devious?"

He saluted her with his pint, then finished it off.

Now she seemed offended.

"Oh, drop the act," he said. "You planted that garbage on his computer. I looked at the download dates. They started right after you moved in. You were giving yourself a trump card for when you wanted out. It would have been perfect, right? Dear husband, give me everything I want or I send you up the river with the child porn I downloaded onto your computer."

Instead of answering, she spit at him.

Eli smiled, glancing at his cell phone resting on the coffee table. "I guess we should begin."

"Begin what? Eli, take this tape off."

"No."

"Why are you treating me like this? Because I left you and married your father?"

He got up and crossed into the kitchen, grabbing himself another bottle of Ten High. It was pure rotgut, but it's what he always drank when he was using. Weird how nostalgia worked.

Crouching down, he removed the revolver from the cabinet under the sink.

"I thought you were a Buddhist," she called from the living room. "A Buddhist wouldn't tie up his girlfriend."

"Ex-girlfriend," he corrected her, ambling back to the couch, his movements feeling liquid and easy. "But you're right. I've left the path. I don't even meditate anymore."

"Why? Too many evil thoughts?"

"Actually," he said, dropping down on the couch, "it started a few months ago. Every time I closed my eyes and concentrated on my breathing, a Bee Gees song would pop into my head. No matter how hard I tried to go with the flow, or how gentle I was with myself, bringing my attention back to my breathing, there the boys would be, 'Jive Talkin'' or whatever. I don't even like the Bee Gees."

She watched him. "Untie me and let me get back to packing. You've had your fun."

"Not enough," he said, placing the revolver on the table.

She looked at it, then looked at him. "What's that for? Come on, Eli. You're scaring me."

"Good."

"I love you, you know that. I always have. Okay, so I married your father, but . . . you were gone. I was lonely. Your father was always there. I needed someone."

He took a single bullet out of the pocket of his shirt and set it next to the gun. "I want answers, Kit. I'm never going to get them unless I force them out of you." He opened the cylinder and showed it to her. "Empty. See?" He fitted the bullet into one of the chambers, then closed the cylinder and gave it a spin. Rising from the couch, he walked over to her and pressed the barrel against her temple. She jerked away, but he grabbed her hair and yanked her upright. "I'm not playing, Kit. My life is a disaster. Before I end it—and I will end it—I want the truth."

"Jesus," she gasped. "All you had to do was ask. I'll tell you anything you want to know."

"No, you won't. You'll lie. You'll make it sound plausible, like you always do, but it will still be a lie."

Now she was pleading. "For the love of God, Eli, I'll tell you anything."

"I think we should leave God out of it. You were in Gideon's condo that night. You were the one who murdered him."

She stared straight ahead and began to shake.

"The truth, Kit."

"Well, I mean . . . I mean . . . I was only trying to help you. You're not a problem solver, but I am. You didn't have the guts to take care of business yourself, so I did it. It was all for you, baby. I couldn't stand the thought that some knuckle-dragging thug would beat the crap out of you in an alley."

He'd wondered if that had been her motive. As hard as he'd tried, he couldn't come up with anything else. Maybe she had loved him a little after all.

"Gideon wasn't supposed to be there," she said. "I panicked."

For some reason, he had a hard time imagining her panicking.

"And yes, I lied about it. If I'd told you the truth, in the shape you were in back then, who knows what you would have done." She hesitated, looking up at him. "Put the gun down now, please."

He considered it. Dropping the gun to his side, he resumed his place on the couch, scooping the newest pint off the coffee table and unscrewing the cap. What she said made sense. It might be difficult to admit, but he believed her. Maybe he wouldn't need the gun. "Okay. Next question. Did you murder my girl-friend?"

"What?" Her eyes grew wide. "Hell, no. Eli, please. Where is this coming from?"

"You did it. I know you did. Tell me the truth."

"I didn't. No way. Yes, I admit to the Gideon thing. I haven't had one single day of peace since it happened. But Harper?" Her eyes pleaded with him.

Eli tilted his head back against the couch cushion. Getting up, he walked over to her. Spinning the cylinder, he gripped her hair again and pressed the business end of the gun to the side of her head.

"Please," she pleaded. "I'm not lying."

He pulled the hammer back with his thumb. "You've got one chance in five that this will be your last breath."

She gaped at him. "You'd never do that to me. You still love me, I know you do."

"I'm counting to three. One."

"You're not that kind of man, Eli."

"Two. Last chance."

"You won't pull the trigger. It's not in you."

"Three." He pulled the trigger.

She screamed. Charlotte sat bolt upright, looked around for a few seconds, then jumped off the chair and made straight for the bedroom.

Kit's eyes pinwheeled. "You're insane," she yelled.

He couldn't argue the point.

Beads of sweat began to appear on her forehead.

"Let's try that question again," said Eli.

Her gaze ricocheted around the room.

"Did you murder Harper?"

"*No.*" As he lifted the gun, she said, "Wait."

If it weren't for the booze, he could never have done this. Even with the booze, he was having a hard time. "Well?"

She swallowed a couple times. "The thing is . . ."

"Yeah?"

"She called me."

"When?"

"A few days before she, ah, died. She said she thought she was pregnant."

"Why would she tell you? Why would she call?"

"Because we talked, a lot more toward the end. She wasn't good enough for you, Eli. She didn't even love you. She said she felt trapped. That living with you was way harder than she'd ever expected. She called you a black hole of need, like I didn't already know that. I hated the way she talked about you. I could talk about you that way because I loved you, but she couldn't. All that stuff about saving the planet, working to end the death penalty, carbon footprints, all her moralizing, and her prissiness about what she ate and didn't eat. She was going to hurt you, Eli. That last day, she called from the hotel where she worked. She was crying, said she had to talk to me. I was the only one who would understand. I suggested a drive up to Taylors Falls, we could talk along the way. I did it for you, Eli. It was *all* for you."

He dropped back down on the couch, pressing his hands to his eyes. Reaching for the bottle, he took a few more swallows of bourbon. Okay, he thought, wiping a hand across his mouth. So he'd heard some of the truth, though he also knew there had to be lies embedded in what she'd said. The part about her undying devotion was the hardest to take. In the last few hours, he'd come to the conclusion that she'd never loved anyone. She wasn't capable of it.

In a soft, childlike voice, she asked, "Will you let me go, baby? We can be together now. I want that more than anything."

He picked up his phone, clicked off the app he'd used for recording the conversation.

"Eli?"

"Shut up. I need to think."

Inside Cordelia's car, Jane watched Peter scan the property. He was jumpy, only partially listening. "Where the hell could she have gone?"

"Maybe she got cold feet about leaving with you," said Jane.

"No. Not possible."

"Call the gallery."

"I told you, she didn't go to the gallery this morning."

"You don't know that for sure. Maybe she changed her mind, and Eli or John Henry gave her a ride."

"This is going nowhere," said Peter. "I'm just wasting my time. I've tried to explain. I don't know why you can't give Kit the benefit of the doubt. She's a good person."

Jane felt sorry for her brother. His feelings for Kit had blinded him to who and what she was. Hooking up with her would be one of the worst decisions he would ever make.

"Call her phone again," said Jane.

Peter unlocked the door and got out.

"Where are you going?" called Cordelia.

As Peter walked up a gravel road, Jane got out and went after him. When she came to the top of a hill, she saw that he'd run ahead and was banging on the door of a small house. A truck was parked next to it. It had to be Eli's place.

"I know you're in there," shouted Peter. "Let Kit go, or I call the police. You've got five seconds."

Just as Jane reached him, Eli burst outside, looking unsteady.

"She's all yours, man," he said, his words slurred.

"What did you do?"

"I got the truth out of her." He held up his cell phone.

Peter shot past him and went inside.

"You recorded the conversation?" said Jane.

"Yeah." He leaned against the rear of the truck, waving the phone triumphantly over his head.

"Did you threaten her?"

"No more than she deserved."

Cordelia finally caught up to them, looking winded. "What did I miss?"

"If you did threaten her, what you got isn't admissible in court," said Jane.

"So?" he said, lifting a pint of Ten High out of his shirt pocket. "I'm not a court. I'm a human being." He took a few swallows. Wiping a hand across his mouth, he added, "I'm not sure she is."

42

Marlo grabbed the ace, tucked it into the cards she was holding, and announced, "Gin. I win again." She laid the cards down.

George tossed his on the bed tray. "The least you could do is let the sad invalid win once in a while."

"But you'd know I was letting you off easy, and you'd hate me for it."

"You think so, do you?" When he coughed, he winced. "Isn't it about time for more pain meds?"

"Another hour. What can I do to help?"

"Don't make me laugh."

She got up, bent over, and kissed him. "Nothing funny about that."

"Bet I don't look like Hugh Grant anymore."

"No, you still do. Your face is a little banged up. But the doctors say you're healing. Every part of you."

Picking up the remote with his good hand, he changed the TV channel. He took a sip of water and then said, "Tell me something. When I was out cold, did you play music for me?"

"The nurses said it would help."

"Aerosmith?"

"Why not? It's . . . lively. I like Aerosmith."

"Uh huh. And, something else. This may sound off the wall, but I swear I heard you discussing baby names."

"Did I? That's odd."

"Is it? Did you?"

"Let me think. Yes, I suppose I may have."

"Any particular reason? You were in and out of the bathroom all morning. If one had a vivid imagination, such as myself, one might conclude that you have a touch of morning sickness."

"Would they?" For Marlo, this was a now-or-never moment. "If the woman in question did have morning sickness, would the man in question be happy about it or sad?"

"Oh, happy. Indeed, without hesitation."

"Really?"

"Yes, but only theoretically."

"What if it wasn't just a theory?"

"I think we should have a baby-name discussion, Marlo. One I can actually be a part of, not floating around somewhere in the ether."

"About theoretical names for a theoretical baby."

"Precisely."

She loved him more in this moment than she ever thought possible. She shuffled the deck. "I was thinking Anastasia, if it was a girl."

"And if it's a boy, how about George the second?"

"Are we officially in negotiations?"

He smiled at her. "I think we are."

When Cordelia returned home that night after spending the afternoon at the police station with Jane, Peter, and eventually Jane's father, she was an exhausted wreck of a woman in need of a Thorn Boilermaker—a glass of black cherry soda and a stiff shot of creme de cacao. She had a little bundle to take up to her bedroom before she came back down to the kitchen.

Peter had spoken to an investigator at the police station for a couple of hours. When he was done, he'd come out to the waiting room where she, Jane, and Ray were having a private conversation. He said he hadn't been asked more than a couple of questions about the night he'd asked Rashad out for a drink. Because the police didn't seem interested in pursuing this line of questioning, Peter appeared to feel emboldened, still resisting the notion that he'd lied on the stand. He called an Uber shortly thereafter and left, though not before asking his dad to call him if he learned anything more.

Cordelia's reaction was far different. She couldn't seem to stop fuming about Kit's pathetic chutzpah. Kit had vehemently pleaded her innocence to anyone who would listen. Both Eli and Kit were booked, though not before Kit had asked to speak to Ray privately. She'd pleaded with him to represent her if the worst happened and she was arrested for murder. Ray, being of sound mind and not given to masochism, declined. The worst part was, Ray indicated that it could be months—or longer—before it all got sorted out. In the meantime, Rashad would stay in prison.

And so, it was dark by the time Cordelia drove Jane home. Now, turning on the light in the breakfast room, ready to dissolve into a heap at the table, she was surprised to find an envelope addressed to Hattie. She fingered it for a moment, then took her glass and headed back upstairs. Would this day never end? Before knocking on Hattie's bedroom door, she gazed up at a sign that read: "The Max Planck Bedroom. Remember, you CAN be two places at once."

"Can I come in?" she called.

"Sure," came Hattie's muffled voice.

Cordelia found her niece sitting on the bed, reading. The room, as usual, was a total disaster. Books, clothes, towels, etc. covered almost every surface.

"I have something for you," said Cordelia, pulling the envelope from the pocket of her wool cardigan. She set her glass down on the nightstand. "This was downstairs on the table in the breakfast room. It has your name on it."

Hattie set the book aside. "Maybe it's my check."

"Check? Skooch over." Cordelia stuffed a pillow behind her head and stretched out.

"Peter said he'd pay for me to join the Planetary Society."

Cordelia had never heard of the Planetary Society, but she knew her niece had a habit of leaning on people to pay for her various scientific interests.

"I had breakfast with him the last couple of mornings. He doesn't think I should eat pie so early in the day."

"Heavens. Where did he get such a silly idea?"

Tearing the envelope open, Hattie smiled and said, "Yup. It's the check. And a note."

"A private note?"

"I don't think so."

"Then read it to me."

Hattie unfolded it. "Dear Hattie. Here's the check. I hope the *Planetary Report* is everything you hope it will be. I'm sorry I couldn't say goodbye to you in person—"

"*Goodbye*," said Cordelia.

"That's what it says."

"Keep going."

302

"—but I'm flying back to London tonight. I'm glad we had a chance to see each other, even if it was only over breakfast. You're a wonderful girl and I'm proud to be part of your family. I want you to know that when you get a little older, I will fly you to England so we can travel the countryside together searching out archeological sites. Start making a list of what you might want to see. Alas, I'm not very good at keeping in touch, but I promise to email you more often. Keep reading those science books, sweetheart. I love you very much. Peter."

Cordelia had tears in her eyes.

"There's a P.S."

"Which says?"

"Look around the house. You may find a new furry friend lurking in the shadows."

Hattie turned to her aunt. "What's he mean by that?"

"Well, I agreed to take care of a sweet little female kitten until her dad gets out of the slammer."

"We have a new kitten?"

"For the moment."

"What if the dad never gets out of the slammer?"

"That would be terribly sad, wouldn't it? I'd like to think he will."

"Sure, but . . . what would happen if he doesn't?"

"I guess we'd have to keep her."

"Really?" She squealed. "Where is she now?"

"On my bed."

Hattie was out the door before Cordelia could even say Max Planck.

43

The following afternoon, Julia's plane was on time, which meant Carol would drop her off at the house sometime around six. By five, Jane was working on dinner, one of Julia's favorites: a simple meatloaf, which would smell wonderful when she walked in the door. Jane also planned to make mashed potatoes, something that had tempted Julia to eat even during some of her worst days on chemo. The champagne was on ice, and the apricot cake was waiting on the counter.

When Julia finally arrived, though, all thoughts of dinner evaporated. They took their joy at being together again up to the bedroom and spent some . . . quality . . . time together. And then, while Julia showered, Jane returned to the kitchen to finish dinner, glad that she'd turned the oven temperature down. The meatloaf was perfect.

They sat at the kitchen table, eating heartily and talking non-stop. Jane had dozens of questions about what Julia had been doing for the last few days, but decided all that could wait. Julia insisted on hearing every last detail about what had happened in the Wise murder case while she'd been gone. By the time Jane got to that day's events, they were on the couch in the living room, cradled in each other arms in front of the fire.

"I called Dad after we found Kit," said Jane. "His trial had recessed for lunch, so I was able to talk to him. He said to phone the police right away, suggested how to handle Kit's jewelry box. He wanted me to stress to the police that Kit was a flight risk. If they didn't detain her, she'd disappear."

"On what basis could they detain her?"

"When I told one of the officers who I was and what I'd been working on, she called someone higher up to come over to the Chenoweth property. I sat with that guy for about an hour. As I was waiting for him, I called Marlo Wise and asked her if she could describe George's watch in more detail. She was able to, and she also mentioned that it was worth at least three thousand dollars. They'd had it appraised a few years back."

"So if Kit took it and had it in her possession, it would be considered theft?"

"Right. The next problem was getting into the Chenoweths' house. The police can't do that without a search warrant. But, as it turned out, Eli's name was on the deed. Kit's wasn't. Don't you wonder why John Henry never changed that?"

"Maybe some part of him saw her for what she was."

"Maybe. Anyway, once Eli realized that he might be arrested, he agreed to cooperate. He took them into the house and, of course, there it all was on the bed in the bedroom, just as I'd left it. I'd described the trophies I suspected Kit had taken from her victims, so the cops knew what they were looking for."

"What about the recording Eli made?"

"The police confiscated it."

"You probably shouldn't tape someone without their permission."

"That's not entirely true," said Jane. "Depends on the state. Some mandate that each party has to consent. Minnesota has a one-person consent law, which means the recording could be legal, except for one small problem: Eli put a gun to her head to get her to talk. Coerced testimony isn't admissible because what the person says may simply reflect their fear. They tell the interrogator what he wants to hear to get out of a bad situation."

"Gee, let me think," said Julia. "Seems to me the Bush administration used coerced interrogations all over the world and swore by them."

"Good point."

"Go on."

"As it turned out, Eli removed the bullet from the revolver before he played his little game of Russian roulette. He showed the cops how he did it. It was pretty clever. He acted like he was slipping it in, but really, he cupped it in his hand. Kit was never in any real danger, though she thought she was, and that's what matters."

"I imagine she looked pretty scared when Peter brought her out of the house."

"Amazingly, no. She came out fighting, insisting that Eli had tried to kill her, that she had nothing to do with any murders, that Eli was looking for someone to pin it on to save his own hide. And on and on. The police took both of them into custody. We all ended up down at the police station. Even Dad eventually arrived."

"But other than the recording, which isn't admissible, and the trophies, what other proof do you have that Kit murdered Gideon?"

"There was hair evidence found in the bathroom that never

matched anyone. I think when they retest it, it will turn out to be Kit's. As far as George goes, I'm hoping we can get our hands on the security video at the gallery for last Saturday morning. That way, we can see who George talked to. Again, I'm sure it will be Kit. It might even jog his memory."

"So with all this new evidence pointing to Kit, will Rashad be set free? Or will he have to be retried?"

"The former, I would think," said Jane. "But my father says that nothing is for sure. Whatever happens, it will take a while— perhaps a very long while."

"That's appalling. What about Peter?"

Jane sighed. "It was a tough day for my brother. But something good came out of it. I think he finally saw Kit for who and what she is. When they first came out of Eli's house, I could tell they'd had words. Peter had lost all his bravado. He kind of shut down after that, stopped talking. Of course, Kit tried to get him to put his arms around her, but he wouldn't."

"Poor guy."

"Yeah. I wish I knew how to help him. He left last night to fly back to London. Never said goodbye to any of us, except for Dad."

"Can he do that? Leave the country? What if the police want to talk to him again?"

"My father talked to him about it, told him that given the amount of time it would take to make any headway in the case, and because the police never asked him to stay in town, going back to England would be okay. He may have to return for a trial, if there is one. Whether or not he gets nailed for perjury in the first trial is something he and Dad will have to sort out. In any case, he's gone. I guess I still hold out hope that he and Sigrid can repair their marriage. Only time will tell." Jane turned to face Julia. "Come on now, it's my turn to ask questions. Tell me why you went to Michigan?"

Julia gazed into the fire. "This is going to be hard."

"Why?"

"Because I don't want you to think I've gone off the deep end."

"Have you?"

Julia squeezed Jane's hand. Hesitating a moment more, she said, "I guess it all started when I had that stroke. I never said anything, but I realized, more than I ever had before, that I'm terrified of dying. Truly terrified. I was talking to a doctor friend a while later, and he asked if he could tell me something I'd probably think was off the wall."

"Such as?"

"He did a lot of work in hospice care. In the last couple of years he'd run into several people who'd turned that paralyzing fear around. He suggested I read an article in *Scientific American*. The title is: 'Psilocybin: A Journey Beyond the Fear of Death?'"

"Magic mushrooms?"

"Yes."

"You took them?"

"It's not the old hippie idea—sitting under a tree and wigging out. The mushrooms are administered in a medical setting, and a trained guide is with you every minute. There's preparation before and a discussion—or in my case, many discussions—afterward. I don't know how to explain what I experienced in a way that won't sound like I've lost my mind. You know I've never been religious. But what I had was the most profound experience of my life. I've always relied on words, but there are no words. Not for this."

It was a lot to take in.

"I'd like you to read the article. As time goes on, I think I may be able to explain some of it, though nothing I say will ever touch the experience."

Jane hesitated. "Okay."

"I know. Just give it some time. Unless you'd like to try it yourself."

"Not interested, Julia."

"Sure. I understand."

"So . . . you said some of your fear is gone. I'm glad. But what about your treatment going forward? Before you left, you suggested you might not continue with the chemo. I mean, if you do discontinue it, it feels to me like you're abandoning hope and just waiting to die."

Julia drew back. "I know this is difficult."

"Then help me understand."

"I want to *live* until I die, Jane, not spend my remaining time being tortured by medical science. All I've done for the last six months is rush around. I stay up late reading new studies, I talk to research doctors all over the world. I'm spending so much time trying to stay alive that I'm not living."

"Sure, but——"

"You think I'm giving up."

Jane took a deep breath, trying to hold back her tears. "Yeah. I do. From my standpoint, it feels to me like you had a bunch of drug-induced hallucinations and now you think you understand the meaning of life."

Julia sat silently for a few minutes. "I can understand that," she said finally. "And maybe you're right. But again, it's my life, so it's my choice."

Jane tipped her head back and closed her eyes.

309

"I've already stopped the chemo. I did it last week. As I expected, I've already begun to feel better. I'll continue with the pain meds and a few others. I know this may sound silly to you, but except for the cancer, I'm really very healthy."

Jane had no idea how to respond.

"Look, I'll leave if you want me to. The last thing I mean to do is hurt you. Either way, here or somewhere else, I will die someday, probably sooner rather than later." She paused, stroking Jane's arm. "I want to travel. Not for work this time, but for fun."

"But your sight?"

"Yes, little by little, it's going. But if you went with me, I could see all these wonderful places again through your eyes. It would be like experiencing them for the first time. I'm not asking you to give up your work. Maybe we could do it every now and then for, say, a week at a time. The memories we'd make would sustain us for a very long time." Looking into Jane's eyes, she said, "Will you think about it?"

"I don't need to. I want to be with you."

"What I said before, I'll say again: All I ask is one good year with you."

"Do you think it's possible?"

"I do. But whatever happens, whatever time we have left, I want you to know I'm grateful. You accepted me back into your life when you didn't have to. You agreed to walk this final path with me. My heart is full because for the first time in my life, I've finally found home."

Holding Julia tight, Jane gazed silently into the fire, watching the logs shift and sparks rise and die in the air.